Wishes come true at Christmas!

Let It Snow

Three fabulous, festive Christmas stories by *New York Times* bestselling authors Debbie Macomber, Sherryl Woods & Robyn Carr

Debbie Macomber is a number one *New York Times* bestselling author. Her recent books include *1022 Evergreen Place, 1105 Yakima Street* and *Hannah's List*. She has become a leading voice in women's fiction worldwide and her work has appeared on every major bestseller list. There are more than a hundred million copies of her books in print. For more information on Debbie and her books, visit www.DebbieMacomber.com.

Sherryl Woods is a member of Romance Writers of America and Sisters in Crime. She spends what little spare time she has gardening—in pots on her balcony in Florida and on every spare patch of land in her yard in Virginia—going to movies and the theatre and travelling to visit friends in far-flung corners of the world.

Sherryl divides her time between Key Biscayne, Florida, where the ocean is at her front door, and Colonial Beach, Virginia, where she can sit on her porch and watch the boats on the Potomac River. 'There is nothing in life that brings me more serenity than the sea,' she says, 'unless it's a good book.'

Robyn Carr is the author of over twelve novels, including the critically acclaimed *Mind Tryst*, and has also written non-fiction and screenplays. Robyn and her husband live in Las Vegas, Nevada.

Let It Snow

Debbie Macomber

SHERRYL WOODS   ROBYN CARR

MILLS & BOON

Mills & Boon, an imprint of Harlequin (UK) Limited,
Eton House, 18-24 Paradise Road, Richmond, Surrey TW9 1SR

LET IT SNOW © Harlequin Enterprises II B.V./S.à.r.l. 2012

Let It Snow © Debbie Macomber 1986
Santa, Baby © Sherryl Woods 2006
Midnight Confessions © Robyn Carr 2010

ISBN: 978 0 263 90243 3

024-1112

Printed and bound by
CPI Group (UK) Ltd, Croydon, CR0 4YY

Let It Snow

DEBBIE MACOMBER

For Joyce Beaman
Fellow author, fortune cookie collector
and, above all, dear friend

One

"Ladies and gentlemen, this is your captain speaking."

Shelly Griffin's fingers compressed around the armrest until her neatly manicured nails threatened to cut into the fabric. Flying had never thrilled her, and she avoided it whenever possible. It had taken her the better part of a month to convince herself that this trip would be perfectly safe. She told herself that of course the Boeing 727 that had taken off without incident from San Francisco almost ninety minutes ago would land unscathed just a little while from now in Seattle. Still, if it wasn't Christmas, if she wasn't so homesick, and if she'd had more than four days off, she would have done anything except fly to get home for the holidays.

"Seattle is reporting heavy snow and limited visibility," the captain continued. "We've been rerouted to

Portland International until the Seattle runways can be cleared."

A low groan filled the plane.

She forced herself to relax. Snow. She could handle snow, right? She wasn't overjoyed at the prospect of having to land twice, but she was so close to home now that she would willingly suffer anything to see a welcoming smile light up her father's eyes.

In an effort to divert her thoughts from impending tragedy, she studied the passengers around her. A grandmotherly type slept sedately in the seat beside her. The man sitting across the aisle was such a classic businessman that he was intriguing. Almost from the moment they'd left San Francisco, he'd been working out of his briefcase. He hadn't so much as cracked a smile during the entire flight. The captain's announcement had produced little more than a disgruntled flicker in his staid expression.

She had seen enough men like him in her job as a reporter in the federal court to catalog him quickly. Polished. Professional. Impeccable. Handsome, too, she supposed, if she was interested—which she wasn't. She preferred her men a little less intense. She managed to suppress a tight laugh. Men? What men? In the ten months she'd been living in the City by the Bay, she hadn't exactly developed a following. A few interesting prospects now and again, but nothing serious.

As the plane made its descent, Shelly gripped the armrest with renewed tension. Her gaze skimmed the emergency exits as she repeated affirmations on the safety of flying. She mumbled them under her breath as the plane angled sharply to the right, aligning its giant bulk with the narrow runway ahead.

Keeping her eyes centered on the seat in front of her, she held her breath until she felt the wheels gently bounce against the runway in a flawless landing. She braced herself as the brakes quickly slowed the aircraft to a crawl.

The oxygen rushed from her lungs in a heartfelt sigh of relief. Somehow the landings were so much worse than the takeoffs. As the tension eased from her rigid body, she looked around to discover the businessman slanting his idle gaze over her. His dark eyes contained a look of surprise. He seemed amazed that anyone could be afraid of flying. The blood mounted briefly in her pale features, and she decided she definitely didn't like his cold attitude, no matter how handsome he was.

The elderly woman sitting next to her placed a hand on Shelly's forearm. "Are you all right, dear?"

"Of course." Relief throbbed in her voice. Now that

they were on the ground, she could feign the composure that seemed to come so easily to the other passengers.

"I hope we aren't delayed long. My daughter's taking off work to meet me."

"My dad's forty minutes from the airport," Shelly offered, hoping that he'd called the airline to check if her flight was on time. She hated the thought of him anxiously waiting for her.

The other woman craned her neck to peek out the small side window. "It doesn't seem to be snowing much here. Just a few flakes. They look a bit like floating goose feathers, don't you think?"

Shelly grinned at the image. "Let's hope it stays that way."

She remained seated while several of the other passengers got up and took advantage of the captain's offer to leave the plane during the delay. The businessman was among those who quickly vacated their seats. But since the captain had said he didn't expect them to be in Portland long, Shelly didn't want to take a chance of missing the flight when it was ready to take off again.

After checking her watch every ten minutes for forty minutes, she was starting to think that they would never leave Oregon. The blizzard had hit the area, and whirling snow buffeted the quiet plane with growing intensity. Her anxieties mounted with equal force. Suddenly her dire musings were interrupted.

"This is the captain speaking." His faint Southern drawl filled the plane. "Unfortunately, Seattle reports that visibility hasn't improved. They're asking that we remain here in Portland for another half hour, possibly longer."

Frustration and disappointment erupted from the remaining passengers, and they all began speaking at once.

"This is the captain again," the pilot added, his tone one of wry humor. "I'd like to remind those of you who are upset by our situation that it's far better to be on the ground wishing you were in the sky than to be in the sky *praying* you were on the ground."

Shelly added a silent amen to that. As it was, she was beginning to feel claustrophobic, trapped inside the plane. She grabbed her purse and reached for her cell, then discovered when she tried to turn it on that she must have forgotten to charge it, because the battery was dead. Unsnapping her seat belt, she stood and headed down the narrow aisle toward the front of the plane.

"Do I have time to make a phone call? My cell is dead," she explained.

"Sure," the flight attendant answered with a cordial smile. "Don't be long, though. The conditions in Seattle could change quickly."

"I won't," Shelly promised, and made her way into the terminal. Thank heavens airports still had payphones, she thought as she found two lonely phones sandwiched between a newsstand and a bagel shop.

She claimed the only unoccupied one, then frowned when she saw the "Out of Order" sign taped over the credit card slot. It wasn't until she was sorting through her purse for change that she noted that the unsympathetic businessman from her flight was sitting at the other phone. Apparently even someone as focused as he seemed to be could forget to charge his phone, too.

"This is Slade Garner again," he announced with the faintest trace of impatience creeping into his voice. "My plane's still in Portland."

Shelly scowled at her wallet. She didn't have change for the phone.

"Yes, yes, I understand the snow's a problem on your end as well," he continued smoothly. "I doubt that I'll make it in this afternoon. Perhaps we should arrange the meeting for first thing tomorrow morning. Nine o'clock?" Another pause. "Of course I realize it's the day before Christmas."

Rummaging in her purse, Shelly managed to dredge up a token for the cable car, a breath mint and a lost button.

Pressing her lips tightly together, she mused about

how coldhearted Slade Garner was to insist on a meeting so close to Christmas. Instantly she felt guilty because her thoughts were so judgmental. Of course he would want to keep his appointment. He obviously hadn't taken this flight for fun. Her second regret was that she realized she had intentionally eavesdropped on his conversation, looking for excuses to justify her dislike of him. Such behavior was hardly in keeping with the Christmas spirit.

Pasting on a pleasant smile, she stepped forward when he replaced the receiver, thinking to claim the working phone, but someone practically knocked her over and got there first.

"Excuse me," she said politely as Slade turned in her direction. He refused to meet her gaze, and for a second she didn't think he'd heard her.

"Yes?" He finally looked her way, his expression bored, frustrated.

"Have you got change, by any chance?"

He uninterestedly checked the contents of his pocket, then looked down at the few coins in his palm. "Sorry." Dispassionately he tucked them back in his pocket and turned away.

She was ready to approach someone else when he turned back to her. His dark brows drew together in a frown, something about her apparently registering in his mind despite his preoccupied thoughts. "You were on the Seattle flight, weren't you?"

"Yes."

"Here." He handed her what change he had.

The corners of her mouth curved up in surprise. "Thanks." He was already walking briskly away, and she was convinced he hadn't even heard her. She didn't know what difference it made that they'd shared the same plane, but without analyzing his generosity any further, she dropped the first coin in the slot, then shifted her weight from one foot to the other while the phone rang, hoping her father—one of the last holdouts against owning a cell—wasn't already at the airport waiting for her. She was pleased when he answered.

"Dad, I'm so glad I caught you."

"Merry Christmas, Shortcake."

Her father had bestowed this affectionate title on her when she was thirteen and her friends had sprouted up around her. To her dismay she had remained at a deplorable five feet until she was seventeen. Then, within six months, she had grown five inches. Her height and other attributes of puberty had been hormonal afterthoughts.

"I'm in Portland."

"I know. When I phoned the airline they told me you'd been forced to land there. How are you doing?"

"Fine." She wasn't about to reveal her fear of flying or

how much she was dreading getting back on that plane. "I'm sorry about the delay."

"It's not your fault."

"But I hate wasting precious time sitting here when I could be with you."

"Don't worry about it. We'll have plenty of time together."

"Have you decorated the tree yet?" Since her mother's death three years before, she and her father had made a ritual of placing the homemade ornaments on the tree together.

"I haven't even bought one. I thought we'd do that first thing in the morning."

She closed her eyes, savoring the warm feeling of love and security that the sound of her father's voice always gave her. "I've got a fantastic surprise for you."

"What's that?" he prompted.

"It wouldn't be a surprise if I told you, would it?"

Her father chuckled, and she could visualize him rubbing his finger over his upper lip the way he did when something amused him. They chatted for another minute, and then she realized she should check on the status of her flight.

"I've missed you, Dad."

"I've missed you, too."

"Take care."

"I will." She was about to hang up, but then… "Dad," she added hastily, her thoughts churning as she focused on a huge advertisement for a rental car agency. "Listen, don't go to the airport until I phone."

"But—"

"I'll be hungry by then, so I'll grab some lunch and be waiting outside for you. That way you won't have to park."

"I don't mind parking, Shortcake."

"I know, but I'd rather do it my way."

"If you insist."

"I do." Her brothers claimed that their father was partial to his only daughter. It was a long-standing family joke that she was the only one capable of swaying him once he'd made a decision. "I insist."

They said their goodbyes, and she disconnected, feeling light-hearted and relieved. Instead of heading back down the concourse toward the plane, she ventured in the opposite direction, taking the escalators to the lower level, where the rental car agencies were located.

To her surprise, she saw Slade Garner talking with a young man at the first agency. Shelly walked past him to the second counter.

"How much would it cost to rent a car here and drop it off in Seattle?" she asked brightly.

The woman on duty hardly looked up from her computer screen. "Sorry, we don't have any cars available."

"None?" Shelly found that hard to believe.

"Lots of people had the same idea you did," the agent explained. "A plane hasn't landed in Seattle in hours. No one wants to sit around the airport waiting. Especially at Christmas."

"Thanks anyway." Shelly hurried down to the third agency and repeated her question.

"Yes, we do," the agent said with a wide grin. "We have exactly one car available." She named a sum that caused Shelly to swallow heavily. But already the idea had gained traction in her mind. Every minute the plane remained on the ground robbed her of precious time with her father. And from what he'd told her, the snow was coming down fast and furiously. It could be hours before the plane was able to take off, if it took off today at all. She freely admitted that another landing at another airport in the middle of the worst snowstorm of the year wasn't her idea of a good time. As it was, her Christmas bonus was burning a hole in her purse. And this was a good cause. Surely there was some unwritten rule that stated every favorite daughter should spend Christmas with her father.

"I'll take the car."

She looked up and saw Slade Garner standing a mere

six inches away. A wide, confident smile spread across his handsome features, and his aura of self-assurance bordered on arrogance.

"I'm already taking it," she said firmly.

"I have to get to Seattle."

"So do I," she informed him primly. And then, in case he decided to remind her that she was indebted to him, she added, "But give me an address and I'll make sure to reimburse you while I'm there."

"I've got an important meeting."

"As a matter of fact, so do I." Turning back to the counter, she picked up a pen and prepared to fill in the rental form.

"How much?" he asked.

"I beg your pardon?"

"How much do you want for the car?" He slipped his hand into the pocket of his coat, apparently prepared to pay her price.

Squaring her shoulders, she exchanged looks with the rental agent, then turned back to Slade and said, "Get your own car."

"There's only one car available. This one."

"And I've got it," she told him with a deceptively calm smile. The more she saw of this man, the more aggravating he became.

His jaw tightened. "I don't think you understand," he

said, and breathed out with sharp impatience. "My meeting's extremely important."

"So is mine. I'm—"

"You could share the car," the agent suggested, causing both Shelly and Slade to turn their eyes his way, shocked by his impromptu peacemaking.

Shelly hesitated.

Slade's brows arched and he met her eyes. "I'll pay the full fee for the car," he offered.

"You mention money one more time and the deal's off," she shot back hotly.

"Don't be unreasonable."

"I'm not being unreasonable. You are."

He rubbed a hand along the back of his neck and forcefully expelled his breath. "Do we or do we not have a deal?"

"I'm not going to Seattle."

He gave her a sharp look of reproach. "I just heard you say Seattle."

"I'm headed for Maple Valley. That's in south King County."

"Fine. I'll drop you off and return the car to the rental office myself."

That would save her one hassle. Still, she hesitated. Two minutes together and they were already arguing.

How would they possibly manage three hours cooped up in the close confines of a car?

"Listen," he argued, his voice tinged with exasperation. "If I make it to Seattle this afternoon, I might be able to get this meeting over with early. That way I can be back home in San Francisco for Christmas."

Without knowing it, he'd found the weakest links in her chain of defense. Christmas and home were important to her.

"All right," she mumbled. "But I'll pay my share of the cost."

"Whatever you want."

For the first time since she'd seen him, Slade Garner smiled.

Two

"What about your luggage?" Slade asked as they strolled down the concourse toward the plane.

"I only have one bag. It's above my seat." Her honey-brown hair curled around her neck, and she absently lifted a strand and looped it over her ear. A farm girl's wardrobe didn't fit in with the formal business attire she needed in San Francisco so she had left most of her clothes with her father. And it hadn't been hard to fit four days' worth of clothes into her carry-on. The brevity of her vacation was turning out to be a blessing in disguise.

Her spirits rose as they neared the plane. She was heading home for Christmas, and she wasn't flying!

"Good. I only have a garment bag with me."

She hesitated. "I do have a tote bag filled with presents."

His gaze collided briefly with hers. "That shouldn't be any problem."

When he saw the monstrosity, he might change his mind, she mused with an inner smile. In addition to a variety of odd-sized gifts, she was bringing her father several long loaves of sourdough bread. The huge package was awkward, and she had required a flight attendant's assistance to fit it in the compartment above her seat. Normally she would have put everything in a second suitcase and checked it, but loaves of bread were so long—sticking out of her bag like doughy antennas—that none of her suitcases had been big enough.

The plane was nearly empty when they boarded, confirming her suspicion that the delay was going to be far longer than originally anticipated. Checking her watch, she discovered that it was nearly noon. The other passengers had probably gone to get something to eat.

Standing on tiptoes, she opened the luggage compartment.

"Do you need help?" Slade asked. A dark gray garment bag was folded neatly over his forearm.

"Here." She handed him her one small bag. She heard him mumble something about appreciating a woman who packed light and smiled to herself.

Straining to stretch as far as she could to get a good grip on her bag of gifts, she heard Slade grumble.

"Look at what some idiot put up there."

"Pardon?"

"That bag. Good grief, people should know better than to try to force a tuba case up there."

"That's mine, and it isn't a tuba case." Extracting the bag containing the bread, so the bigger bag would be easier to extricate, she handed it down to him.

Slade looked at it as if something were about to leap out and bite him. "Good heavens, what is this?"

What was it? What was wrong with his eyes? Bread had to be the most recognizable item in the world.

"A suitcase for a snake," she replied sarcastically.

The beginnings of a grin touched his usually impassive features as he gently moved in front of her. "Let me get that thing down before you drop it on your head."

She stepped aside so he could put the bread and their carry-ons on her empty seat..

"Suitcase for a snake, huh?" Unexpectedly he smiled again.

The effect on her was dazzling. She had the feeling that this man didn't often take the time to enjoy life. Only minutes before she'd classified him as cheerless and intense. But when he smiled, the carefully guarded facade cracked and she felt she was being given a rare glimpse of the intriguing man inside. And he fascinated her.

By the time they'd arranged things with the airline, the courtesy van from the rental agency had arrived to deliver them to their vehicle.

"I put everything in my name," Slade said on a serious note as he unlocked their car.

The snow continued to fall, creating a picturesque view and making her happier than ever that she wasn't getting back on that plane. "That's fine." He'd taken the small carry-on from her, leaving her to cope with the huge bag filled with Christmas goodies.

"It means I'll be doing all the driving."

After another glance at the snowstorm, she was grateful.

"Well?" He looked as though he expected an argument.

"Do you have a driver's license?"

Again a grin cracked the tight line of his mouth, touching his eyes. "Yes."

"Then there shouldn't be any problem."

He paused, looking down at her, and smiled again. "Are you always so witty?"

Shelly chuckled, experiencing a rush of pleasure at her ability to make him smile. "Only when I try to be. Come on, loosen up. It's Christmas."

"I've got a meeting to attend. Just because it happens to fall close to a holiday doesn't make a bit of difference."

"Yeah, but just think, once you're through, you can hurry home and spend the holidays with your family."

"Right."

The jagged edge of his clipped reply was revealing. She wondered if he had a family.

As they deposited their luggage in the trunk of the rented Taurus, she had the opportunity to study him. The proud, withdrawn look revealed little of his thoughts; there was an air of independence about him. Even after their minimal conversation, she realized that he possessed a keen and agile mind. He was a man of contrasts—pensive yet decisive, his highly organized façade covering his sense of humor.

The young man at the rental desk had given Slade a map of the city and highlighted the route to the nearest freeway entrance ramp, apologizing for the fact that the car's built-in GPS was broken. Since that explained why the car was available at all, neither she nor Slade had objected.

Now Slade pulled the map from his pocket and handed it to her. "Are you ready?"

"Forward, James," she teased, climbing into the passenger seat and rubbing her bare hands together to generate some warmth. When she'd left San Francisco that morning, she hadn't dressed for snow.

With a turn of the key, Slade started the engine and adjusted the heater. "You'll be warm in a minute."

Shelly nodded, burying her hands in her jacket pockets. "You know, if it gets much colder, we might get snow before we reach Seattle."

"Very funny," he muttered dryly, snapping his seat belt into place. Hands gripping the wheel, he hesitated. "Do you want to call your husband before we hit the road and I need you to navigate?"

"I'm visiting my dad," she corrected him. "I'm not married. And no. If I told him what we're doing, he'd only worry."

Slade shifted gears, and they pulled onto the road.

"Do you want to contact...your wife?"

"I'm not married, either."

"Oh." She prayed that her tone wouldn't reveal her satisfaction at the information. It wasn't often that she found herself so fascinated by a man. The crazy part was that she wasn't entirely sure she liked him, but he certainly attracted her.

"I'm engaged," he added.

"Oh." She swallowed convulsively. So much for that. "When's the wedding?"

The windshield wipers hummed ominously. "In approximately two years."

Shelly nearly choked in an effort to hide her shock.

"Margaret and I have professional and financial goals we hope to accomplish before we marry." He drove with his back suddenly stiff, his expression turning chilly. "Margaret feels we should save fifty thousand dollars before we think about marriage, and I agree. We both feel that having a firm financial foundation is the basis for a lasting marriage."

"I can't imagine waiting two years to marry the man I loved."

"But then you're entirely different from Margaret."

As far as Shelly was concerned, that was the nicest thing anyone had said to her all day. "We do agree on one thing, though. I feel a marriage should last forever." But for her, love had to be more spontaneous and far less calculated. "My parents had a marvelous marriage," she said, filling the silence. "I only hope that when I marry, my own will be as happy." She went on to explain that her parents had met one Christmas and been married less than two months later on Valentine's Day. Their marriage, she told him with a sad smile, had been blessed with love and happiness for nearly twenty-seven years before her mother's unexpected death. It took great restraint for her not to mention that her parents had barely had twenty dollars between them when they'd taken their vows. At the time her father had been studying veterinary medicine, with only two years of vet school behind him. They'd managed without a huge bank balance.

From the tight lines around his mouth, she could tell that Slade found the whole story trite.

"Is your sweet tale of romance supposed to touch my heart?"

Stung, she straightened and looked out the side window at the snow-covered trees that lined the side of Interstate 5. "No. I was just trying to find out if you had one."

"Karate mouth strikes again," he mumbled.

"Karate mouth?" She was too stunned by his unexpected display of wit to do anything more than repeat his statement.

"You have the quickest comeback of anyone I know." But he said it with a small smile, and admiration flashed unchecked in his gaze before he turned his attention back to the freeway.

Shelly was interested in learning more about Margaret, so she steered the conversation away from herself. "I imagine you're anxious to get back to spend Christmas with Margaret." She regretted her earlier judgmental attitude toward Slade. He had good reason for wanting his meeting over with.

"Margaret's visiting an aunt in Arizona over the holidays. She left a couple of days ago."

"So you won't be together." The more she heard about

his fiancée, the more curious she was about a woman who actively wanted to wait two years for marriage. "Did she give you your Christmas gift before she left?" The type of gift one gave was always telling, she felt.

He hesitated. "Margaret and I agreed to forgo giving gifts this year."

"No presents? That's terrible."

"I told you. We have financial goals," he growled irritably. "Wasting money on trivialities simply deters us from our two-year plan. Christmas gifts aren't going to advance our desires."

At the moment Shelly sincerely doubted that good ol' Margaret and Slade *had* "desires."

"I bet she's just saying she doesn't want a gift," Shelly said. "She's probably secretly hoping you'll break down and buy her something. It doesn't have to be something big. Any woman appreciates roses."

Slade gave an expressive shrug. "I thought flowers would be a nice touch myself, but she claims they make her sneeze. Besides, roses at Christmas are ridiculously expensive. A total waste of money, when you think about it."

"Total," Shelly echoed under her breath. She was beginning to get a clearer and far less flattering picture of Slade Garner and his insanely-practical fiancée.

"Did you say something?" A hint of challenge echoed in his cool tone.

"Not really." Leaning forward, she fiddled with the radio, trying to find some decent music. "What's Margaret do, by the way?"

"She's a systems analyst."

Shelly arched both eyebrows in mute comment. That was exactly the type of occupation she would have expected from a nuts-and-bolts person like Margaret. "What about children?"

"What about them?"

She realized that she was prying, but she couldn't help herself. "Are you planning a family?"

"Of course. We're hoping that Margaret can schedule a leave of absence in eight years."

"Eight years?" She looked at him assessingly. "You'll be nearly thirty!" The exclamation burst from her lips before she could hold it back.

"Thirty-one, actually. Do you disapprove of that, too?"

She swallowed uncomfortably and paid an inordinate amount of attention to the radio, frustrated because she couldn't find a single radio station. "I apologize. I didn't mean to sound so judgmental. It's just that—"

"It's just that you've never been goal oriented."

"But I have," she argued. "I've always wanted to be a court reporter. It's a fascinating job."

"I imagine that you're good at anything you put your mind to."

The unexpected compliment caught her completely off guard. "What a nice thing to say."

"If you put your mind to it, you might figure out why you can't get the radio working."

Her gaze flickered automatically from Slade to the dial. Before she could comment, he reached over and pushed a button. "It's a bit difficult to hear anything when the radio isn't turned on."

"Right." She'd been too preoccupied with asking about Margaret to notice. Color flooded into her cheeks at her own stupidity. Slade flustered her as no man had in a long time. She had the feeling that, in a battle of words, he would parry her barbs as expertly as a professional swordsman.

She found a station playing Christmas carols, and music filled the car. Warm and snug, she leaned back against the headrest and hummed along, gazing at the falling flakes.

"With the snow and all, it really feels like Christmas," she murmured, fearing more questions would destroy the tranquil mood.

"It's caused nothing but problems."

"I suppose, but it's so lovely."

"Of course *you* think it's lovely. You're sitting in a warm chauffeur-driven car, listening to 'Silent Night.'"

"Grumble, grumble, grumble," she tossed back lightly. "Bah, humbug!"

"Bah, humbug," he echoed, and then, to her astonishment, he laughed.

The sound of it was rich and full, and she couldn't stop herself from laughing with him. When the next song was a Bing Crosby Christmas favorite, she sang along. Soon Slade's deep baritone joined her clear soprano in sweet harmony. The lyrics spoke of dreaming, and her mind conjured up her own longings. Despite his rough edges, she found herself comfortable with this man, when she'd expected to find a dozen reasons to dislike him. Instead, she'd discovered that she was attracted to someone who was engaged to another woman. A man whose responses showed he was intensely loyal. That was the usual way her life ran. She was attracted to a man she couldn't have, experiencing feelings that would lead nowhere. She wasn't even entirely sure that her insights about him were on base. As uncharitable as it sounded, she might be overestimating his appeal simply because she considered him too good for someone like Margaret.

Disgusted with herself, she closed her eyes and rested her head against the window. The only sounds were the soft melodies playing on the radio and the discordant swish of the windshield wipers. Occasionally a gust of wind would cause the car to veer slightly. She decided to ignore her troublesome feelings and lost herself in thoughts of Christmas.

The next thing she knew, she was being shaken by a gentle hand on her shoulder. "Shelly."

With a start she bolted upright. "What's wrong?"

Slade had pulled over to the shoulder of the freeway. The snow was so thick that she couldn't see two feet in front of her.

"I don't think we can go any further," he announced.

Three

"We can't stay *here*," Shelly insisted, looking at their precarious position beside the road. Snow was whirling in every direction. The ferocity of the storm shocked her as it whipped and howled around them. While she'd slept, the storm had worsened drastically. She found it little short of amazing that Slade had been able to steer the car at all.

"Do you have any other suggestions?" he asked, and breathed out sharply.

He was angry, but his irritation wasn't directed at her. Wearily she lifted the hair from her neck. "No, I guess I don't."

Silence seeped around them as Slade turned off the engine. Gone was the soothing sound of Christmas music, the hum of the engine and the rhythmic swish of the wipers. Together they sat waiting for nature's fury to lessen so they could get going again. Staring out at the surrounding area between bursts of wind and snow, she guessed that they weren't far from Castle Rock and Mount St. Helens.

After ten minutes of uneasiness, she decided to be the first to break the gloom. "Are you hungry?" She stared at the passive, unyielding face beside her as she spoke.

"No."

"I am."

"Have some of that bread." He cocked his head toward the back seat, where she'd stuck the huge loaves of sourdough.

"I couldn't eat Dad's bread. He'd never forgive me."

"He'd never forgive you if you starved to death, either."

Glancing down at her pudgy thighs, Shelly sadly shook her head. "There's no chance of that."

"What makes you say that? You're not fat. In fact, I'd say you were just about perfect."

"Me? Perfect?" A burst of embarrassed laughter slid from her throat. Reaching for her purse, she removed her wallet.

"What are you doing?"

"I'm going to pay you for saying that."

Slade chuckled. "What makes you think you're overweight?"

"You mean aside from the fat all over my body?"

"I'm serious."

She shrugged. "I don't know. I just feel chubby. Since leaving home, I don't get enough exercise. I couldn't very well bring Sampson with me when I moved to San Francisco."

"Sampson?"

"My horse. I used to ride him every day."

"If you've gained any weight, it's in all the right places."

His gaze fell to her lips, and her senses churned in quivering awareness. He stared into her dark eyes and blinked, as if not believing what he saw. For her part, she studied him with open curiosity. His eyes were smoky dark, his face blunt and sensual. His brow was creased, as though he was giving the moment grave consideration. Thick eyebrows arched heavily over his eyes.

Abruptly he pulled his gaze away and leaned forward to start the engine. The accumulated snow on the windshield was brushed aside with a flip of the wiper switch. "Isn't that a McDonald's up ahead?"

Shelly squinted to catch a glimpse of the world-famous golden arches through a momentary break in the storm. "Hey, I think it is."

"The exit can't be far, then."

"Do you think we can make it?"

"I think we'd better," he mumbled.

She understood. The car had become their private cocoon, unexpectedly intimate and far too tempting. Under normal circumstances they wouldn't have given each other more than a passing glance. What was happening now was magical, and far more exhilarating than the real life that seemed very far away right now.

With the wipers beating furiously against the window, Slade inched the car toward the exit, which proved to be less than a half mile away.

Slowly they crawled down the side road that paralleled the freeway. With some difficulty he was able to find a place to park in the restaurant lot. Shelly sighed with relief. This was the worst storm she could remember. Wrapping her coat securely around her, she reached for her purse.

"You ready?" she blurted out, opening her door.

"Anytime."

Hurriedly he joined her, tightly grasping her elbow as they stepped together toward the entrance. Pausing just inside the door to stamp the snow from their shoes, they glanced up to note that several other travelers were stranded there, as well.

They ordered hamburgers and coffee, and sat down by the window.

"How long do you think we'll be here?" she asked, not really expecting an answer. She needed reassurance more than anything. This Christmas holiday hadn't started out on the right foot. But of one thing she was confident: their plane hadn't left Portland yet.

"Your guess is as good as mine."

"I'll say two hours, then," she murmured, taking a bite of her burger.

"Why two hours?"

"I don't know. It sounds reasonable. If I thought it would be longer than that I might start to panic. But, if worse comes to worst, I can think of less desirable places to spend Christmas. At least we won't starve."

He muttered something unintelligible under his breath and continued eating. When he finished, he excused himself and returned to the car for his briefcase.

She bought two more cups of coffee and propped her feet on the seat opposite her. Taking the latest issue of *Mad* from her purse, she was absorbed in the magazine by the time he returned. Her gaze dared him to comment on her reading material. Her love of *Mad* was a long-standing joke between her and her father. He even read each issue himself so he could tease her about the contents. Since moving, she'd fallen behind by several issues and wanted to be prepared when she saw her dad again. She didn't expect Slade to understand her tastes.

He gave her little more than a glance before reclaiming his seat and briskly opening the *Wall Street Journal*.

Their reading choices said a lot about them, she realized. Rarely had two people been less alike. A lump grew in her throat. She liked Slade. He was the type of man she would willingly give up *Mad* for.

An hour later she contentedly set the magazine aside and reached in her purse for the romance novel she kept tucked away. It wasn't often that she was so at ease with a man. She didn't feel the overwhelming urge to keep a conversation going or fill the silence with chatter. They were comfortable together.

Without a word she went to the counter and bought a large order of fries and placed it in the middle of the table. Now and then, her eyes never leaving the printed page, she blindly reached for a fry. Once her groping hand bumped another, and her startled gaze collided with Slade's.

"Sorry," he muttered.

"Don't be. They're for us both."

"They get to be addictive, don't they?"

"Sort of like reading the *Wall Street Journal?*"

"I wondered if you'd comment on that."

She laughed. "I was expecting you to mention *my* choice."

"*Mad* is exactly what I'd expect from you." He said it in such a way that she couldn't possibly be offended.

"At least we agree on one thing."

He raised his thick brows in question.

"The fries."

"Right." Lifting one, he held it out for her.

She leaned toward him and captured the fry in her mouth. The gesture was oddly intimate, and her smile faded as her gaze met his. It was happening again. That heart-pounding, room-fading-away, shallow-breathing syndrome. Obviously this…feeling…had something to do with the weather. Maybe she could blame it on the season of love and goodwill toward all mankind. Apparently she was overly endowed with benevolence this Christmas. Given the sensations she was already experiencing, heaven only knew what would happen if she spied some mistletoe.

Slade raked his hand through his well-groomed hair, mussing it. Quickly he diverted his gaze out the window. "It looks like it might be letting up a little."

"Yes, it does," she agreed without so much as checking the weather. The French fries seemed to demand her full attention.

"I suppose we should think about heading out."

"I suppose." A glance at her watch confirmed that it was well into the afternoon. "I'm sorry about your appointment."

He looked at her blankly for a moment. "Oh, that. I knew when we left that there was little likelihood I'd be able to make it in time today. Luckily I've already made arrangements to meet tomorrow morning."

"It's been an enjoyable break."

"Very," he agreed.

"Do you think we'll have any more problems?"

"We could, but there are enough businesses along the way that we don't need to worry about getting stranded."

"In other words, we could hit every fast-food spot between here and Seattle."

He responded with a soft chuckle. "Right."

"Well, in that case, bring on the French fries."

By the time they were back on the freeway, Shelly saw that the storm had indeed lessened, though it was far from over. And when the radio issued a weather update that called for more snow, Slade groaned.

"You could always spend Christmas with me and Dad," she offered, broaching the subject carefully. "We'd like to have you. Honest."

He tossed her a disbelieving glare. "You don't mean that."

"Of course I do."

"But I'm a stranger."

"I've shared French fries with you. It's been a long time since I've been that intimate with a man. In fact, it would be best if you didn't mention it to my dad. He might be inclined to reach for his shotgun."

It took a minute for Slade to understand the implication. "A shotgun wedding?"

"I *am* getting on in years. Dad would like to see me married off and producing grandchildren. My brothers have been lax in that department." For the moment she'd forgotten about Margaret. When she remembered, she felt her exhilaration rush out of her with all the force of a deflating balloon. "Don't worry," she was quick to add. "All you need to do is tell Dad about your fiancée and he'll let you off the hook." Somehow she managed to keep her voice cheerful.

"It's a good thing I didn't take a bite of your hamburger."

"Are you kidding? That would have put me directly into your last will and testament."

"I was afraid of that," he said, laughing good-naturedly.

Once again she noticed how rich and deep the sound

of his laughter was. It had the most overwhelming effect on her. She discovered that, when he laughed, nothing could keep her spirits down.

Their progress was hampered by the still-swirling snow, and finally their forward movement became little more than a crawl. She didn't mind. They chatted, joked and sang along with the radio. She discovered that she enjoyed his wit. Although a bit dry, under that gruff, serious exterior lay an interesting man with a warm but subtle sense of humor. Given any other set of circumstances, she would have loved to get to know Slade Garner better.

"What'd you buy your dad for Christmas?"

The question came so unexpectedly that it took her a moment to realize that he was speaking to her.

"Are you concerned that I have soup in my bag?"

He scowled, momentarily puzzled. "Ah, to go with the bread. No, I was just curious."

"First I got him a box of his favorite chocolate-covered cherries."

"I should have known it'd be food."

"That's not all," she countered a bit testily. "We exchange the normal father-daughter gifts. You know. Things like stirrup irons, bridles and horse blankets. That's what Dad got me last Christmas."

He cleared his throat. "Just the usual items every father buys his daughter. What about this year?"

"Since Sampson and I aren't even living in the same state, I imagine he'll resort to the old standbys, like towels and sheets for my apartment." She was half hoping that, at the mention of her place in San Francisco, Slade would turn the conversation in that direction and ask her something about herself. He didn't, and she was hard-pressed to hide her disappointment.

"What about you?" she asked into the silence.

"Me?" His gaze flickered momentarily from the road.

"What did you buy your family?"

He gave her an uncomfortable look. "Well, actually, I didn't. It seemed simpler this year just to send them money."

"I see." She knew that was perfectly acceptable in some cases, but it sounded so cold and uncaring for a son to resort to a gift of money. Undoubtedly, once he and Margaret were married, they would shop together for something appropriate.

"I wish now that I hadn't. I think my parents would have enjoyed fresh sourdough bread and chocolate-covered cherries." He hesitated for an instant. "I'm not as confident about the stirrups and horse blankets, however."

As they neared Tacoma, Shelly was surprised at how

heavy the traffic had gotten. The closer they came to Maple Valley, the more anxious she became.

"My exit isn't far," she told him, growing impatient. "Good grief, you would expect people to stay off the roads in weather like this."

"Exactly," he agreed without hesitation.

It wasn't until she heard the soft timbre of his chuckle that she realized he was teasing her. "You know what I mean."

He didn't answer as he edged the car ahead. Already the night was pitch-dark. Snow continued to fall with astonishing vigor. She wondered when it would stop. She was concerned about Slade driving alone from Maple Valley to Seattle.

"Maybe I should phone my dad," she suggested, momentarily forgetting that her cell was dead.

"Why?"

"That way he could come and pick me up, and you wouldn't—"

"I agreed to deliver you to Maple Creek, and I intend to do exactly that."

"Maple Valley," she corrected.

"Wherever. A deal is a deal. Right?"

A rush of pleasure assaulted her vulnerable heart. Slade wasn't any more eager to put an end to their adventure than she was.

"It's the next exit," she informed him, giving him the directions to the ten-acre spread on the outskirts of town. Taking out a pen and paper, she drew a detailed map for him so he wouldn't get lost on the return trip to the freeway. Under the cover of night, there was little to distinguish one road from another, and he could easily become confused.

Sitting straighter, she excitedly pointed to her left. "Turn here."

Apparently in preparation for his departure for the airport, her father had plowed the snow from the long driveway.

The headlights cut into the night, revealing the long, sprawling ranch house that had been Shelly's childhood home. A tall figure appeared at the window, and almost immediately the front door opened.

Slade had barely put the car into Park when Shelly threw open the door.

"Shortcake!"

"Dad." Disregarding the snow and wind, she flew into his arms.

"You little… Why didn't you tell me you were coming by car?"

"We rented it." Remembering Slade, she looped an arm around her father's waist. "Dad, I'd like you to meet Slade Garner."

Her father stepped forward. "Don Griffin," he said, and extended his hand. "So you're Shelly's surprise. Welcome to our home. I'd say it was about time my daughter brought a young man home for her father to meet."

Four

Slade extended his hand to Shelly's father and grinned. "I believe you've got me confused with sourdough bread."

"Sourdough bread?"

"Dad, Slade and I met this morning on the plane." Shelly's cheeks brightened in a self-conscious pink flush.

"When it looked like the flight wasn't going to make it to Seattle, we rented the car," Slade explained further.

A curious glint darkened Don Griffin's deep blue eyes as he glanced briefly from his daughter to Slade and ran a hand through is thick thatch of dark hair. "It's a good thing you did. The last time I phoned the airline, I learned your plane still hadn't left Portland."

"Slade has an important meeting first thing tomorrow." Her eyes were telling him that she was ready to make the break. She could say goodbye and wish him every happiness. Their time together had been too short for any regrets. Hadn't it?

"There's no need for us to stand out here in the cold discussing your itinerary," her father inserted and motioned toward the warm lights of the house.

Slade hesitated. "I should be getting into Seattle."

"Come in for some coffee first," her father invited.

"Shelly?" Slade sought her approval. The unasked question in his eyes pinned her gaze.

"I wish you would." *Fool!* her mind cried out. It would be better to sever the relationship quickly, sharply and without delay, before he had the opportunity to touch her tender heart. But her heart refused to listen to her mind.

"For that matter," her father continued, seemingly oblivious to the undercurrents between Slade and Shelly, "stay for dinner."

"I couldn't. Really." Slade made a show of glancing at his wristwatch.

"We insist," Shelly said quickly. "After hauling this bread from here to kingdom come, the least I can offer you is a share of it."

To her astonishment Slade grinned, his dark eyes crinkling at the edges. The smile was both spontaneous and personal—a reminder of the joke between them. "All right," he agreed.

"That settles it, then." Don grinned and moved to the rear of the car while Slade extracted Shelly's suitcase and the huge tote bag. "What's all this?"

"Presents," she said.

"For me?"

"Well, who else would I be bringing gifts for?"

"A man. It's time you started thinking about a husband."

"Dad!" If her cheeks had been bright pink previously, now the color deepened into fire-engine red. In order to minimize further embarrassment, she returned to the car and rescued the bread. Her father carried the gifts inside, while Slade brought up the rear with her carry-on.

The house contained all the warmth and welcome that she always associated with home. She paused in just inside the open doorway, her gaze skimming over the crackling fireplace and the large array of family photos that decorated the mantel. Ol' Dan, their thirteen-year-old Labrador, slept on the braided rug and did little more than raise his head when Don and Slade entered the house. But on seeing Shelly, the elderly dog got slowly to his feet and with difficulty ambled to her side, tail wagging. She set the bread aside and fell to her knees.

"How's my loyal mangy mutt?" she asked, affectionately ruffling his ears and hugging him. "You keeping Dad company these days?"

"Yeah, but he's doing a poor job of it," her father complained loudly. "Ol' Dan still can't play a decent game of chess."

"Do *you* play?" Slade asked her father as his gaze scanned the living room for a board.

"Forty years or more. What about you?"

"Now and again."

"Could I interest you in a match?"

Slade was already unbuttoning his overcoat. "I'd enjoy that, sir."

"Call me Don, everyone does."

"Right, Don."

Within a minute the chessboard was out and set up on the coffee table, while the two men sat opposite each other on matching ottomans.

Suspecting that the contest could last a while, she checked the prime rib roasting in the oven and added large potatoes, wrapping each in aluminum foil. The refrigerator contained a fresh green salad and her favorite cherry pie from the local bakery. There were also some carrots in the vegetable drawer; she snatched a couple and put them in her pocket.

After grabbing her denim jacket with its thick wool padding from the peg on the back porch and slipping into her cowboy boots, she made her way out to the barn.

The scent of hay and horses greeted her, and she

paused, taking in the rich, earthy odors. "Howdy, Sampson," she said, greeting her favorite horse first.

The sleek black horse whinnied a welcome as she approached the stall, then accepted the proffered carrot without pause.

"Have you missed me, boy?"

Pokey, an Appaloosa mare, stuck her head out of her stall, seeking a treat, too. Laughing, Shelly pulled another carrot from her pocket. Midnight, her father's horse and Sampson's sire, stamped his foot, and she made her way down to his stall.

After stroking his sleek neck, she took out the brushes and returned to Sampson. "I suppose Dad's letting you get fat and lazy now that I'm not around to work you." She glided a brush down his muscled flank. "All right, I'll admit it. Living in San Francisco has made *me* fat and lazy, too. I haven't gained any weight, but I feel flabby. I suppose I could take up jogging, but it's foggy and rainy and—"

"Shelly?"

Slade was standing just inside the barn door, looking a bit uneasy. "Do you always carry on conversations with your horse?"

"Sure. I've talked out many a frustration with Sampson. Isn't that right, boy?"

Slade gave a startled blink when the horse answered

with a loud snort and a toss of his head, as if agreeing with her.

"Come in and meet my favorite male," she invited, opening the stall door.

Hands buried deep in his pockets, Slade shook his head. "No, thanks."

"You don't like horses?"

"Not exactly."

Having lived all her life around animals, she had trouble understanding his reticence. "Why not?"

"The last time I was this close to a horse was when I was ten and at summer camp."

"Sampson won't bite you."

"It's not his mouth I'm worried about."

"He's harmless."

"So is flying."

Surprised, Shelly dropped her hand from Sampson's hindquarters.

Slade strolled over to the stall, a grin lifting the edges of his mouth. "From the look on your face when we landed, one would assume that your will alone was holding up the plane."

"It was!"

He chuckled and tentatively reached out to rub Sampson's ebony forehead.

She went back to grooming the horse. "Is your chess match over already?"

"I should have warned your father. I was on the university chess team."

Now it was her turn to look amused. She paused in midstroke. "Did you wound Dad's ego?"

"I might have, but he's regrouping now. I came out here because I wanted to have a look at the famous Sampson before I headed for Seattle."

"Sampson's honored to make your acquaintance." *I am, too,* her heart echoed.

Slade took a step in retreat. "I guess I'll get back to the house. No doubt your dad's got the board set for a rematch."

"Be gentle with him," she called out, trying to hide a saucy grin. Her father wasn't an amateur when it came to the game. He'd been a member of the local chess club for years, and she wondered just what his strategy was tonight. Donald Griffin seldom lost at any game.

An hour later she stamped the snow from her boots and entered the kitchen through the back door. She shed the thick coat and hung it back on its peg, then went to check the roast and the baked potatoes. Both were done to perfection, and she turned off the oven.

Seeing that her father and Slade were absorbed in their game, she stepped up behind her father and slipped her arms around his neck, resting her chin on the top of his head.

"Dinner's ready," she murmured, not wanting to break his concentration.

"In a minute," he grumbled.

Slade moved his bishop, leaving his hand on the piece for a couple of seconds. Seemingly pleased, he released the piece and relaxed. As though sensing her gaze on him, he lifted his incredibly dark eyes, which locked with hers. They stared at each other for long, uninterrupted moments. She felt her heart lurch as she basked in the warmth of his look. She wanted to hold on to this moment, forget San Francisco, Margaret, the snowstorm. It felt paramount that she capture this magic with both hands and hold on to it forever.

"It's your move." Don's words cut into the stillness.

"Pardon?" Abruptly Slade dropped his eyes to the chessboard.

"It's your move," her father repeated.

"Of course." Slade studied the board and moved a pawn.

Don scowled. "I hadn't counted on your doing that."

"Hey, you two, didn't you hear me? Dinner's ready." She was shocked at how normal and unaffected her voice sounded.

Slade got to his feet. "Shall we consider it a draw, then?"

"I guess we better, but I demand a rematch someday."

Shelly's throat constricted. There wouldn't be another day for her and Slade. They were two strangers who had briefly touched each other's lives. Ships passing in the night and all the other clichés she had never expected would happen to her. But somehow she had the feeling that she would never be the same again. Surely she wouldn't be so swift to judge another man. Slade had taught her that, and she would always be grateful.

The three of them chatted easily during dinner, and Shelly learned things about Slade that she hadn't thought to ask. He was a salesman, specializing in intricate software programs, and was meeting with a Seattle-based company, hoping to agree on the first steps of a possible distribution agreement. It was little wonder that he'd considered his meeting so important. It was. And although he hadn't mentioned it specifically, she was acutely aware that if his meeting was successful, he would be that much closer to achieving his financial and professional goals—and that much closer to marrying coldly practical Margaret.

Shelly was clearing the dishes from the table when Slade set his napkin aside and rose. "I don't remember when I've enjoyed a meal more, especially the sour-dough bread."

"A man gets the feel of a kitchen sooner or later," Don said with a crusty chuckle. "It took me a whole year to learn how to turn on the oven."

"That's the truth," she added, sharing a smile with her father. "He thought it was easier to use the microwave. The problem was, he couldn't quite get the hang of that, either. Everything came out the texture of beef jerky."

"We survived," her father grumbled, affectionately looping an arm around Shelly's waist. The first eighteen months after her mother's death had been the most difficult for the family, but life went on, and almost against their wills they'd adjusted.

Slade paused in the living room to stare out the window. "I can't remember it ever snowing this much in the Pacific Northwest."

"Rarely," Don agreed. "It's been three winters since we've had any snow at all. I'll admit this is a pleasant surprise."

"How long will it be before the snowplows are out?"

"Snow*plow*, you mean?" Don said with a gruff laugh. "King County is lucky if they have more than a handful. There isn't that much call for them." He walked to the picture window and held back the draperies with one hand. "You know, it might not be a bad idea if you stayed the night and left first thing in the morning."

Slade hesitated. "I don't know. If I miss this meeting, it'll mean having to wait over the Christmas holiday to reschedule."

"You'll have a better chance of making it safely to Seattle in the morning. The roads tonight are going to be treacherous."

Slade slowly expelled his breath. "I have the distinct feeling you may be right. Without any streetlights, Lord knows where I'd end up."

"I believe you'd be wise to delay your drive. Besides, that will give us time for another game."

Slade's gaze shifted to Shelly and softened. "Right," he concurred.

The two men were up until well past midnight, engrossed in one chess match after another. After watching a few games, Shelly decided to say good-night and go to bed.

Half an hour later Shelly lay in her bed in her darkened room, dreading the approach of morning. In some ways it would have been easier if Slade had left immediately after dropping her off. And in other ways it was far better that he'd stayed.

She fell asleep with the bright red numbers of the

clock insidiously counting down the minutes to six o'clock when Slade would be leaving. There was nothing she could do to hold back time.

Before even being aware that she'd fallen asleep, she was startled into wakefulness by the discordant drone of the alarm.

Tossing aside the covers, she automatically reached for the thick housecoat she kept at her father's. Pausing only long enough to run a comb through her hair and brush her teeth, she rushed into the living room.

Slade was already dressed and holding a cup of coffee. "I guess it's time to say goodbye."

Five

Shelly ran a hand over her weary eyes and blinked. "You're right," she murmured, forcing a smile. "The time has come."

"Shelly—"

"Listen—"

"You first," Slade said, and gestured toward her with his open hand.

Dropping her gaze, she shrugged one shoulder. "It's nothing, really. I just wanted to wish you and Margaret every happiness."

His gaze softened, and she wondered if he knew what it had cost her to murmur those few words. She did wish him happiness, but she was convinced that he wouldn't find it with a cold fish like Margaret. Forcefully she directed her gaze across the room. For all her good intentions, she was doing it again—judging someone else. And she hadn't even met Margaret.

When she turned back his eyes delved into hers. "Thank you."

"You wanted to say something?" she prompted softly.

He hesitated. "Be happy, Shelly."

A knot formed in her throat as she nodded. He was telling her goodbye, *really* goodbye. He wouldn't see her again, because it would be too dangerous for them both. Their lives were already plotted, their courses set. And whatever it was that they'd shared so briefly, it wasn't meant to be anything more than a passing fancy.

The front door opened and her father entered, brushing the snow from his pant legs. A burst of frigid air accompanied him, and she shivered.

"As far as I can see you shouldn't have a problem," Don said to Slade. "We've got maybe seven to ten inches of snow, but there're plenty of tire tracks on the road. Just follow those."

Unable to listen anymore, she headed into the kitchen and poured herself a cup of hot black coffee. Clasping the mug with both hands, she braced her hip against the counter and closed her eyes. Whatever Slade and her father were saying to each other didn't matter to her. She was safer in the kitchen, where she wouldn't be forced to watch him leave. The only sound that registered in her mind was the clicking of the front door opening and closing.

Slade had left. He was gone from the house. Gone from her life. Gone forever. She refused to mope. He'd touched her heart, and she should be glad. For a long time she'd begun to wonder if there was something physically wrong with her because she couldn't respond to a man. Slade hadn't so much as kissed her, but she'd experienced a closeness to him that she hadn't felt with all the men she'd dated in San Francisco. Without even realizing it, he had granted her the priceless gift of expectancy. If he was capable of stirring her restless heart, then so would another.

Humming softly, she set a skillet on the burner and laid thick slices of bacon across it. This was the day before Christmas, and it promised to be a full one. She couldn't be sad or filled with regrets when she was surrounded by everything she held dear.

The door opened again, and her father called cheerfully, "Well, he's off."

"Good." She hoped her tone didn't give away her feelings.

"He's an interesting man. I wouldn't mind having someone like him for a son-in-law." He entered the kitchen and reached for the coffeepot.

"He's engaged."

He sighed, and there was a hint of censure in his voice when he spoke. "That figures. The good ones always seem to be spoken for."

"It doesn't matter. We're about as different as any two people can be."

"That's not always bad, you know. Couples often complement each other that way. Your mother was the shy one, whereas I was far more outgoing. Our lives would have been havoc if we'd had identical personalities."

Silently Shelly agreed, but to admit as much would reveal more than she wanted to. "I suppose," she murmured softly, and turned over the sizzling slices of bacon.

A few minutes later she was sliding the eggs easily from the hot grease onto plates when there was a loud pounding on the front door.

Her gaze rose instantly and met her father's.

"Slade," they said simultaneously.

Her father rushed to answer the door, and a breathless Slade stumbled into the house. She turned off the stove and hurried out to meet him.

"Are you all right?" Her voice was laced with concern. Heart pounding, she looked him over for any obvious signs of injury.

"I'm fine. I'm just out of breath. That was quite a hike."

"How far'd you get?" Don asked.

"A mile at the most. I was gathering speed to make it to the top of an incline when the wheels skidded on a patch of ice. The car, unfortunately, is in a ditch."

"What about your meeting?" Now that she'd determined that he was unscathed, her first concern was the appointment that he considered so important to his future.

"I don't know."

"Dad and I could take you into town," she offered.

"No. If I couldn't make it, you won't be able to, either."

"But you said this meeting is vital."

"It's not important enough to risk your getting hurt."

"Not to mention my truck has been acting up, so I took it in for servicing," her father said, then smiled. "But there's always the tractor."

"Dad! You'll be lucky if the old engine so much as coughs. You haven't used that antique in years." As far as she knew, it was collecting dust in the back of the barn.

"It's worth a try," her father argued, looking to Slade. "At least we can pull your car out of the ditch."

"I'll contact the county road department and find out how long it'll be before the plows come this way," Shelly said. She didn't hold much hope for the tractor, but if she could convince the county how important it was to clear the roads near their place, Slade might be able to make his meeting somehow.

Two hours later, Shelly was dressed in dark cords and a thick cable-knit sweater the color of winter wheat as she paced the living room carpet. Every few minutes she paused to glance out the large front window for signs of either her father or Slade. Through some miracle they'd managed to fire up the tractor, but how much they could accomplish with the old machine was pure conjecture. If they were able to rescue Slade's car from the ditch, then there was always the possibility of towing it up the incline so he could try again to make it into the city.

The sound of a car pulling into the driveway captured her attention, and she rushed onto the front porch just as Slade was easing the Taurus to a stop. He climbed out of the vehicle.

"I called the county. The road crew will try to make it out this way before nightfall," she told him, rubbing her palms together to ward off the chill. "I'm sorry, Slade, it's the best they could do."

"Don't worry." His gaze caressed her. "It's not your fault."

"But I can't help feeling that it is," she said, following him into the house. "I was the one who insisted you bring me here."

"Shelly." He cupped her shoulder with a warm hand. "Stop blaming yourself. I'll contact Walt Bauer, the man I was planning to see. He'll understand. It's possible he didn't make it to the office, either."

Granting him the privacy he needed to make his call, she donned her coat and walked to the end of the driveway to see if she could locate her father. Only a couple of minutes passed before she saw him proudly steering the tractor, his back and head held regally, like a benevolent king surveying all he owned.

Laughing, she waved.

He pulled to a stop alongside her. "What's so funny?"

"I can't believe you, sitting on top of a 1948 Harvester like you own the world."

"Don't be silly, serf," he teased.

"We've got a bit of a problem, you know." She realized she shouldn't feel guilty about Slade, but she did.

"If you mean Slade, we talked about this unexpected delay. It might not be as bad as it looks. To his way of thinking, it's best not to appear overeager with this business anyway. A delay may be just the thing to get the other company thinking."

It would be just like Slade to say something like that, she thought. "Maybe."

"At any rate, it won't do him any good to stew about it now. He's stuck with us until the snowplows clear the roads. No one's going to make it to the freeway unless they have a four-wheel drive. It's impossible out there."

"But, Dad, I feel terrible."

"Don't. If Slade's not concerned, then you shouldn't be. Besides, I've got a job for you two."

Shelly didn't like the sound of that. "What?"

"We aren't going to be able to go out and buy a Christmas tree."

She hadn't thought of that. "We'll survive without one." But Christmas wouldn't be the same.

"There's no need to. Not when we've got a good ten acres of fir and pine. I want the two of you to go out and chop one down like we used to do in the good old days."

It didn't take much to realize her father's game. He was looking for excuses to get her together with Slade.

"What's this, an extra Christmas present?" she teased.

"Nonsense. Being out in the cold would only irritate my rheumatism."

"What rheumatism?"

"The one in my old bones."

She hesitated. "What did Slade have to say about this?"

"He's agreeable."

"He is?"

"Think about it, Shortcake. He's stuck here. He wants to make the best of the situation."

It wasn't until they were back at the house and Slade had changed into borrowed jeans and a flannel shirt, along with a pair of heavy boots, that she truly believed he'd fallen in with her father's scheme.

"You don't have to do this, you know," she told him on the way to the barn.

"Did you think I was going to let you traipse into the woods alone?"

"I could."

"No doubt, but there isn't any reason why you *should*. Not when I'm here."

She brought out the old sled from a storage room in the rear of the barn, wiping away the thin layer of dust with her gloves.

He located a saw, and she eyed him warily.

"What's wrong now?"

"The saw."

"What's the matter with it?" He tested the sharpness by carefully running his thumb over the jagged teeth and raised questioning eyes to her.

"Nothing. If we use that rusty old thing, we shouldn't have any trouble bringing home a good-sized rhododendron."

"I wasn't planning to chop down a California redwood."

"But I want something a bit larger than a poinsettia."
She grabbed an axe and headed for the door.

He paused, then followed her out of the barn. "Are
you always this difficult to get along with?"

Dragging the sled along behind her in the snow, she
turned and said, "There's nothing wrong with me. It's
you."

"Right," he growled.

Shelly realized that she was acting like a shrew, but
her behavior was a defense mechanism against the attraction she felt for Slade. If he was irritated with her,
it would be easier for her to control her own feelings
for him.

"If my presence is such an annoyance to you, I can
walk into town."

"Don't be silly."

"She crabs at me about cutting down rhododendrons
and *I'm* silly?" He appeared to be speaking to the sky.

Plowing through the snow, Shelly refused to look
back. She started determinedly up a small incline toward the woods. "I just want you to know I can do this
on my own."

He laid his hand on her shoulder, stopping her in her
tracks. "Shelly, listen to me, would you?"

She hesitated, her gaze falling on the long line of trees
ahead. "What now?"

"I like the prospect of finding a Christmas tree with you, but if you find my company so unpleasant, I'll go back to the house."

"That's not it," she murmured, feeling ridiculous. "I have fun when I'm with you."

"Then why are we arguing?"

Against her will she smiled. "I don't know," she admitted.

"Friends?" He offered her his gloved hand.

She clasped it in her own and nodded wordlessly at him.

"Now that we've got that out of the way, just how big a tree were you thinking of?"

"*Big.*"

"Obviously. But remember, it's got to fit inside the house, so that sixty-foot fir straight ahead is out."

"But the top six feet isn't," she teased.

Chuckling, Slade draped his arm across her shoulder. "Yes, it is."

They were still within sight of the house. "Don't worry. I don't want to cut down something obvious."

"How do you mean?"

"In years to come, I don't want to look out the back window and see a hole in the landscape."

"Don't be ridiculous. You've got a whole forest back here."

"I want to go a bit deeper into the woods."

"Listen, Shortcake, I'm not Lewis and Clark."

Shelly paused. "What did you call me?"

"Shortcake. It fits."

"How's that?"

His gaze roamed over her, his eyes narrowing as he studied her full mouth. It took every ounce of control, but she managed not to moisten her lips. A tingling sensation attacked her stomach, and she lowered her gaze. The hesitation lasted no longer than a heartbeat.

His breath hissed through his teeth before he asked, "How about this tree?" He pointed to a small fir that barely reached his waist.

She couldn't keep from laughing. "It should be illegal to cut down anything that small."

"Do you have a better suggestion?"

"Yes."

"What?"

"That tree over there." She marched ahead, pointing out a seven-foot pine.

"You're being ridiculous. We wouldn't be able to get that one through the front door."

"Of course we'd need to trim it."

"Like in half," he mocked.

She refused to be dissuaded. "Don't be a spoilsport."

"Forget it. This tree would be a nice compromise." He

indicated another small tree that was only slightly bigger than the first one he'd chosen.

Without hesitating, she reached down and packed a thick ball of snow. "I'm not willing to compromise my beliefs."

He turned to her, exasperation written all over his features, and she let him have it with the snowball. The accuracy of her toss astonished her, and she cried out with a mixture of surprise and delight when the snowball slammed against his chest, spraying snow in his face.

His reaction was so speedy that she had no time to run before he was only inches away. "Slade, I'm sorry," she said, taking a giant step backward. "I don't know what came over me. I didn't mean to hit you. Actually, I was aiming at that bush behind you. Honest."

For every step she retreated, he advanced, packing a snowball between his gloved hands.

"Slade, you wouldn't," she implored him, arms wide in surrender.

"Yes, I would."

"No!" she cried, and turned, running for all she was worth. He overtook her almost immediately, grabbing her shoulder and turning her to face him. She stumbled, and they went crashing together to the snow-covered ground.

His heavy body pressed her deeper into the snow.

"Are you all right?" he asked urgently, fear and concern evident in the tone of his voice as he tenderly pushed the hair from her face.

"Yes," she murmured, breathless. But her lack of air couldn't be attributed to the fall. Having Slade this close, his warm breath fanning her face, was responsible for that. Even through their thick coats she could feel the pounding rhythm of his heart echoing hers.

"Shelly." He ground out her name like a man driven to the brink of insanity. Slowly he slanted his mouth over hers, claiming her lips in a kiss that rocked the very core of her being. In seconds they were both panting and nearly breathless.

Her arms locked around his neck, and she arched against him, wanting the kiss to go on and on.

"Shelly…" he said again as his hands closed around her wrists, pulling free of her embrace. He sat up with his back to her. All she could see was the uneven rise and fall of his shoulders as he dragged in air.

"Don't worry," she breathed in a voice so weak that it trembled. "I won't tell Margaret."

Six

"That shouldn't have happened," Slade said at last.

"I suppose you want an apology," Shelly responded, standing and brushing the snow from her pants. In spite of her efforts to appear normal, her hands trembled and her pulse continued to hammer away madly. From the beginning she'd known that his kiss would have this effect on her, and she cursed her traitorous heart.

He stared, clearly shocked that she would suggest such a thing. "*I* should be the one to apologize to *you*."

"Why? Because you kissed me?"

"And because I'm engaged."

"I know." Her voice rose several decibels. "What's in a kiss, anyway? It wasn't a big deal. Right?" *Liar,* her heart accused, continuing to beat erratically. It had been the sweetest, most wonderful kiss of her life. One that would haunt her forever.

"It won't happen again," he said without looking at her. He rose and held himself stiffly, staying a good two feet away from her. His facade slipped tightly into place, locking his expression right before her eyes. She was reminded of the man she'd first seen on the plane—that polished, impeccable businessman who looked at the world with undisguised indifference.

"As I said, it wasn't a big deal."

"Right," he answered. Her dismissive attitude toward his kiss didn't appear to please him. He stalked in the direction of the trees and stopped at the one he'd offered as a compromise. Without soliciting her opinion, he began sawing away at its narrow trunk.

Within minutes the tree toppled to the ground, stirring up the snow. She walked over, prepared to help him load the small fir onto the sled, but he wouldn't let her.

"I'll do it," he muttered gruffly.

Offended, she folded her arms and stepped back, feeling awkward. She knew she would feel better if they could discuss the kiss openly and honestly.

"I knew it was going to happen." She'd been wanting him to kiss her all morning, in fact.

"What?" he barked, heading in the direction of the house, tugging the sled and Christmas tree behind him.

"The kiss," she called after him. "And if I was honest, I'd also admit that I wanted it to happen. I was even hoping it would."

"If you don't mind, I'd rather not talk about it."

He was making her angrier every time he opened his mouth. "I said *if* I was being honest, but since neither of us is, then apparently you're right to suggest we drop the issue entirely."

This time he ignored her, taking long strides and forcing her into a clumsy jog behind him. The north wind whipped her scarf across her mouth, and she tucked it more securely around her neck. Then she turned and walked backward, so the bitter wind stopped buffeting her face.

Unexpectedly her boot hit a small rock hidden under the snow, and she momentarily lost her balance. Flinging her arms out in an effort to catch herself, she went tumbling down the hill, somersaulting head over heels until she lay spread-eagled at the base of the slope.

Slade raced after her, falling to his knees at her side, his eyes clouded with emotion. "Do you have to make a game out of everything?"

What was he talking about? She'd nearly killed herself, and he was accusing her of acrobatics in the snow. She struggled to give him a sassy comeback, but the wind had been knocked from her lungs and she discovered that she couldn't speak.

"Are you all right?" He looked genuinely concerned.

"I don't know," she whispered tightly. Getting the appropriate amount of oxygen to her lungs seemed to require all her energy.

"Don't move."

"I couldn't if I wanted to."

"Where does it hurt?"

"'Where doesn't it?' would be a more fitting question." Then, giving the lie to her previous answer, she levered herself up on one elbow and wiggled her legs. "I do this now and then so I can appreciate how good it feels to breathe," she muttered sarcastically.

"I said don't move," Slade barked. "You could've seriously injured something."

"I did," she admitted. "My pride." She got slowly to her feet, then bowed mockingly before him and said, "Stay tuned for my next trick when I'll single-handedly leap tall buildings and alter the course of the mighty Columbia River."

"You're not funny."

"There goes my career in comedy, then."

"Here." He tucked a hand under her elbow. "Let me help you back to the house."

"This may come as a shock to you, but I'm perfectly capable of walking on my own."

"Nothing you do anymore could shock me."

"That sounds amazingly like a challenge."

His indifference visibly melted away as he stared down at her with warm, vulnerable eyes. "Trust me, it isn't." He claimed her hand, lacing his fingers with hers. "Come on, your father's probably getting worried."

Shelly sincerely doubted it. What Slade was really saying was that things would be safer for them both back at the house. Temptation could more easily be kept at bay with someone else present.

He let go of her hand and placed his palm at the small of her back, and they continued their short sojourn across the snowy landscape.

The house looked amazingly still and dark as they approached. Only a whisper of smoke drifted into the clear sky from the chimney, as though the fire had been allowed to die. She had expected to hear Andy Williams crooning from the stereo and perhaps smell the lingering scent of freshly popped popcorn.

Instead, they were greeted by an empty, almost eerie silence.

While Slade leaned the tree against the side of the house, she ventured inside. A note propped against the sugar bowl in the middle of the kitchen table commanded her attention. She walked into the room and picked it up.

Sick horse at the Adlers' place. Ted W came for me and will bring me home. Call if you need me.
Love,
Dad.

She swallowed tightly, clenching the paper in her hand as the back door shut.

"Dad got called out to a neighbor's. Sick horse," she announced without turning around. "Would you like a cup of coffee? The pot's full, although it doesn't look too fresh. Dad must have put it on before he left. He knew how cold we'd be when we got back." She realized she was babbling and immediately stopped. Without waiting for his response, she reached for two mugs.

"Coffee sounds fine." His voice was heavy with dread. The same dread she felt pressing against her heart. Her father was the buffer they needed, and now he was gone.

She heard Slade drag out a kitchen chair, and she placed the mug in front of him. Her thick lashes fanned downward as she avoided his gaze.

Reluctantly she pulled out the chair opposite his and joined him at the table. "I suppose we should put up the tree."

He paused, then said, "We could."

From all the enthusiasm he displayed, they could have been discussing income taxes. Her heart ached, and she felt embarrassed for having made the suggestion. No doubt Margaret had her tree flocked and decorated without ever involving Slade.

Her hands tightened around the mug, the heat burning the sensitive skin of her palms.

"Well?" he prompted.

"I think I'll wait until Dad's back. We—every year since Mom died, we've done it together. It's a fun time." The walls of the kitchen seemed to be closing in on them. With every breath she drew, she became more aware of the man sitting across from her. They'd tried to pretend, but the kiss had changed everything. The taste of him lingered on her lips, and unconsciously she ran her tongue over them, wanting to recapture that sensation before it disappeared forever.

His eyes followed her movement, and he abruptly stood and marched across the kitchen to place his half-full mug in the sink.

"I'll see to the fire," he offered, hastily leaving the room.

"Thank you."

After emptying her own mug in the sink, she joined

him, standing in the archway between the kitchen and living room.

She watched as he placed a small log in the red coals, and in moments flames were sizzling over the dry bark. Soon the fire crackled and hissed, hungry flames attacking the fresh supply of wood. Ol' Dan got slowly off the couch where he'd been sleeping and lay down in front of the fire with a comfortable sigh.

"I wonder what's happening with the road crew," Slade said.

"They could be here anytime."

They turned simultaneously toward the phone and collided. She felt the full impact of the unexpected contact, and her breath caught somewhere between her lungs and her throat, but not from pain.

"Shelly." His arms went around her faster than a shooting star. "Did I hurt you?"

One hand was trapped against his broad chest, while the other hung loosely at her side. "I'm fine," she managed, her voice as unsteady as his. Still, he didn't release her.

Savoring his nearness and warmth, she closed her eyes and pressed her head to his chest, listening to the beat of his heart beneath her ear.

Slade went utterly still, and then his arms tightened around her and he groaned her name.

Could anything that felt this wonderful, this good, be wrong? Shelly knew the answer, and her head buzzed with a warning. Even though her eyes were closed, she could see flashing red lights. Slade had held and kissed her only once, and he had instantly regretted it. He'd even refused to talk about it, closing himself off from her. This couldn't end well.

Yet all the logical arguments melted away like snow in a spring thaw when she was in his arms. His lips moved to her hair, and he breathed in deeply, as though to capture her scent.

"Shelly," he pleaded, his voice husky with emotion. "Tell me to stop."

The words wouldn't form. She knew that she should break away and save them both the agony of guilt. But she couldn't.

"I want you to hold me," she whispered. "Just hold me."

His arms tightened even further, anchoring her against him, and his lips nuzzled her ear, shooting tingles of pleasure down her spine. From her ear he found her cheek, her hair. For an eternity he hesitated.

The phone rang and they broke apart with a suddenness that made her lose her balance. Slade's hand on her shoulder steadied her. Brushing the hair from her face, she drew a steadying breath and picked up the phone.

"Hello." Her voice was barely above a whisper.

"Shelly? Are you all right? You don't sound like yourself."

"Oh, hi, Dad." She glanced up guiltily at Slade. His returning look was heavy with his own unhappiness. He brushed a hand through his hair and walked to the picture window, and she returned her attention to the call. "We got the tree."

"That's good." Her father paused. "Are you sure everything's fine?"

"Of course I'm sure," she answered, somewhat defensively. "How are things at the Adlers'?"

"Not good. I may be here awhile. I'm sorry to be away from you, but Slade's there to keep you company."

"How...long will you be?"

"A couple of hours, three at the most. You and Slade will be all right, won't you?"

But her father didn't sound any more convinced than she felt when she replied, "Oh, sure."

She replaced the receiver. Without the call as a buffer, the air in the room seemed to vibrate with Slade's presence. He turned around and met her gaze. "I've got to get to Seattle. Bauer said he's going to be at the office late anyway, finishing up some things so he can enjoy Christmas without work hanging over his head. I've really got to get there."

What he was really saying was that he had to get away from her. "I know," she told him. "But how?"

"How'd your dad get to that sick horse?"

"The Adlers' neighbor, Ted Wilkens, has a pickup with a plow blade. He came for Dad."

"Would it be possible for him to take me into Seattle?"

Shelly hadn't thought of that. "I'm not sure. I'll call."

"Although…it's Christmas Eve." He sounded hesitant, so different from the man she'd overheard on the phone yesterday, the man who hadn't cared about setting up a meeting for Christmas Eve.

"They're good people," she said, reaching for the phone. Slade paced nearby while she talked to Connie Wilkens.

"Well?" He studied her expectantly as she hung up the phone.

"Ted's out helping someone else, but Connie thinks he'll be back before dark. She suggested that we head their way, and by the time we arrive, Ted should be home."

"You're sure he won't mind?"

"Positive. Ted and Connie are always happy to help out their friends."

"They really are good people—like you and your dad," he murmured softly.

She laced her fingers together in front of her. "We're

neighbors, although they're a good four miles from here. And friends." She scooted down in front of Ol' Dan and petted him in long, soothing strokes. "I told Connie that we'd start out soon."

Slade's brow furrowed as her words sank in. "But how? The tractor?"

"I couldn't run that thing if my life depended on it."

"Shelly, we can't trek that distance on foot."

"I wasn't thinking of walking."

"What other way is there?"

A smile graced her soft features until it touched her eyes, which sparkled with mischief. "We can always take the horses."

Seven

"You have to be kidding!" Slade gave her a look of pure disbelief.

"No," Shelly insisted, swallowing a laugh. "It's the only possible way I know to get there. We can go up through the woods, where the snow isn't as deep."

Rubbing a hand over his eyes, Slade stalked to the far side of the room, made an abrupt about-face and returned to his former position. "I don't know. You seem to view life as one big adventure after another. I'm not used to…"

"Pokey's as gentle as a lamb," she murmured coaxingly.

"Pokey?"

"Unless you'd rather ride Midnight."

"Good grief, no. Pokey sounds more my speed."

Doing her best to hold back a devilish grin, she led the way into the kitchen.

"What are you doing now?"

"Making us a thermos of hot chocolate."

"Why?"

"I thought we'd stop and have a picnic along the way."

"You're doing it again," he murmured, but she noticed that an indulgent smile lurked just behind his intense dark eyes. He was a man who needed a little fun in his life, and she was determined to provide it. If she was only allowed to touch his life briefly, then she wanted to bring laughter and sunshine with her. Margaret would have him forever. But these few hours were hers, and she was determined to make the most of them.

"It'll be fun," she declared enthusiastically.

"No doubt Custer said the same thing to his men," he grumbled as they put their coats and boots back on, and he followed her out to the barn.

"Cynic," she teased, holding the barn door for him.

Reluctantly he preceded her inside.

"How do you feel about a lazy stroll in the snow, Pokey?" she asked as she reached the Appaloosa's stall and petted the horse's nose. "I know Sampson's ready anytime."

"Don't let her kid you, Pokey," Slade added from behind her. "Good grief, now you've got *me* doing it."

"Doing what?"

"Talking to the animals."

"Animals often share human characteristics," she said. "It's only natural for people to express their feelings to the animals that share their lives."

"In which case we're in trouble. Pokey is going to have a lot to say about how I feel when I climb on her back."

"You'll be fine."

"Sure, but will Pokey?"

"You both will. Now stop worrying."

When Shelly brought out the tack, Slade just stared at her, hands buried deep in his pockets, but then he stepped up and did what he could to help her saddle the two horses. Mostly he circled her awkwardly, looking doubtful.

When she'd finished, she led the horses out of the barn. Holding on to both sets of reins, she motioned for him to mount first. "Do you need any help?" she asked. He looked so different from the staid executive she'd met in Portland that she had trouble remembering that he really was the same person. The man facing her now was clearly out of his element, nothing like the unflappable man on the airplane.

"I don't think so," he said, reaching for the saddle and trying to follow Shelly's directions. Without much difficulty he swung himself onto Pokey's back. The horse barely stirred.

Looking pleased with himself, he smiled down at Shelly. "I suppose you told her to be gentle with me."

"I did," she teased in return. Double-checking the cinch, she asked, "Do you need me to adjust the stirrups or anything?"

"No." He shifted his weight slightly and accepted the reins she handed him. "I'm ready anytime you are."

She mounted with an ease that spoke of years in the saddle. "It's going to be a cold ride until we get under the cover of the trees. Follow me."

"Anywhere."

She was sure she must have misheard him. "What did you say?" she asked, twisting around in the saddle.

"Nothing." But he was grinning, and she found him so devastatingly appealing that it demanded all her willpower to turn around and lead the way.

They quickly reached the path that took them through the woods. Gusts of swift wind blew the snow from the trees. The swirling flakes were nearly as bad as the storm had been. Even Pokey protested at having to be outside.

"Shelly," Slade said, edging the Appaloosa to Sampson's side. "This may not have been the most brilliant idea. Maybe we should head back."

"Don't be ridiculous."

"I don't want you catching cold on my account."

"I'm as snug as a bug in a rug," she said, using one of her father's favorite expressions.

"Liar," he purred softly.

"I want you to have something to remember me by." She realized she must sound like some lovesick romantic. He would be gone soon, and she had to accept that she probably would never see him again.

"Like what? Frostbite?"

She laughed. The musical sound was carried by the wind and seemed to echo in the trees around them. "How can you complain? This is wonderful. Riding along like this makes me want to sing."

He grumbled something unintelligible under his breath.

"What are you complaining about now?"

"Who says I'm complaining?"

She grinned, her head bobbing slightly with the gentle sway of Sampson's gait. "I'm beginning to know you."

"All right, if you insist on knowing, I happen to be humming. My enthusiasm for this venture doesn't compel me to burst into song. But I'm doing the best I can."

Holding an unexpectedly contented feeling to her heart, she tried not to think about what would happen when they reached the Wilkens place. She was prepared to smile at him and bid him farewell, freely sending him out of her life. But that would have been easier before he'd held her in his arms and she'd experienced the gentle persuasion of his kiss. So very much easier.

Together, their horses side by side, they ambled along, not speaking but singing Christmas songs one after the other until they were breathless and giddy. Their voices blended magically in two-part harmony. More than once they shared a lingering gaze. But Shelly felt her high spirits evaporating as they neared the landmark that marked the half-way point of their journey.

"My backside is ready for a break," Slade announced unexpectedly.

"You aren't nearly as anxious to scoff at my picnic idea now, are you?" she returned.

"Not when I'm discovering on what part of their anatomy cowboys get calluses." A grin curved his sensuous mouth.

They paused in a small clearing, looping the horses' reins around the trunk of a nearby fir tree.

While she took the hot chocolate and some homemade cookies from her saddlebags, he exercised his stiff legs, walking around as though he were on stilts.

"We'll have to share the cup," she announced, holding out the plastic top of the thermos. She stood between the two horses, munching on a large oatmeal cookie.

Slade lifted the cup to his lips and hesitated as their eyes met. He paused, slowly lowering the cup without breaking eye contact.

Her breath came in shallow gasps. "Is something wrong?" she asked with difficulty.

"You're lovely."

"Sure." She forced a laugh. "My nose looks like a maraschino cherry and—"

"Don't joke, Shelly. I mean it." His voice was gruff, almost harsh.

"Then thank you."

He removed his glove and placed his warm hand on her cold face, cupping her cheek. The moment was almost unbearably tender, and she swallowed the surging emotion that clogged her throat. It would be the easiest thing in the world to walk into his arms, lose herself in his kiss and love him the way he deserved to be loved.

As if reading her thoughts, Sampson shifted, bumping her back and delivering her into Slade's arms. He dropped the hot chocolate and hauled her against him like a man in desperate need.

"I told myself this wouldn't happen again," he whispered against her hair. "Every time I hold you, it becomes harder to let you go."

Her heart gave a small leap of pleasure at his words.

She didn't want him to let her go. Not ever. Everything felt right between them. Too right and too good.

How long he held her, Shelly didn't know. Far longer than was necessary and not nearly long enough. Each second seemed to stretch, sustaining her tender heart for the moment when she would have to bid him farewell.

Not until they broke apart did she notice that it was snowing again. Huge crystalline flakes filled the sky with their icy purity.

"What should we do?" he asked, looking doubtful.

Her first instinct was to suggest that they return to the house, but she hesitated. The thought of their inevitable goodbye became more difficult to bear every minute.

"We're going back," he said, answering his own question.

"Why?"

"I'm not leaving you and your father to deal with the horses. It's bad enough that I dragged you this far." Placing his foot in the stirrup, he reached for the saddle and remounted. "Come on, before this snow gets any worse."

"But we can make it to the Wilkens place."

"Not now." He raised his eyes skyward and scowled. "It's already getting dark."

Grumbling, she repacked her saddlebags, tugged Sampson's reins free of the tree trunk and lifted her body onto his back with the agile grace of a ballerina.

* * *

The house was in sight when Slade finally spoke again. "Once we get back, I need to contact Margaret. She'll be waiting. I told her I'd call Christmas Eve."

Shelly's heart constricted at the mention of the other woman's name. Until now, unless she'd asked about Margaret, Slade hadn't volunteered any information about his fiancée. Now he had freely thrust her between them.

"She's a good woman," he said when Shelly stayed silent.

She didn't know who he was trying to convince. "I didn't think you'd love a woman who wasn't."

"I've known Margaret a lot of years."

"Of course you have." And he'd only known *her* a few days. She understood what he was saying. It was almost as if he were apologizing because Margaret had prior claim to his loyalties and his heart. He didn't need to. She'd accepted that from the beginning.

When they left the cover of the woods, she spoke, managing to keep her voice level and unemotional. "You'll never get a cell signal way out here, not in this weather. You go in and use the phone," she said, surprised that her voice could remain so even. "I'll take care of the horses so you can make your call in private, and I'll call the Wilkenses when I'm done."

"I won't talk long."

"Don't cut the conversation short on my account."

He wiped his forearm across his brow. The movement brought her attention to the confusion in his eyes. "I won't."

By then they were at the barn, where she dismounted slowly, lowering both booted feet to the ground. He did the same, but she avoided his gaze as she opened the barn door and led the horses through. The wind followed her inside the dimly lit building. The cold nipped at her heels.

With a heavy heart she lifted the saddle from Pokey's back before she noticed Slade's dark form blocking the doorway. Her hands tightened around the smooth leather. "Is there a problem?"

"No."

After cross-tying Pokey in the aisle, Shelly turned back to Slade, only to find that he'd left.

Taking extra time with the horses, she put off entering the house as long as possible. Removing the gloves from her hands one finger at a time, she walked in the back door to discover Slade sitting in the living room staring blindly into the roaring fire. She walked quickly to the phone and called the Wilkenses. Connie was glad to hear from her and admitted that after a full day driving neighbors around in the snow, Ted was exhausted.

"I don't know about you," she called out cheerfully after hanging up the phone, "but I'm starved." The tip of her tongue burned with questions that pride refused to let her ask. She was dying to know what Slade had said to Margaret, if anything, about his current circumstances. "How about popcorn with lots of melted butter?"

He joined her, a smile lurking at the edges of his full mouth. His eyes were laughing, revealing his thoughts. He really did have wonderful eyes, and for a moment Shelly couldn't look away.

"I was thinking of something more like a triple-decker sandwich," he admitted.

"You know what your problem is, Garner?" It was obvious he didn't, so she took it upon herself to tell him. "No imagination."

"Because I prefer something meatier than popcorn?"

She pretended not to hear him—easy to do with her head buried in the open refrigerator. Without comment she brought out a variety of fixings and placed them on the tabletop.

She peeled off a slice of deli ham, tore it in two and gave Slade half. "How about a compromise?"

He looked dubious, as if he were sure she was about to suggest a popcorn sandwich. "I don't know..."

"How about if you bring in the tree while I fix us something to eat?"

"That's an offer I can't refuse."

Singing softly as she worked, Shelly concocted a meal neither of them was likely to forget. Sandwiches piled high with three different kinds of meat, sliced dill pickles and juicy green olives. In addition, she set out Christmas cookies and thick slices of fudge that she found sitting around the kitchen.

Slade set the tree in the holder, dragged it through the front door and stood it in the corner. "The snow's stopped," he told her when she carried in their meal.

"That's encouraging. I was beginning to think we'd be forced to stay until the spring thaw." Of course, she wouldn't have minded, and her smile was wistful.

Sitting Indian-style in front of the fireplace, their backs resting against the sofa, they dug into the sandwiches. But she found herself giving most of hers to Ol' Dan, having discovered that she had little appetite. Never had she been more aware of a man. They were so close that, when she lowered her sandwich to the plate, her upper arm brushed against his. But neither one of them made any effort to move, and she found that the contact, although impersonal, was soothing. She paused, trying to capture this moment of peacefulness.

"This has been a good day," he murmured, his gaze following hers as he stared out the living room window.

"It's certainly been crazy."

Without replying immediately, he reached for her hand, entwining their fingers. "I don't know when I've enjoyed a day more." His dark gaze flickered over her and rested on her mouth. Abruptly he glanced away, his attention on the piano at the far side of the room. "Do you play?"

She sighed expressively. "A little. Dad claimed that my playing was what kept the mice out of the house."

He raised one dark brow with a touch of amusement. "That bad?"

"See for yourself." She rose and walked to the piano, lifted the lid of the bench seat and extracted some Christmas music.

When she pressed her fingers to the keys, the discordant notes were enough to make her wince, and cause Ol' Dan to lift his chin and cock his head curiously. He howled once.

"I told you I wasn't any good," she said with another dramatic sigh. Staring at the music, she squinted and sadly shook her head.

Slade joined her. Standing directly behind her, he laid his hands on her shoulders, leaning over to study the music.

"I think I may have found the problem," she stated seriously. Dimples formed in her cheeks as she tried not to smile. Turning the sheet music right side up, she leaned forward to study the notes a second time and tried again. This time a sweet melody flowed through the house.

Chuckling, Slade tightened his hands around her

shoulders and spontaneously lowered his mouth to her cheek. "Have I told you how much fun you are?"

"No, but I'll accept that as a compliment."

"Good, because it was meant as one."

She continued to play, hitting a wrong note every once in a while and going back to repeat the bar until she got it right. Soon his rich voice blended with the melody. Her soprano tones mixed smoothly with his, although her playing faltered now and again.

Neither of them heard the front door open. "Merry Christmas Eve," Don announced.

Shelly froze with her hands above the keys and turned to look at him. "Welcome home. How's the Adlers' horse?"

Her father wiped a weary hand over his face. "She'll make it."

"What about you?" He was clearly exhausted. His pants were caked with mud and grit.

"Give me half an hour and I'll let you know."

"I can make you a sandwich if you're hungry."

"All I want right now is a hot shower." He paused to scratch Ol' Dan's ears. "Keep playing. You two sound good together."

"I thought we were scattering the mice to the barn," Slade teased.

Don scratched the side of his head with his index finger. "Say that again?"

"He's talking about my piano playing," she reminded her father.

"Oh, that. I don't suppose you play?"

"As a matter of fact, I do," Slade admitted.

"You do?" Shelly was stunned. "Why didn't you say something earlier? Here." She slid off the bench. "Trade places."

He claimed her position and ran his large, masculine hands over the keys with a familiarity that caused her heart to flutter. His fingers moved over the keys with reverence. Stroking, enticing the instrument, until the music practically had the room swaying. She felt tears gather in the corner of her eyes. Slade didn't play the piano; he made love to it.

When he'd finished, he rested his hands in his lap and slowly expelled his breath.

She sank into an easy chair. "Why didn't you tell me you could play like that?"

A smile brightened his eyes. "You didn't ask."

Even her father was awestruck and, for the first time in years, at a complete loss for words.

"You could play professionally. You're magnificent." Her soft voice cracked with the potency of her feelings.

"I briefly toyed with the idea at one time."

"Why didn't—"

"I play for enjoyment now." The light dimmed in his eyes, and the sharp edge of his words seemed to say that the decision hadn't come easy. And it clearly was not one he was willing to discuss, even with her.

"Will you play something else?" her father asked, his shower apparently on hold.

Judging by the look he shot her father, Slade appeared to regret admitting that he played the piano. She could tell that music was his real love, and he'd abandoned it. Coming this close again was probably pure torture for him. "Another time, perhaps."

Except that there wouldn't be another time, not for them. "Please," she whispered, rising to stand behind him, then placing her hands on his shoulders in a silent plea.

He covered her hand with his as he looked up into her imploring gaze. "All right, Shelly. For you."

For half an hour he played with such intensity that his shoulders sagged with exhaustion when he'd finished.

"God has given you a rare gift," her father said, his voice husky with appreciation. He glanced down at his mud-caked clothes. "Now, if you'll excuse me, I'll go take that shower before I start attracting flies."

As her father left the room, she moved to Slade's side, sitting on the bench beside him. Unable to find the words to express herself, she simply traced the sculptured line of his jaw as tears blurred her vision. The tightness in her chest made her breathing shallow and difficult.

He lifted a hand and stopped her, then brought her

fingers to his lips and gently kissed her palm. She bit her bottom lip to hold back all the emotion stored in her heart.

A lone tear escaped and trickled down her pale cheek. Slade gently brushed it aside, his finger cool against her heated skin. He bent down and found her mouth with his. She realized that, without speaking a word, he was thanking her. With her, he'd allowed his facade to crumble. He'd opened his heart and revealed the deep, sensitive man inside. He was free now, with nothing more to hide.

Wrapping her arms around him, she kissed him in return, telling him in the only way she could how much she appreciated the gift of seeing his true self.

"Merry Christmas, Shortcake," her father greeted her on the tail end of a yawn.

Shelly stood in front of the picture window, cupping her coffee mug. Her gaze rested on the sunrise as it blanketed the morning with the bright hues of another day. She tried to force a smile when she turned to her father, but it refused to come. She felt chilled and empty inside.

"Where's Slade?" he asked.

"The snowplows came during the night," she whispered through the pain. "He's gone."

Eight

"Gone? Without saying goodbye?" A look of disbelief filled her father's eyes.

"He left a note." She withdrew it from her pocket and handed it to him. The message was only a few lines. He thanked them for their hospitality, and wished her and her father much happiness. And then said goodbye. Without regrets. Without second thoughts. Without looking back.

Her father looked up from the note and narrowed his eyes as he studied her. "Are you okay?"

"I'm fine."

He slowly shook his head. "I've never seen you look at a man the way you looked at Slade. You really liked him, didn't you?"

I love him! her heart cried. "He's a wonderful man. I

only hope Margaret and that computer firm realize how lucky they are."

"They don't, you know," he whispered, slipping an arm around her shoulders and hugging her close. She offered him a feeble smile in return. "He might come back."

She knew differently. "No." He'd made his choice. His future had been charted and defined as precisely as a road map. Slade Garner was a man of character and strength. He wouldn't abandon Margaret and all that was important to him for a two-day acquaintance and a few stolen kisses. He'd shared his deepest desires and secrets with her, opened his heart and trusted her. She shouldn't wish for more. But she did. She wanted Slade.

Christmas Day passed in a blur. Her brothers and their families were there, and somehow she managed to smile and talk and eat, with no one but her father any the wiser about her real feelings. She flew back to San Francisco the following afternoon, still numb, still aching, but holding her head up high and proud.

Her tiny apartment in the Garden District, although colorful and cheerfully decorated, did little to boost her drooping spirits.

Setting her suitcase on the polished hardwood floor, she kicked off her shoes and reached for the phone.

"Hi, Dad. I'm home." Taking the telephone with her, she sank into the overstuffed chair.

"How was the flight?"

"Went without a hitch."

"Just the way you like it." He chuckled, then grew serious. "I don't suppose…?"

"No, Dad." She knew what he was asking. He had thought that Slade would be in San Francisco waiting for her. She knew better. Slade wouldn't want to think of her. Already he'd banished any thought of her to the furthest corner of his mind. Perhaps what they'd shared was an embarrassment to him now.

She spoke to her father for a few minutes longer, then claimed exhaustion and said goodbye. After she hung up she sat with the receiver cradled in her lap, staring blindly at the wallpaper.

Starting the next day she worked hard at putting her life back on an even keel. She went to work each day and did her utmost to forget the man who had touched her so profoundly.

Her one resolution for the New Year was simple: Find a man. For the first time since moving to San Francisco, she was lonely. Oh, she had friends and plenty of things to do, but nothing to take away the ache in her soul.

Two days before New Year's Eve, she stepped off the bus and on impulse bought flowers from a vendor on the street corner, then headed inside her building.

The elderly woman who lived across the hall opened her door as Shelly approached. "Good afternoon, Mrs. Lester," she said, pulling a red carnation from the bouquet and handing it to her neighbor.

"Now, isn't that a coincidence." Mrs. Lester chuckled. "I've got flowers for you."

Shelly's heart went still.

"The delivery boy asked me to give them to you." She stepped back inside, then stepped out and handed Shelly a narrow white box. "Roses, I suspect."

"Roses?" Shelly felt the blood drain from her face. She couldn't get inside her apartment fast enough. Closing the door with her foot, she walked across the room and set the box on a table. Inside she discovered a dozen of the most perfect roses she'd ever imagined. Each bud was identical to the others, their color brilliant.

Although she went through the box twice, she found no card. It was foolish to think Slade had sent them. Surely he wouldn't be so cruel as to say goodbye, only to invade her life again. Besides, he'd claimed roses were stupidly expensive, and she couldn't argue with that. They were, especially this time of year.

She was still puzzling over who could have sent them

when the doorbell rang. She opened the door, and a deliveryman handed her a second long narrow box, identical to the first.

"Sign here." He offered her his pen.

Shelly scribbled her name across the bottom of the delivery order, then carried the second box to the kitchen table and opened it. Another dozen red roses, and again there was no card.

No sooner had she arranged all twenty-four flowers in her one and only tall vase when the doorbell chimed again. It was a deliveryman from another flower shop with another dozen roses.

"Are you sure you have the right address?" she asked.

"Shelly Griffin?" He read off her street address and apartment number, and raised expectant eyes to her.

"That's me," she conceded.

"Sign here."

She did. And for a third time discovered—with no surprise whatsoever at this point—that there was no card.

Without another vase to hold them, she emptied her tall jar of dill pickles into a bowl, rinsed out the jar and used that. With the first roses already brightening her living room, she left these to grace the kitchen.

Whoever was sending her so many flowers was either very rich or else extremely foolish, she thought.

Hands pressed against her hips, she surveyed the small apartment and couldn't decide if it resembled a flower shop or a funeral parlor.

When the doorbell chimed again, she sighed expressively. "Not again," she groaned aloud, turning the dead bolt and opening the door.

But instead of opening it to yet another delivery, she came face-to-face with Slade. He was so tall, so incredibly good-looking, that her breath became trapped in her lungs.

"Slade."

"Hello, Shelly." His eyes delved into hers, smiling and warm. "Can I come in?"

"Of…of course." Flustered, she stepped aside.

"Do you realize you only have on one shoe?"

"Why are you here?" she demanded. With her hands behind her back, she leaned against the closed front door, desperately wanting to believe everything she dared not even think about.

"I've missed you."

She closed her eyes to the tenderness in his voice. Words had never sounded sweeter. "Did you reschedule your meeting?" When he nodded, she asked, "How did it go?"

"Fine. Better than I expected."

"That's nice." She studied him, still unsure.

"I got a hefty bonus, but I may have offended a few friends."

"How did you do that?"

"They were hoping I'd accept a promotion."

"And you aren't?" A promotion sounded like something Margaret would love.

"No, I resigned this afternoon."

"Resigned? What did…Margaret have to say about that?"

"Well—" He took a step closer, stopping just short of her but near enough to reach out and touch her if he wanted to. "—Margaret and I aren't exactly on speaking terms."

"Oh?" Her voice went incredibly weak.

"She didn't take kindly to some of my recent decisions."

I'll just bet, Shelly mused. "And what are those decisions…the most recent ones?"

"I decided to postpone the wedding."

She couldn't fault his fiancée for being upset about that. "Well, I can't say that I blame her. When—when's the new date?"

"Never."

"Never?" She swallowed tightly. "Why not?"

"Why not?" He smiled. "Because Margaret doesn't haul sourdough bread on an airplane or look forward to getting a horse blanket for Christmas or laugh at every opportunity or do any of the things that make life fun."

Speechless, she stared at him, love shining from her eyes.

"Nor does she believe I'll ever make a decent living as a pianist," he continued. "Hell, I'm nearly thirty now. It could be too late."

"But...?"

"But—" He smiled and reached for her, bringing her into the loving circle of his arms. "—I'm going to give it one whopper of a try. I'm no prize, Shelly Griffin. I don't have a job, and I'm not even sure the conservatory will renew the offer they made me once upon a time, but for the first time in too many years, I've got a dream."

"Oh, Slade," she whispered and pressed her face to his broad chest. "I would consider it the greatest honor of my life to be a part of that dream."

"You couldn't help but be," he whispered, lifting her mouth to his. "You're the one who gave it to me."

* * * * *

Santa, Baby

SHERRYL WOODS

Dear Friends,

The holidays have always been an incredibly special time for my family. From childhood I remember the pre-holiday baking, the hiding of gifts—with me trying to hunt them down—midnight Christmas Eve church services, the excitement of opening presents on Christmas morning, the visits to grandparents. There were a few bah-humbug types in the family, but for the most part all of us rejoiced in the season. So, as the holidays approach this year, I wish all of you the joy of the season, the warmth of shared times with family and friends, and a few dozen holiday cookies with not a calorie in them.

All best,

Sherryl

One

Amy Riley had a fever of 102, globs of oatmeal all over her face, hair that desperately needed washing, a screaming baby and a five-year-old who was regarding her with such reproach that she wanted to sit down and cry herself. It was not a promising start to the holidays.

"But, Mom, you said we could go to the mall today and see Santa," Josh whined. "You promised."

Amy clung to her patience by a thread. "I know, sweetie, but I'm sick. I'm sorry."

"But it's Christmas Eve," he persisted, clearly not hearing or at least not caring about the state of her health. "We *have* to go today. If we don't, how will Santa know what to bring us? He doesn't even know where we live now. What if he takes our presents to Michigan and we're not there?"

"He won't," Amy assured him.

"But how do you *know?*"

"Because I sent him a letter," she claimed in desperation.

"What if he didn't get it? Mail gets lost all the time."

"He got it," she reassured him, thinking of the small stash of gifts in her closet. Tomorrow morning, they would provide proof for her doubting son, but today he'd just have to take her word for it.

Thanks to the expense of relocating, she hadn't been able to afford much this year, but she was determined Josh would have at least a few packages from Santa to open on Christmas morning, along with a handful from her folks and the one from his dad that she'd picked out just in case Ned didn't bother sending anything. Unless a miracle occurred and something turned up in an overnight delivery on Christmas morning, she'd pegged her ex's lack of consideration exactly right.

With Josh in her face this morning, she had to keep reminding herself that it wasn't his fault that she and his father had gone through a nasty divorce and that she'd packed up with him and his baby sister and moved to a suburb outside of Charlotte, NC, far from family and friends back in Michigan. Everyone had tried to talk her into waiting until after the holidays, but the thought of spending one more minute in the same town as her ex had been too much. Maybe by next year the wounds would have healed and she and the kids could spend the holidays with her folks, but this year staying there a few weeks longer or making a quick trip back had been out of the question. Amy hadn't had the stomach or the money for it.

She'd convinced herself that things would be better after the first of the year when she started her new job at the headquarters of the same bank she'd worked for back home. At the time she'd been offered the transfer, it had seemed like a godsend, a way to get a fresh start with the promise of some financial security in the very near future.

This morning, though, she was regretting the hasty decision. Money was tight and emotions were raw. She was far from home with no new support system in place. And if it was tough for her, it was a thousand times worse for Josh, who felt cheated not to be with family for Christmas.

But, she reassured herself, Josh was an outgoing kid. He would make new friends in kindergarten. In a few more weeks tantrums like the one he was pitching now would be a thing of the past. They just had to survive till then.

"I hate this place," Josh declared, pressing home a

point with which she was already far too familiar. Not a day had gone by in the last week when he hadn't expressed a similar sentiment.

Fighting for patience, Amy lowered the now-quiet baby into her portable playpen, then sat her son in her lap and gave him a squeeze. "It's going to get better," she promised him.

He nestled under her chin in an increasingly infrequent display of affection. "When?" he asked plaintively.

"Soon," she vowed. No matter what it took, she would make this work.

"There's not even any snow in this dumb place. At home, we always had snow for Christmas and Dad would take me out on my sled." He sighed dramatically. "I miss Dad."

"I know you do, sweetie. And I'm sure he misses you, too," she said, though she was sure of no such thing.

Ned had been all too eager to see them gone so he could get on with his new life with another woman and the baby that was already on the way by the time his divorce from Amy was final. He rarely spared more than a couple of minutes for his calls to his son and even those brief bits of contact had become less routine. Ned was an out of sight, out of mind kind of guy, which was pretty much how he'd gotten involved with a woman he'd met on his business travels. Amy—and his marriage—had definitely been out of sight and out of mind during those trips.

Amy resolved not to dwell on her many issues with her ex today. Even though she felt awful, she was going to do whatever she could to make this first Christmas in their new home memorable for Josh. Emma was still too young to notice much more than the bright lights on their skinny little tree, but Josh needed more. He needed to believe that life in North Carolina would eventually be much like his old life in Michigan. Perhaps even better.

She tousled his dark brown hair, which badly needed a trim. "We can bake cookies later," she told him. "We'll play all the Christmas CDs and tonight I'll make hot chocolate with lots and lots of marshmallows and we can watch Christmas movies on TV. How about that?"

"Sure," he said wearily. "But it won't be Christmas if I don't get to see Santa. We *always* go on Christmas Eve."

Amy bit back her own sigh. That's what came of creating a tradition for your children. They clung to it tenaciously, even when circumstances changed. And seeing Santa was such a little thing for him to ask for. He hadn't requested a million presents. He didn't make a lot of demands. He even helped with Emma as much as he could. He'd rock her to sleep in her carrier or even show her his picture books accompanied by dramatic reenactments of the stories. He was a great big brother and, most of the time anyway, a big help to Amy.

How many more years would he want to climb up on Santa's lap, anyway, she asked herself. How much longer before he stopped believing?

Maybe if she took a couple more aspirin and a hot shower, she could manage the trip to the mall, she thought without much enthusiasm. Her head throbbed just thinking about the crowds. Still, one look into her son's disappointed eyes and she knew she had to try.

"Will you stay right here and watch your sister?" she asked Josh. "Keep her entertained, okay?"

"How come?"

"So I can take a shower," she told him without elaborating or making another promise she might not be able to keep.

Josh's eyes lit up in sudden understanding, anyway. "And then we'll go see Santa?" he asked excitedly.

"*Maybe* we'll go see Santa," she cautioned. "If I feel better."

He threw his arms around her neck and squeezed. "You will, Mom. I know you will."

He scrambled down, knelt beside the playpen and peered through the mesh at Emma. "We're going to see Santa, Em. You're gonna love him. He's this jolly old guy, who goes ho-ho-ho real loud." He demonstrated, holding his tummy, as he bellowed ho-ho-ho. "He's all dressed in red, and you tell him what you most want for Christmas and then, if you've been good all year, he brings it to you. Santa's the best." He grinned up at Amy. "Next to Mom, of course."

Amy couldn't help grinning back at her budding young diplomat. How could she resist giving him anything he asked for, especially this Christmas? She just hoped she didn't throw up all over jolly old St. Nick.

Nick DiCaprio was not having a good week. Hell, he wasn't having a good life. The police department psychologist had informed his superiors on Monday that he was burned out, that he had anger management issues, that letting him go back on active duty in the immediate future would be irresponsible.

Well, duh! After being forced to stand by helplessly while a deranged man had terrorized his own kid to get even with his ex-wife, who wouldn't have anger issues? Nick had wanted to pound heads together that awful day, especially those of the SWAT team who wouldn't allow him to intervene. He couldn't imagine that talking that whole disastrous scenario to death with some shrink was going to improve his mood.

As if all that psychobabble weren't annoying enough, it was Christmas Eve. The whole world was all caught up in the commercialized holiday frenzy. If he heard one more Christmas song, he was going to turn on the gas and stick his head in the oven. Or just get blind, stinking drunk. Yeah, he thought, that was better. Saner. The stupid shrink would be delighted to know he wasn't completely self-destructive.

When his phone rang, he ignored it. There wasn't a single person in the universe he wanted to talk to this morning. Not one. There were even more he wanted to avoid completely, namely his family, almost all of whom seemed to be possessed by unrelenting holiday cheer. The answering machine clicked on.

"Nick, answer the phone!" his baby sister commanded, sounding frantic. "Dammit, I know you're there. Pick up. I'm desperate."

Nick sighed. When Trish hit a panic button, the whole world was going to suffer right along with her. She'd be over here banging on his door, if he didn't answer the phone. Or, worse, using the key he'd given her for emergencies to barge in and turn his world as topsy-turvy as her own apparently was.

He yanked the phone out of its cradle and barked, "What?"

"Thank God," she said fervently, oblivious to his sour mood. "Nick, I need you at the mall right now!"

"Not in a hundred million years," he said at once. "Are you crazy?"

Just because her duties as a mall events coordinator required Trish to be at a shopping mall on Christmas Eve didn't mean he intended to get within ten miles of the place. He wouldn't have done it when he was in a good mood. Today, it would border on turning him homicidal.

"I'm not crazy," she insisted. "I'm desperate. Santa called in sick. If you ask me he took one look outside at the lousy weather and decided to stay home in front of a warm fire, but the bottom line is it's Christmas Eve and I don't have a Santa."

"Hire another one," he said without sympathy. "Gotta go."

"Don't you dare hang up on me, Nicholas DiCaprio. If you do, I swear I will tell Mom and Dad all about this burnout thing."

Nick hesitated. The only thing worse than having Trish nagging him to death would be to have his parents all over his case. They weren't that happy about his decision to become a cop in the first place. They'd see this so-called burnout thing as the perfect excuse to harangue him about getting off the force for good. If his sister was annoyingly persistent, his protective mother was qualified to drive him right over the brink into insanity.

"What about Rob?" he suggested, referring to their older brother. "He'd make an excellent Santa. He loves the holidays."

"Rob and Susan are taking the kids to cut down a tree today. It's their Christmas Eve tradition, remember?"

Nick groaned. How could he have forgotten that? Last year he'd gone along. It had taken the entire day, because everyone in the family, including one-year-old Annie, had a vote and there hadn't been a single tree on which they could all agree. How they could gauge Annie's vote, when she only knew one discernible word—mama—was beyond him. By three in the afternoon, he'd vowed not only to never begin any Christmas traditions, but to never have a family.

"And Stephen?" he asked hopefully. His younger brother had no traditions that Nick had ever noticed. No family, either. In fact, he was the DiCaprio black sheep, but surely Trish could corral him for the day. She was the only one in the family who seemed to understand his need for rebellion. In return Stephen did things for her that no one else could persuade him to do. She could even coerce him into showing up for holiday meals and tolerating their mother fussing over him.

"I actually spoke to Stephen. He's a little hung over,"

she admitted. "I don't think that's a good quality for a Santa."

Nick regretted not getting drunk when he'd had the chance. "Okay, fine," he said, his tone grim. "What exactly do you need from me?"

"Isn't that obvious? I need you to substitute for Santa," Trish said sweetly, obviously sensing victory. "It won't be hard. Just a few ho-ho-ho's for the kids. Listen to their gift lists. Don't make any promises. Get your picture taken. That's all."

"How long?"

"I need you here ASAP and the mall's open till six. It's a few hours, Nick. How bad can it be?"

It sounded like hell. "Come on, Trish. This is so not me. There has to be someone else," he pleaded. "Don't they have agencies for this kind of thing? Rent-a-Santa or something?"

"Are you nuts? It's Christmas Eve. All the good Santas are already working. I don't have time to hunt down the last remaining qualified Santa in all of North Carolina. And why should I, when you have absolutely nothing to do today? Please, Nick. You're good with kids."

Once upon a time he had considered himself to be good with kids. He'd been a doting uncle to Rob's kids, taking the older boys to ball games, even babysitting Annie a time or two. But after what had happened with freckle-faced Tyler Hamilton less than a month ago, Nick didn't trust himself to be within a hundred miles of a child. He didn't even want to be anywhere near Rob's kids this Christmas, at least not without backup.

Still, despite his reservations, somewhere deep down inside—very deep down—he wondered if this wouldn't be a chance for some sort of redemption. He hadn't been able to do much to help Tyler, so he could spend all day today making up for it.

No, he thought wearily, this was more like payback. Like some sort of giant cosmic joke, asking a man with his complete and total lack of holiday cheer to spend a whole day faking it for the sake of a bunch of greedy little brats.

"You'll owe me," he told his sister eventually.

"No question about it," she agreed. "Won't that be a nice change?"

"I beg your pardon."

"I have a list of the favors I've done for you, big brother, beginning with getting you your dream date with Jenny Davis."

"You did not get me a date with Jenny," he snapped, thinking of the redheaded teenager who'd been able to twist his insides into knots at seventeen.

"Did, too. She wouldn't give you the time of day, till I told her what a terrific guy you are. I also offered to loan her my cashmere sweater and to give her my new Kenny Chesney CD."

"You bribed her?" he demanded incredulously. If that wasn't the most humiliating piece of news he'd heard lately, he thought with a shake of his head.

"It was the least I could do for my favorite brother," she said.

"Well, given how badly that relationship turned out, I wouldn't be bringing it up now, if I were you," he muttered. Jenny, whom he'd dated all through his senior year in high school only to be dumped by her the day before prom, had been the first in a long string of disastrous mistakes he'd made when it came to women. At least Trish hadn't had a hand in any of the rest. He'd made those absurd choices all on his own.

"Not to worry, Nicky. My list of the favors I've done for you goes on and on. I keep it posted right beside my desk for times like this," she said cheerfully. "See you in an hour. Come to my office. I have Santa's costume here. This is going to be fun."

"Torture," he mumbled. "It's going to be torture."

"What?"

"Nothing. I'll see you in an hour."

"Love you, Nicky."

Normally he would have echoed his sister's sentiment, but at the moment he was more inclined to throttle her.

Two

The parking lot at King's Mall was already a zoo by the time Amy had showered, dried her hair, packed up the kids and found it after taking several wrong turns. A line of cars waited at the entrance and more inched up and down each aisle looking fruitlessly for someone who might be about to leave. Heavy, dark clouds were looming overhead, almost completely blocking the sun. She couldn't be sure if they were threatening rain or even snow. Though snowfall here was rare, it certainly felt cold and raw enough for it to Amy.

Just a year ago, when she'd been eight months pregnant with Emma and totally exhausted, she'd still felt the excitement of the last-minute holiday crush. Today, all she felt was tired, and the gloomy sky wasn't helping.

"Over there," Josh shouted from the backseat. "Mom, see that lady with all the bags? She's gonna leave. You can get there."

Amy spotted the woman two aisles over. "Sweetie, there are already half a dozen cars waiting for that space. Don't worry. We'll find one. It's always like this on Christmas Eve. We just have to be patient."

"What if Santa's not even here?" Josh asked worriedly. "I mean, he's in Michigan, right? How can he be in two places at once?"

"He's here. I called."

"Maybe he gets off early on Christmas Eve, you know, so he can start flying all over the world. We usually go first thing in the morning back home, then Dad and me shop to buy your presents."

Amy bit back a grin at her pint-size worrier. That, at least, was a trait he'd gotten from her. It probably wasn't the best one she could have shared. "I checked on that, too," she told him. "Santa will be here till the mall closes at six."

"What time is it now?"

"Two-thirty. We have lots of time."

"Not if we don't find a parking place *soon*," Josh warned grimly.

Amy was forced to admit, she was beginning to have her doubts about that ever happening, too. People were nuts. Two cars were currently in a standoff over a space in the next aisle, both so determined to grab it that the poor driver trying to get out couldn't even move.

"People in Michigan were nicer," Josh declared from the back.

"No, they weren't. These people are nice, too. Everyone gets a little stressed out on Christmas Eve." A fat drop of rain splatted on the windshield and her mood deteriorated even further. She envisioned whatever bug she'd had this morning turning into pneumonia.

"I'll bet Santa won't come see them," Josh predicted direly. "Not when they say bad words and stuff. Look at that guy over there. He said something bad and he did that thing with his finger that you told me never, ever to do."

Amy regretted that her five-year-old had ever seen that gesture, but unfortunately it had been one of his father's routine actions behind the wheel. She'd been forced to discuss its inappropriateness on numerous occasions.

"I think that's enough play-by-play commentary on the parking lot," she told Josh just as a space right in front of her opened up. The driver even backed up in a way that guaranteed Amy would be the one to get it, then waved cheerfully as she drove off.

"See, she was nice," she told her cynical son. "Now

let's get your sister into her stroller and go see Santa before it really starts raining."

Unloading the stroller, then getting Emma settled into it took time. Emma liked being carried. She hated the stroller...or thought she did. She kicked and screamed until Amy thought her head would split. Once she was in, though, and they were moving, Emma beamed up at Amy with the sort of angelic smile that made Amy wonder if she'd imagined all those heart-wrenching sobs only moments before. That was the joy of Emma. She could switch moods in a heartbeat.

As they reached the mall entrance, Amy gazed directly into Josh's eyes. "No running off, okay?" she said sternly. "You don't know this mall, so you have to stay with me and hold on to my hand."

"Mom!" he protested. "I'm not a baby."

"It's either that or we go right back home," she said in her most authoritative, no-nonsense tone. "I don't want you getting lost on Christmas Eve."

He rolled his eyes, but he took her hand. As soon as they were inside, he began to hurry her along past the shoe stores, lingerie shop, dress boutiques, cell phone kiosks and jewelry stores. Amy thought it was ironic that with all the big-name chain stores in the mall, it seemed every bit as familiar as anyplace they'd shopped back home. Maybe that's why Josh thought he knew where he was going.

When she was tempted to linger in front of a toy store, Josh barely spared a glance at the games in the window, then tugged her back into motion.

"Mom, come on," he urged. "Santa's gotta be right up here. See all those people? He's there. I know it! Hurry."

"Sweetie, he's not going anywhere. Slow down."

"We gotta get in line, Mom," he countered. "I'll bet it's really, really long."

Before Amy could argue with that, with some sort of child's radar, Josh spotted Santa.

"There he is," he shouted. "See, Mom. He's right there in the middle of all those Christmas trees! It's like a whole Santa's workshop around him." His eyes lit up. "Wow! That is totally awesome! It's better than anything I ever saw in Michigan! Did you bring the camera? We gotta send pictures to Dad."

His excitement was contagious. Even Emma seemed captivated by the glittering sea of lights ahead.

"I gotta see," Josh declared.

And with that he let go of Amy's hand and bolted into the frenzied crowd that was swirling all around between Amy and Santa.

It took less than a second for him to disappear in the crush of people. Excitement and anticipation died. Panic clawed its way up the back of Amy's throat. Instinctively, she gathered Emma out of her stroller and clung to her as she shouted over and over for Josh, pushing her way through the crowd, the stroller abandoned.

Most people were oblivious to her cries, but finally a young woman stopped, alarm on her face.

"What's happened?" she asked, placing a comforting hand on Amy's arm. "Can I help?"

Amy was shaking so hard, she couldn't seem to form a coherent sentence.

"It's okay," the young woman soothed. "Take a deep breath and tell me. I'm Trish DiCaprio." She gestured toward her name tag. "I work for the mall. What can I do to help?"

"My son," Amy whispered. "He spotted Santa and took off and now I can't find him. There are so many people and we don't know anyone here and he's never been in this mall before." She was babbling now, but she couldn't seem to stop.

"When did you lose track of him?"

"A minute ago at the most."

"Then he can't have gone far. It's going to be okay," Trish reassured her. "My brother is playing Santa. In real life he's a cop. He'll know exactly what to do. I'll talk to him and we'll find your son in no time. Will you be okay right here for a minute till I can get to him?"

Amy nodded. She was clinging so tightly to Emma that the baby began to whimper. Someone appeared at her side just then with the stroller. Dazed, Amy stared at it, wondering where on earth she'd left it.

"I saw your boy take off and then you ran after him and left this behind," the woman said, her voice gentle. Her blue eyes were filled with concern. "Are you okay? Shall I stay with you till that young woman comes back?"

Tears stung Amy's eyes at the kindness in the woman's expression. "Thank you for rescuing the stroller. I don't know what I was thinking."

"You were just trying to catch up with your boy. What's his name?"

"Josh."

"Oh, my," the woman said with a smile. "I have a Josh, too. Of course, he's all grown-up now." She gave a rueful shake of her head. "My kids used to pull this kind of stunt on me all the time when they were small. Trust me, they all turned up. Now they have children of their own putting them through the same thing. What do they call that? Karma, isn't it?" She patted Amy's shoulder. "Don't you worry. Your boy will be back any minute. He'll probably find you before they can even get a search going."

She spoke with such conviction that Amy felt her

panic slowly ease. "You're very kind. I really appreciate it. If you need to get your shopping finished, I'll be okay now."

"I have time," she said. "I'm Maylene Kinney, by the way. I'll just wait with you till that nice young woman comes back with help. I heard you say that you're new to Charlotte. Is that right?"

Amy nodded.

"What's your name?"

"Amy. Amy Riley."

"Well, welcome, Amy. I know this isn't the way to get off to a good start in a new place, but you will laugh about it someday, I promise you that." She smiled. "Maybe not till that boy of yours is grown and his son is doing something just as bad, but you will laugh."

Maylene's soft, Southern voice and friendly chitchat kept the panic at bay, at least for now, but Amy couldn't seem to stop searching the crowd for some sign of Josh. She ought to be looking for him, not just standing around waiting. She was always so careful to make sure he stayed in sight, to hold tight to his hand in unfamiliar surroundings. Now he could be anywhere, with anyone. This was her worst nightmare come true.

Her imagination immediately went into overdrive, envisioning every dire fate she'd ever read about. This time when the tears started, she couldn't seem to stop.

Apparently sensing her mother's despair, Emma began to howl, too. Maylene put an arm around Amy's shoulder and murmured reassurances.

"I can't do this," Amy said finally. "I shouldn't be standing around crying. I have to do something constructive. I should be looking for Josh."

"You will," Maylene said. "Help will be here any second. They'll know exactly what to do. If you go running around every which way and getting lost yourself, what good will that do?"

Amy knew she was right. She drew in a deep breath and accepted the wad of tissues Maylene handed her. "You're right. I have to be smart about this."

But she'd never felt so helpless in her life.

If Nick had to utter one more ho-ho-ho, he was going to scream. It had been 9:00 a.m. by the time he was decked out in this ridiculous red suit with all the fat man pillows stuffed into it. The stupid beard itched like crazy and the too-big hat kept sliding down over his eyes. If he was fooling one single person in this mall into thinking he was Santa Claus, he'd eat the oversize hat. Even the littlest kids were eyeing him with skepticism.

Even so, the line waiting to see him was endless. It had been nonstop since he'd settled onto Santa's red velvet throne, which he intended to tell his sister was uncomfortable as hell. No wonder Santa hadn't reported for duty.

He'd managed to eat two cookies and sneak a sip of a soda for lunch before Trish had snatched them out of his hands to have his picture taken with a dad and three teenage boys. He was so hungry he was about to snatch a candy cane out of the pile being handed out to the kids. And he was just about blind from the flash-bulbs going off in his eyes. Every parent clearly wanted to record the scene.

At least the job didn't require much acting on his part. Aside from trying to inject an unaccustomed note of cheer into his voice, his dialogue was pretty much lim-ited to the ho-ho-ho's and asking what the tiny monsters wanted Santa to bring them. He'd done okay with that, he thought. None of them had run off screaming that he was an impostor. Not yet, anyway.

"You go on being a good girl," he told the shy imp sitting rigidly on his knee. "If you do everything your mommy and daddy tell you to do, Santa will bring you that doll you've been asking for."

Her sky-blue eyes went wide. "Really?" she asked with such amazement that Nick wondered if he'd made a serious blunder. Never promise anything, Trish had warned him. Why hadn't he listened? He cast an anx-ious glance toward her mother, who gave him a surreptitious wink. He sighed with relief. Thank goodness he hadn't set the kid up for disappointment.

Just then his sister, who'd been suspiciously absent since she'd parked him here in Santa's workshop, except for the photo-op with some contest winners, appeared at his side. He immediately noted the complete lack of Christmas cheer in her expression. She looked pale and even more harried than she had earlier.

"Something up?" he asked.

She leaned down and whispered, "We have a problem, Nicky. I've got a panicky mom back there who can't find her little boy."

Nick's gut began to churn. "Call security and the cops."

"I've already called security," Trish told him. "But I'm worried she's going to pass out or something. She just needs some reassurance that everything possible is being done. Can't you help? It would make me feel a lot better if you would. You're trained to deal with situations like this. And I'd rather not call the police in unless it's absolutely necessary."

"Why the hell not?"

"I'd just rather not, okay?"

He gave her a hard look. "Are you worried about how this would play out on TV or something?"

She frowned at his scathing tone. "Don't look at me

like that, Nicky. It's part of my job to worry about things like that."

A missing child scenario barely a month in the past played itself out in Nick's mind. That one hadn't come to a good end. He didn't want to be in the middle of another one with a tragic outcome. And, goodness knows, he knew how stories like that played in the media. He'd seen his face on the front page of the papers and on the six o'clock news too damn many times.

"Then let security deal with it. Let them be heroes," he repeated firmly, not even trying to hide his reluctance to be involved in any capacity. Trish had to know what she was asking of him was too much. He didn't give a hoot how many favors he owed her.

"But I already told her you're a policeman," Trish pressed. "I know you're not on duty right now, but she's so scared, Nicky. Put yourself in her place. It's Christmas Eve and her little boy is lost. They just moved here, so she's all alone. It's no wonder she's freaking out. Please, you have to do something. Go into your professional mode. Ask the right questions, organize the search. That will calm her down until security can find her son. I'm sure it won't take that long."

Nick wasn't nearly as optimistic as his sister. In a crowd like this, with everyone focused on last-minute shopping, how many people would even notice a little boy on his own? His stomach continued to churn. He poked a hand in his pocket in search of the antacids he usually had with him. Unfortunately, he hadn't transferred them to Santa's costume.

"What about the line?" he asked, preferring even another hundred kids to one desperate mom whose child had gone missing in this mob scene.

"I'll tell them Santa has to take a break," Trish said at once. "It happens. They won't freak out or anything."

She regarded him with that same imploring look that had lured him into doing whatever she wanted when they were kids. It might work a hundred percent of the time on Stephen, but Nick was pretty much a sucker for that look, too.

Even in the face of his continued silence, Trish didn't let up.

"Security will be here any minute, but I need a real cop in charge, Nicky. You said it yourself. Please," Trish begged.

He compared his own credentials with those of the average mall security staffer and resigned himself to the inevitable. Even if it weren't his sister's neck on the line, he only had one choice. He'd been brought up to help anyone in need. His police training had ingrained the concept. Just because he was a burned-out mess, that hadn't changed.

"You get me out of here without all hell breaking loose and I'll calm this woman down and help her look for her kid." He gave Trish a fierce look. "If we don't have any luck in the next half hour, I want every cop in Charlotte combing this place, okay? I don't care what kind of PR nightmare it creates."

Trish threw her arms around him and kissed his cheek. "Thank you, Nicky. I'll make the announcement about your break right now, then I'll take you to her."

Nick figured his good deeds for the day ought to be racking up big points by now. Maybe his debt to Trish was paid. Maybe with any luck, as soon as he'd located the boy, he could scamper right on out the back door of the mall without one more ho-ho-ho.

Just as that cheerful prospect occurred to him, he caught a glimpse of the restless parents and disappointed kids as they were greeted with the news that Santa was taking a break and knew that plan was out the window.

He might be the lousiest Santa in the history of Christmas, but he was all these kids had. Heaven help them.

Three

While she was waiting for that woman—Trish something-or-other—Amy called for Josh until she was nearly hoarse, even though Maylene Kinney told her she was only hurting her vocal cords.

"Kids only hear what they want to hear," Maylene admonished. "You save your voice so you can tell him how much you love him the second he turns up."

"Right now I just want to kill him," Amy said, though she knew the older woman was right. No matter how terrified and furious she was, she could hardly wait to hold Josh in her arms again.

How could she have lost him so quickly? She'd known precisely where he was headed—to see Santa. He had to be somewhere in this mob scene of frantic shoppers and impatient children right around Santa's village, but there'd been no sign of him for what seemed like an eternity.

Finally the harried-looking young woman who'd spoken to her a few minutes earlier returned with Santa in tow. He was tall, at least six feet, and well rounded, thanks to plenty of fake padding. She couldn't guess his age, because of the fake white hair and beard, but if he and Trish were brother and sister, then surely he wasn't that old, late twenties or early thirties, maybe. Right around her age. Maybe he even had children of his own and would be able to empathize with her distress.

"Ma'am, this is my brother," Trish told Amy. "Don't be put off by the costume. He's really a terrific detective. He'll help you find your son. You'll be back together in no time."

Amy gazed into Santa's dark blue eyes behind their fake, round little glasses and felt an odd *zing* that was totally inappropriate under the circumstances. She had the oddest desire to fling her arms around this man who was offering to help her find Josh and hold on for dear life. After all, Santa Claus represented all that was good and hopeful in the world. Add to that the fact that *this* Santa was an experienced detective and he was everything she needed in this particular crisis.

"I'm Nick DiCaprio," he told her, his somber expression far from the jolly persona usually expected from Santa.

Her mouth dropped as the irony struck her. "St. Nick?"

His face relaxed and a faint smile touched his lips, then vanished. "Hardly. Trish had a last-minute emergency and, after a lot of sisterly persuasion and blackmail, I agreed to fill in for Santa. Trust me, no one would confuse me with any kind of saint."

The young woman beside him nudged him in the ribs. "Don't be modest, Nicky. You have a few saintly traits." She smiled at Amy, then gave her an oddly speculative look. "For one thing, Nicky is one of the last genuine good guys. You can't tell it now, but he's really handsome. Hot, even. And he stays in great shape."

Santa—rather Nick—frowned and cut her off before she could cover any more of his masculine attributes. "I think maybe she's more interested in my professional qualifications, Trish."

"I already told her you're an excellent policeman," she said quickly, then turned to Amy. "He has lots of commendations. If anyone can find your son—"

"Why don't you tell me about your son," he interrupted, his tone gruff. He still seemed uncomfortable, even though his sister's unsolicited praise had turned professional. "Trish, let me borrow your clipboard and notepad." He glanced back at Amy. "What's your name?"

"Amy Riley."

"And the boy's name?"

"Josh Riley."

"Age?"

"He's five."

"Height? Hair color?"

Amy rattled off the statistics, growing more impatient by the second. She knew he needed the basic information but why weren't they looking already? By now Josh could have been swept along to the other end of the mall.

"What's he wearing?"

Increasingly exasperated, she tersely described the bright red jacket, jeans and Spiderman T-shirt Josh had put on that morning and the red and green scarf he had around his neck.

"I know you think we're wasting time, Mrs. Riley," Nick said as if he'd read her mind. "But with thousands of kids running around the mall today, it's best to know exactly what your son looks like. Giving a good description to the security staff will save a lot of time in the long run."

"I have a picture," Amy said, hurriedly pulling his last school picture from her purse. It had been taken just a couple of months before they'd left Michigan. She choked up at the sight of Josh's precious gaping smile and that untamed cowlick of brown hair that refused to stay put no matter how much gel she used to slick it down.

Handing the picture to Nick, she said, "He needs a haircut now, but this was taken not too long ago."

"Cute kid," Nick said, then turned to his sister. "Trish, how far does the sound from that PA system travel?"

"It's just for the immediate vicinity," she told him. "Some of the department stores have their own. I could write up an announcement and ask them to make it ASAP."

"Do that, and we'll give this one a try, in the meantime. Keep it simple, Trish. Ask Josh Riley to come to see Santa." He glanced at Amy. "Think that would get his attention?"

"Oh, yes," Amy said eagerly. "He was so anxious to see you, I mean Santa. That's why he took off in the first place. I wasn't moving fast enough to suit him. He wanted to see you up close, then get in line."

"Have you checked the line?" he asked.

"Front to back," Amy confirmed. "He's not in it. I just don't understand why he would have wandered away."

"Because that's what little boys do," Nick offered. "They're easily distracted and often far too fearless for their own good. Trish, let's try the PA and see what happens, then do whatever you have to do to get the cooperation of the stores."

But even after several announcements, there was still no sign of Josh. Amy gazed up at Santa. Despite the beard and makeup designed to give him a jolly look, there was no mistaking the fact that his expression was troubled.

"He really is lost, isn't he?" she whispered, her voice choked.

Nick nodded, but he took her hand in his and gave it a squeeze. "Don't you dare lose it on me now, Mrs. Riley."

"Amy," she told him.

"Okay, Amy. Hang in there. We're going to find your boy."

"Of course, you will," Maylene added.

It was the first time she'd spoken since Nick's arrival. Amy knew she'd stayed close by in case she was needed, but she hadn't intruded. Amy was grateful for her presence. With Maylene around, she didn't feel quite so alone.

"I believe I know your mother, Nick," Maylene continued. "We belong to the same Red Hat Society." She beamed at Amy. "Laura DiCaprio is always bragging about her son the policeman." She smiled at Nick. "Your mother is very proud of you."

Nick seemed as surprised by that as he'd been put off by his sister's glowing comments.

"Weren't you involved in a high-profile case just recently?" Maylene asked, her brow furrowing as she apparently tried to recall the details.

"Let's not get into that," Nick said curtly.

Maylene looked taken aback by his sharp tone, but then something must have come to her because she nodded. "I'm sorry. You're absolutely right," she said hurriedly. "I don't know what I was thinking. You need to be concentrating on finding Josh."

"That's exactly right," Nick said, his sympathetic gaze pinned on Amy. "You okay?"

"I'll be a lot better when we find Josh."

"It won't be much longer," Nick reassured her. "I can see some of the security guys coming now. We want to get this search organized the right way. Once security fans out through the mall, it shouldn't take any time at all."

Oddly enough, Amy believed him. There was something solid and reassuring about a detective who would be willing to take the time to play Santa in a mall filled with last-minute shoppers and hyperactive children. It said a lot about his character that he'd helped out his sister, when most men wouldn't have wanted to be within a hundred miles of the mall today. Of course, he had mentioned something about Trish needing to blackmail him to get his cooperation, but still...

With his warm, comforting hand wrapped around

hers, Amy finally let herself start to relax. Nick might be a reluctant substitute for the real Santa Claus, but perhaps he was capable of performing at least one minor miracle and reuniting her with her little boy.

By the time Nick accepted the fact that Josh Riley was nowhere near Santa's village, a dozen mall security officers including the less experienced extras hired during the holidays, had arrived. Familiar with the mall's various wings, Nick hastily organized them into an efficient search party, showed them the picture of the boy, gave them a description of his clothes, and sent them to the areas of the mall most likely to draw an adventurous five-year-old.

All the while, he was aware of Amy regarding him with her big, soulful eyes that were shadowed by fear. Tyler Hamilton's mom had looked at him exactly like that, trusted him to bring back her boy. Nick shuddered at the memory of those harrowing hours, which Maylene Kinney had almost revealed at a most inopportune moment. Thank goodness the woman's memory had temporarily failed her. When the incident had come back to her, she'd covered well. Meanwhile, Amy seemed too distracted to notice the byplay between them. He didn't want her to start asking a lot of questions about why Nick had been in the news recently.

None of them could afford to go back and think about that tragedy right now. Amy needed to believe in him. And he had to stay focused on this mom and this boy. He refused to consider the possibility that this was anything more than a missing child. Anything else took him down a road he couldn't bring himself to travel.

That didn't mean that he didn't understand the urgency of finding Josh before his mom freaked out completely or before the situation turned into something worse. Any location that attracted a lot of children also had the potential to draw those who preyed on them.

With the security staff fanning out, he turned back to Amy.

"Let me take the baby, okay? Then we can leave the stroller here with Trish," he said lightly. The little sweetheart with her blond curls and pink bow in her hair immediately beamed at him in a way that made his heart ache.

"Who's this angel?" he asked, responding to that smile with one of his own.

"Her name's Emma," Amy said. "She's eleven months old. Are you sure you want to hold her? I can keep her."

"I don't mind. I have a niece who's not much older," he told her.

He gently patted the baby's back till she settled down again. She felt good in his arms. There was something about holding an innocent baby, smelling that powdery scent, feeling that weight relax against his chest, that always affected him and made him yearn for something that he rarely acknowledged was missing from his life.

Feeling the start of that yearning somewhere deep inside, he snapped his attention back to the current crisis.

"Is there any store in the mall that your son especially likes?" he asked.

She shook her head. "We've never been here before. We just moved to town a couple of weeks ago and we're getting settled. I wasn't even sure exactly where the mall was. I got lost getting here. We probably shouldn't have come, but it's been a family tradition to see Santa on Christmas Eve and I didn't want to disappoint Josh. It's hard enough on him since his dad's back in Michigan."

"You're divorced?" A glance at her ring finger confirmed the absence of a wedding band.

She nodded and Nick's sense of dread magnified.

"You're absolutely sure your husband's in Michigan?" he asked, his voice filled with tension.

Amy regarded him with confusion. "Of course. Why?"

"What were the terms of custody?"

"I have full custody. Josh will spend summers with his dad. What does that have to do with anything?"

"And your husband agreed to that willingly?"

"He was eager to have us leave," Amy explained. "Why are you asking all these questions about my ex-husband? He has nothing to do with this."

Nick regarded her with a penetrating look. "Are you sure about that? He wouldn't try to snatch Josh away from you?"

"No. Never," she said fiercely. "I told you, he was glad we were leaving, so he could move on with his new wife. I don't understand what you're trying to get at."

Nick recalled that Mitzi Hamilton hadn't believed her ex-husband was capable of taking their son, either. They'd wasted precious time searching for a stranger, only to determine that Tyler had been taken by his own dad, a man intent on revenge. How the hell was Nick supposed to know if Amy Riley was telling him the truth about this situation?

He looked into her eyes and tried to read her expression. She looked a bit confused, maybe even troubled by his questions, but she seemed totally sincere.

"You're absolutely certain your ex-husband wouldn't change his mind, come looking for Josh?"

"Not a chance," Amy said. She pulled a cell phone from her purse. "I could call him, if you want."

"Do it," Nick commanded. "At home, not on his cell phone."

"Why?"

"If you call his cell phone, he could be anywhere. I want to know for a fact he's in Michigan."

She looked shaken by his persistence, but she dialed. "Ned," she said eventually. "It's Amy." Her gaze locked with Nick's. "I..." Her voice trailed off, as if she'd suddenly realized that she needed an excuse for calling. Clearly she wasn't anxious to tell her ex-husband the truth, that their son was missing. After a noticeable hesitation, she said, "I was just wondering if you'd sent a gift for Josh. Nothing's come yet."

Nick sagged with relief at the evidence that Josh's dad wasn't involved in his disappearance. He barely listened to the rest of Amy's brief conversation.

When she'd hung up, she frowned at him. "Satisfied?"

He nodded. "Sorry. I had to be sure, Amy."

"Something tells me I need to know why all of this mattered so much."

He shook his head. "Just covering all the bases."

"I'm not sure I believe that," she said, studying him intently.

Nick hated seeing the doubts in her eyes, but he knew there would only be more if he explained. "Just trust me, okay?"

"I don't have much choice, do I?" she muttered wearily. She met his gaze. "Now what?"

Nick tried to think like a five-year-old boy on the day

before Christmas. "Would Josh go to a store to buy a present for his dad?"

Amy frowned. "I don't think so. We sent a present last week."

"What about you? Would he want to find a last-minute gift for you?"

Her eyes, an unusual shade of amber, shimmered with unshed tears. "I don't think so. I don't think he has any money. All he wanted to do today was see Santa. He didn't even want to waste time looking in the windows at the toy store. He was so upset this morning when I didn't feel well and said we couldn't come. I felt so awful about letting him down that I got dressed and came anyway." The tears spilled over and ran down her cheeks. "We should have stayed at home. I should have known something bad would happen."

"Come on now, Amy. You couldn't predict something like that. Stop beating yourself up. This isn't your fault."

"I just don't understand why he didn't come straight here. I swear to you that he's never done anything like this before."

"With kids, it seems as if there's a first time for everything," Nick said. "My nieces and nephews are always catching their parents off guard."

"That's what Maylene said." She glanced around. "Where is she?" Regret clouded her eyes. "She must have left. I should have wished her a merry Christmas. She was so kind to me."

Nick regarded her with wonder. What kind of woman worried about wishing someone a merry Christmas in the middle of her own crisis? "I imagine she knew you had other things on your mind. And you know her name. You can always give her a call tonight and let her know Josh is home safe and sound."

"Do you think he will be?" she asked.

"I know it," he assured her, because he couldn't very well tell her anything else. There would be time enough for a reality check if the boy didn't turn up in the next few minutes.

Suddenly her expression turned frantic again. "You don't think he'd go outside and try to find the car, do you?"

Nick sure as hell hoped not. The parking lot would make a kidnapping a thousand times easier, to say nothing of the other dangers from careless drivers trying to snag a parking place in their rush to finish up last-minute shopping. "What do you think?" he countered.

"No," she admitted. "He was totally focused on Santa, but where on earth could he be? He saw where you were."

"It's one thing to see the whole Santa's workshop thing from a distance," Nick explained. "But the closer he got, probably all he could really see were people. That's what happens with kids. They're intrepid. They rush off and the next thing you know they're lost in a sea of legs."

"I should have held on to him," she lamented, looking miserable. "I tried. I told him not to let go of my hand."

"I'm sure you did," he soothed. "Tell you what. Why don't you and I take a walk?"

She regarded him with bemusement. "A walk? Why? He'll come here first. I told you all he cares about is seeing Santa."

"Which is why we're going for a walk," Nick told her. "We'll see if we can help him spot Santa a little more easily. When I came out here this morning, I was like some sort of kid-magnet walking through the mall. If Josh is anxious to see Santa, maybe he'll see the commotion and find us."

"But what if he comes back here, thinking you'll be in the workshop seeing kids?" she asked worriedly. "He was in such a rush to get in line."

"But he didn't, did he? Which means something else caught his attention," Nick suggested, then turned to his sister who'd rejoined them after making her announcements and contacting the stores in the mall to get them to make the same announcement. "Trish will watch for him, just in case, though, right Trish?"

"Of course, I will," Trish said at once. "I'll keep his

picture with me, so he won't be scared if I approach him. Nicky, you have your cell phone?"

He nodded.

"Then I'll call you the second he shows up here," Trish volunteered, giving Amy a sympathetic look.

Nick studied his sister. She was a warm and generous woman and she seemed okay with his plan, but it had to be throwing her whole Santa photo-op thing off-kilter. As frantic as she'd been this morning over finding a Santa replacement, he couldn't help wondering if she was holding back her own emotions over this turn of events.

"Is me taking off for a little while longer going to be a problem?" he asked her.

She looked at Amy's pale face and immediately shook her head. "This is more important. I'll manage. If anyone complains I'll tell 'em Santa got stuck in the workshop elevator."

Nick grinned at her quick thinking. Her inventiveness was one of the traits that had made her perfect for this job.

"That'll work," he said just as Emma gave his beard a hard tug. "Hey there, sweet thing," he said, extricating her tiny fist from his beard. "Don't be giving away my disguise right here. We're likely to be mobbed by angry kids if they figure out they're being duped by a fake Santa."

A faint smile crossed Amy's lips, but it didn't take the worry from her eyes. She was trying so hard to hold it all together, but she had to be close to the edge. She was in a strange city, recently divorced, her kid had wandered off on Christmas Eve and a cop had been asking her all sorts of uncomfortable questions. Nick had to admire the strength it must be taking for her not to come unglued.

She gazed up at him just then, her heart in her eyes. There was no mistaking the fact that she was counting on him, that she trusted him to find her boy.

Seeing that expression on her face made Nick want to thrust Emma back in her mother's arms and take off, but he knew he couldn't. Trish had dragged him into this and now he had to see it through, for Amy's sake and maybe even for his own.

Something told him, as well, that Amy Riley could get under his skin if he gave her half a chance. He immediately sent that errant thought right back to wherever it had come from. His sense of timing obviously sucked. He could hardly hit on a woman, when he was supposed to be finding her child.

"Where are we going?" she asked him as they set off, their pace slow because of the wall-to-wall throng of people.

"Everyplace and no place," he explained. "The goal is just to draw lots and lots of attention, so maybe Josh will find us."

As a plan, it lacked finesse, but Nick was a pro at using whatever unorthodox tactics were handed him. And finding a kid who wanted to see Santa by putting Santa directly into his path seemed to be as smart a strategy as any.

Four

Santa was definitely a kid-magnet, just as Nick had predicted, Amy concluded with wonder. They were instantly surrounded by children everywhere they went. She couldn't help wondering if Nick himself weren't a babe-magnet under that padded red costume. His sister had certainly hinted at as much and he didn't seem all that put off by being the center of attention.

Nor did the throngs of children seem to rattle him any more than Emma's attempt to unmask him had. Despite his grumblings about being coerced into taking the Santa job, he handled their awestruck silences or chattered barrage of questions with equal aplomb. He hunkered down to speak with them, listening carefully as if each child was the most important one in the world. Amy couldn't miss their childish delight after getting a private moment with Santa on Christmas Eve. Despite his patience with each child, they made good progress. Nick's gaze was watchful every second.

"Do you have kids?" she asked curiously, during a rare moment when Nick wasn't being besieged.

He seemed to freeze at the question. "No. Why?"

"You're wonderful with Emma and with all these kids who keep stopping you," Amy told him. "I'm impressed. You never seem to lose patience."

"Just playing a role," he said tersely. "What would it do for Santa's reputation if I were a grouch? Just because I'm not into the holiday thing this year, why ruin some poor kid's Christmas?"

Amy didn't entirely buy the explanation. She had a hunch he was trying to hide a tender heart, though she couldn't imagine why he would want to.

"You said you have nieces and nephews, though. Trish's kids?"

"No, our older brother's. He has three boys and a girl."

"And she's the one who's about Emma's age?"

"A little older." He gave her a penetrating look. "Why all the questions?"

Amy shrugged. "Just making small talk, I suppose, anything to keep my mind off the fact that we haven't found Josh yet." She'd strained her eyes scanning the crowds, but so far she hadn't even caught a glimpse of any boy who looked like Josh wandering around lost and alone.

"I have to admit it's getting to me, Nick," she confessed, then voiced her greatest fear, "What if we don't find him?"

Nick's expression immediately turned sympathetic. She was growing to hate that look, the pity that couldn't quite cover his own worry. And he was worried. She could see it in his strained expression whenever he thought she wasn't looking.

"Don't tell me he'll turn up any minute," she snapped before he could respond. "He hasn't yet."

"Come on, Amy," he chided. "Don't give up so easily. We haven't been looking that long."

She glanced at her watch and realized it really had been little more than a half hour since this nightmare had begun. She felt as if her whole life—and Josh's— had played out in her mind since she'd last seen him. She'd formed some sort of bond with this man in the Santa suit, a closer bond of trust than she'd had with her husband toward the end. Maybe that just proved that all kinds of emotions were heightened in a crisis.

"You're right, but it seems like an eternity. Don't worry, though, I'll never give up," she said fiercely. "In the meantime, you placating and patronizing me is getting on my nerves."

"I'm sorry," he apologized, his eyes filled with un-mistakable regret.

She drew in a deep breath. "No, I'm sorry. I know you're doing everything you can. I'm just scared."

"Of course you are. You have every right to be, but we are going to find him, Amy."

She heard a giggle just then and glanced up to see Emma trying to snatch Santa's hat off. Nick grabbed it just in time, but not before she caught a glimpse of black curly hair under the white wig Emma had tugged askew along with the red velvet hat.

"Are you sure you don't want me to take her?" she asked Nick. "She has to be distracting you."

"Emma's fine right where she is," he assured her. "Be-sides, she's actually part of the bait."

"Bait?"

"With me holding her, she's high enough in the air for Josh to spot her. If I know anything about kids, he will not be happy that baby sister got to Santa first."

Amy recognized the truth in that. "You really must be a terrific detective."

He seemed taken aback by the comment. It wasn't the first time he'd seemed surprised or embarrassed when his expertise as a cop was touted. Amy couldn't imag-ine why it seemed to throw him. Was he just naturally modest or had something happened to make him question himself? Did it have something to do with that high-profile case Maylene had mentioned? Nick had gotten very uptight when she'd brought it up.

"Why do you say that?" he asked. "We haven't found your son yet."

The question only confirmed her reading that he was thrown by any praise of his professional skills. She was tempted to ask him why, but instead she merely answered the question.

"Maybe not, but you're obviously clever and intuitive about people," she told him. "At least you have my son pretty well nailed down. You seem to know how he thinks."

For an instant, the somber expression faded and his eyes twinkled behind his wire-rimmed glasses. "You met Trish. I'll bet there's the same age difference between her and me as there is between Josh and little Emma here. I was not happy when she came along. Having two brothers was bad enough, but a girl? I was not ready for that."

"But Josh loves Emma," Amy countered. "He's a terrific big brother."

"On the surface," Nick responded. "Underneath there are bound to be a few minor insecurities about having the whole order of his universe disrupted."

"Somehow I can't imagine you being insecure about the arrival of a baby sister," she scoffed.

"I was five," he said with a shrug. "It didn't take much to shake my world. The fact that my folks wanted a girl so badly was very apparent to me. After three boys and a whole lot of trucks and sports equipment, suddenly the house was filled up with dolls and frilly dresses and way too much pink."

She smiled at the image and at his exaggerated shudder of disdain. "How did your brothers react? Were you the only one green with envy?"

"Rob—he's the oldest—was okay. He was nine and already into sports and barely noticed a new baby in the house. Stephen, who's between me and Trish in age, seemed to take it in stride, too. He just ignored her, though I have to wonder in retrospect if that wasn't the moment he started to rebel to get attention."

"What did you do?"

"I alternated between being fascinated by this tiny creature with all her pink ruffles and bows and hating her guts because she was taking up all of my mom's time. I hadn't felt that way when Stephen came along. He seemed to fit right in." He gave her a wry grin. "Must have been all that girlie-girl stuff."

Amy regarded him with amusement. "And now? Do you still have mixed feelings?"

"Yes, but the princess back there rules the world. Otherwise, can you think of any reason a sane man would agree to step in as Santa on Christmas Eve?"

"Not many," Amy agreed. "Unless the pay was very, very good."

"No pay. I'm here as a favor," he said, then added, "At least it's a favor if you don't take into account her particular techniques."

"Blackmail?"

Nick nodded. "Afraid so."

"Care to explain?"

"Not at the moment."

"Then I think I'll just go on believing that Trish has you wrapped around her finger," Amy replied. "I like what that says about you."

"That I'm a wuss?" he asked, clearly amused.

"No, that you love your sister. What about the rest of your family? Are you close to all of them, too?"

"Yeah, I guess so," he admitted. "I spend a lot of time with my folks, just so my mom can nag me about being a policeman. It bothers her a lot, so I make sure she sees me enough to know that I'm still all in one piece, but not so much that her commenting drives me insane."

"That's why you were so surprised when Maylene said your mom brags about you being a cop," she concluded.

"Exactly. I never wanted to be anything else, but she

and my dad did everything they could to dissuade me. I've been on the force for nearly ten years now and they still take every opportunity to suggest other career options. If I complain about anything work related, they're all over it. My charming sister used that to get me here today."

Amy studied him curiously. "How? Are we back to the blackmail?"

He smiled, though he looked as if he regretted saying anything about it. "Maybe I'll tell you sometime, but not today. We need to concentrate on finding Josh."

Amy could hardly argue with that. The whole time they moved slowly through the mall, she was scanning the faces of the children who were staring in wide-eyed wonder at Santa. Where was Josh? Why hadn't someone found him by now or why hadn't he found them?

Just then Nick's cell phone rang. He answered it, then glanced around as if to get his bearings. "Got it," he said eventually. He explained exactly where they were located. "We'll start in that direction."

"What?" Amy demanded, her heart in her throat.

"Security found a boy wandering around by himself. He says his name is Josh."

Amy's heart turned over. "He's okay?"

"He's scared and crying, but otherwise he's just fine."

"Where is he?"

"All the way down at the other end of the mall. Security's going to pick us up in a golf cart and take us to him. In the meantime, let's start heading that way."

Amy took off at a run in the direction he'd pointed.

"Hey," he said, catching up to her. "Stick with me. I'm the one the guard's watching for, remember?"

"Of course," she said. "I'm sorry."

He touched her shoulder. "It's okay. Here he comes now."

The golf cart cruised to a stop beside them and Amy climbed in. Still holding Emma, Nick sat on the seat in back.

"Were you there when they found him?" Nick asked the security officer.

"No. I just got a call to come pick you up."

The golf cart made slow progress, especially when kids spotted Santa riding in it. In fact, at times Amy wanted to leap out and run ahead to get there faster, but she restrained herself. As Nick had pointed out, the driver knew where they were going. She didn't. She'd only waste precious time if she got lost herself.

Her heart was pounding so hard in anticipation of seeing her son, she thought it would burst. Apparently Nick sensed her restlessness.

"We're almost there," he told her, his gaze locked with hers.

The golf cart made a sharp turn to the left down another corridor, then slowed.

Amy glanced around frantically looking for Josh, but rather than spotting him, she saw only a very young security officer walking their way, his expression chagrined.

"I'm so sorry," he said, barely able to look her in the eye.

"What?" Amy demanded, her heart sinking. "He ran away again?"

"What happened?" Nick demanded.

The officer shook his head. "It was the wrong boy," he admitted, looking miserable. "His name *was* Josh, but not two seconds after I called you, his folks turned up." His gaze met Amy's, then shifted away. "I'm so sorry, ma'am. I've already put out a call. Everyone's searching again. We didn't lose more than a couple of minutes."

The last faint shred of strength Amy possessed seemed to snap in that instant. Tears tracked down her cheeks and her chest heaved with sobs. She was barely aware of Nick shoving Emma unceremoniously into the arms of the startled security guard. Then he was gathering her close.

"Come on, Amy," he murmured. "I know how strong you are. Don't fall apart now. It's going to be okay. This was just a small setback."

"I know," she whispered in a choked voice, but she couldn't seem to stop the tears or to let go of him. Nick might think she was strong, but he was wrong. She needed to absorb some of his strength before they went back to search some more. "I'll be fine in a minute, okay?"

"Okay," he said gently. He rubbed her back as he had Emma's earlier. There was nothing sensual about the gesture. It was meant only to calm, but it had been so long since anyone had touched her so tenderly that she wanted the contact to go on forever.

Not once during her divorce had she let herself lean on anyone, not her family, not her friends. She'd wanted all of them to see that she was handling it all right. But this…this was too much to expect. She didn't have any reserves of strength left. She needed someone else to share the burden. Nick, a virtual stranger to whom she owed no apologies, filled a terrible void in her life. So what if she held on for just a short while?

With her face buried against his padded chest, she could smell the faint scent of mothballs—the costume, no doubt—and a mix of clean aftershave and mint mouthwash. The velvet texture of the Santa suit felt good against her cheek, though she couldn't help wondering how his fake beard would feel. The lyrics of an old Christmas song about mommy kissing Santa Claus came to mind and made her smile.

"What's that for?" Nick asked, tucking a finger under a chin and looking into her eyes.

Amy blushed. "What?"

"The smile," he reminded her. "Not two minutes ago you were soaking my costume with your tears."

"I just remembered something," she said evasively. "It isn't important."

His gaze locked with hers and something simmered in the air between them. "It is if it put a smile back on your lips," he said quietly.

She didn't want him talking about her lips or looking at them or thinking about them. Frantically she searched for something to throw him off track. "I was just thinking about how mad Josh will be that he didn't get to ride in the golf cart."

Nick didn't look as if he believed her, but he didn't press her on it. "Then we'll see that he gets a ride. You ready to go for another stroll through the mall?"

Amy blotted up her tears with the last of the tissues Maylene had given her and forced a bright smile. "Absolutely," she said. She looked at the damp spots on Nick's costume and winced. "Sorry about that."

"No big deal." He shrugged. "It'll dry out."

When he would have taken Emma back from the security officer, Amy put her hand on his arm and felt the muscle clench. "I'm sorry we've caused such an uproar."

"You have nothing to be sorry for," he said tersely, his expression suddenly distant. "But let's not waste any more time, okay?"

Startled by his abrupt change in mood, she merely nodded, then set out to keep pace with him when he strode off with Emma back in his arms. One of these days she might not mind trying to unravel the many contradictions in Nick DiCaprio, but now certainly wasn't the time. With his quick withdrawal still fresh in her mind, she couldn't help wondering if the timing would ever be right.

Nick had just descended straight into hell. He'd had a woman in his arms who'd felt exactly right there, but unless he found her son and did it soon, she would wind up hating him. He imagined Tyler Hamilton's mother didn't have a lot of nice things to say about him these days and for good reason. He'd failed her—and her boy—and this whole episode with Amy Riley was beginning to feel the same way…as if it were skidding downhill at a breakneck pace.

The emotional roller coaster of thinking her son had been found, only to realize it had been another lost child had to have been devastating. It had nearly torn him apart watching the hope in her eyes fade and the despair return.

"Let's stop back at Santa's village," he said, praying that maybe there would be news there. Of course Trish had promised to call if Josh turned up, but Nick was starting to run out of ideas except for the kind that didn't bear thinking about. He'd have to start considering those possibilities soon enough.

"Sure, whatever you think," Amy agreed, once again sounding defeated.

Nick didn't even try to dream up some lie just to bolster her spirits. She obviously knew as well as he did that the longer Josh was missing, the more danger he might be in. Besides, he was fresh out of good cheer and he wasn't sure he could fake it. He was almost as worried as Amy must be by now.

A minute later as they approached Santa's workshop, Trish spotted them and met them before they could get too close and cause a stir. Her worried gaze shifted from him to Amy, then back again.

"Nothing?" Trish asked.

"Not yet," Nick admitted.

Trish turned to Amy. "I am so sorry about the false alarm. You must have been heartbroken. Would you like to go freshen up or anything? Get something to drink or eat? You could get off your feet for a few minutes in my office, while Nicky continues the search for Josh."

"I'm okay," Amy insisted. "I have to keep looking." She faced Nick. "But shouldn't you go back to work? Santa's been missing a long time now. The kids must be losing patience and driving their parents nuts."

"I'll go back, but not until we've found your son," he said.

"But all those kids." She gestured toward the line that still snaked down the mall's main corridor. "They're going to be so disappointed."

"They'll survive," he insisted. He gave his sister a speculative look. "But with some extra padding, Trish, you could probably pull off the Santa thing yourself."

Amy chuckled at his outrageous suggestion, which was what he'd hoped for.

The sound made his spirits lift fractionally. He grinned at her. "I wasn't kidding."

Trish frowned at him. "Well, it's not going to happen, big brother, so get over that idea. You're going to find Josh any second, then get right back into Santa mode. If I didn't know for a fact that Amy really does have a son and it's obvious that she's worried sick about him, I'd suspect you of putting her up to this just to help you sneak away from Santa duty."

Amy's eyes widened. "Would he do that?"

"In a heartbeat," Trish confirmed. "I could tell you stories about my brother—"

Nick decided these two had bonded enough. "Amy doesn't have time to listen to you go on and on about how badly I've mistreated you and how I've misbehaved through the years," he said. "Her son's missing, remember?"

Amy's intrigued expression immediately faded, but she cast a last glance over her shoulder as Nick led her away. "Later," she told Trish. "I want to hear everything."

"That's a promise," his traitorous sister replied.

Nick shook his head. If he had his way, these two wouldn't spend five minutes alone together. It was a toss-up whether his sister would sell him out...or just try to sell him. He'd seen that matchmaking glint in her eyes a few other times over the years, beginning way back with Jenny Davis. It never boded well.

Five

Nick tucked his hand under Amy's elbow and started away from Santa's village, then hesitated. As much as he hated it, there was something that had to be done. He'd waited too long as it was. To wait any longer would be totally irresponsible. He could only imagine what his bosses would have to say if this whole search blew up in his face because he'd been trying to prove something to himself. He had to stop thinking about his shattered ego and do what was best for the boy.

"Wait here a sec, okay?" he told Amy, as he held Emma out to Amy. "There's something I forgot to tell Trish."

"Sure," she said, taking the protesting Emma from him.

Warmed by the baby's reaction to parting with him,

he slipped back through the crowd and found his sister. En route, his good spirits had given way to grim reality. Trish apparently sensed his mood.

"What's up?" she asked, regarding him with concern.

"I didn't want to say this in front of Amy, but I think it's time to call in the police," he told her. "I don't like the fact that we haven't had any sightings of the boy at all. I'd think even on a day as crazy as today someone would have noticed a kid alone and stopped a security guard."

Trish's worry turned to dismay. "You don't think...?"

Nick cut her off before she could voice the thought. "I'm trying not to jump to any conclusions. Maybe Josh is just a self-possessed kid who isn't the least bit afraid to wander around in a strange place alone, but it's not likely. Most kids start to worry when their mom's been out of sight for this long. I don't want to upset Amy any more than she is already, but I'd feel better if there were some more professional cops on the scene or at least watching things in the parking lot to see if anything looks suspicious out there."

"You're absolutely right. I'll call nine-one-one," Trish said at once, clearly grasping the urgency.

"Tell the dispatcher I'm on the scene in an unofficial capacity and that I need some backup over here."

His sister nodded and pulled her cell phone out of her pocket.

Nick felt awful for Trish. He knew how important this job was to her and that a Christmas Eve story with an unhappy ending was the last thing she needed, but he didn't have a choice. Josh's safety came first. If they did everything right, there was still hope that the ending would be the happy one they all wished for.

"I know this is exactly what you were hoping to avoid, Trish, but I don't want to take chances. I hope you understand that."

"Of course I do," she said readily. "Without a doubt, finding Josh is far more important than the mall's PR. I'd never forgive myself if something were to happen to that boy and we hadn't done everything we could to find him."

"Tell me about it," Nick agreed grimly.

She gave him a penetrating look. "You holding up okay, Nicky? I know this can't be easy for you and I'm sorry I put you in this position. Maybe when your backup gets here, you can walk away and let them handle this."

"No way," he said tersely. "Amy's counting on me."

"That's what worries me," Trish said gently. "I know how you'll react if you think you've let her down."

"I'll be fine," Nick insisted. "Or I will be, as long as we find that boy safe and sound."

* * *

Amy bounced Emma in her arms and tried not to lose her patience as she waited for Nick to return. She kept consoling herself that they weren't the only ones searching for Josh, but she needed to be doing *some*thing, *not just standing idly by while others looked for her son.*

"Sorry that took so long," Nick apologized as he joined her. "Let's try this corridor over here on the left. We didn't go this way earlier."

"Your sister must be tearing her hair out over having Santa disappear on the busiest day of the season," Amy said. "I could look by myself."

"I thought we'd settled that. I still think we'll have a better chance of finding him if I'm with you. Do you have another picture of Josh in your wallet? I think we should start showing it to some of the shop employees. Maybe they've spotted him if he's been doing some shopping. A kid that age on his own would definitely leave an impression."

"I really don't think he has the money to shop," she said, though Nick's plan was probably as good as anything else they'd tried.

"No telling what a kid might have saved up for Christmas," Nick countered. "Is he a thoughtful boy?"

Amy recalled the breakfast he'd tried to make her for Mother's Day and the brightly painted lump of clay with an imprint of his hand he'd given her for her birthday. "He tries to be."

"Then he might have spotted something he wanted to buy for you," Nick said. "Have you mentioned anything in particular you want?"

Amy shook her head.

"Nothing?" he asked as if it were impossible for a woman not to want something.

"I've been totally focused on getting settled in our new place," she said with a shrug. "And I've never much cared about accumulating things."

"You haven't spotted a sweater in a newspaper ad or some earrings you might have mentioned around Josh?"

She glanced down at her comfortable, well-worn jeans and the warm red sweater she'd owned for four years at least. "I've never exactly been a fashion plate," she told Nick. "I dress better than this for work, but my wardrobe's not fancy. Just some suits and blouses. I can't imagine Josh shopping for those."

Nick surveyed her with an appreciative once-over that heated her cheeks. "You look good to me," he said, his gaze lingering on the soft red wool clinging to her chest. Then he jerked his gaze away. "Okay, then," he said, his voice a little choked. "If not clothes, what about candy? Do you have a weakness for chocolate?"

Amy laughed. "Do you know a woman who doesn't?

But I'm happy with a bag of mini candy bars from the grocery store. I don't crave the gourmet stuff. It's definitely not in our budget."

"Still, a kid might spot those big gold boxes of chocolates and check them out," he said, turning into a candy boutique.

Amy reluctantly followed him inside, where she was immediately assailed by the rich scent of fine chocolate. She couldn't help staring at the selection of truffles in the glass case, the piles of elegantly wrapped holiday boxes on the display tables. Her mouth watered despite her claim that ordinary candy satisfied her cravings. The last time she'd indulged in anything this decadent had been before her marriage when Ned brought one of the small boxes for her as a Valentine's Day gift. It was one of those rare thoughtful gestures that had convinced her he was the right one for her.

She was so absorbed in reading the labels on the trays of individual candies that she was barely aware of Nick chatting with the salesclerk, then showing the woman a picture of Josh. Only when they were back outside did she notice the small gold bag in his hand.

"Here," he said. "You need to keep your strength up."

Startled, she met his gaze. "But I told you I don't have to have the decadent kind of chocolate."

He grinned. "Maybe not, but you were practically drooling all over the case. I had to buy something."

She was too tempted by the decadent scent of that chocolate to turn him down. She opened the bag and found four different candies inside. She took a deep breath just to savor the aroma.

He watched her with amusement. "I hear they're even better when you actually eat them."

She held out the bag. "Would you like one?" she asked politely.

Chuckling, he replied, "I am not risking life and limb by trying to take one of those away from you."

"I offered," she said, though she drew the bag back.

"But the look in your eyes is daring me to accept," he teased.

Embarrassed, she held out the bag again. "No, really. Have one."

"Watching you enjoy them will be treat enough for me," he said.

She couldn't totally hide her relief. She reached in the bag, drew out one with a dark chocolate coating. If she remembered correctly, it had a chocolate raspberry filling. Very slowly she bit into it, then closed her eyes as the flavors burst on her tongue.

"Oh, my," she murmured.

When she opened her eyes again, Nick was regarding her with an odd expression. In fact, he looked a little dazed.

"What?" she asked.

"Just thinking what it would be like," he began, then cut himself off. "Never mind. We need to keep looking for Josh."

"Nick?"

He grabbed her hand. "Come on, Amy. There are a lot of stores left to cover."

He moved so quickly, she practically had to run to keep up with him. Emma jiggled in his arms, giggling happily at the unexpected adventure. He whipped in and out of half a dozen stores before he finally slowed down again.

Amy regarded him wearily. "I feel as if we're just spinning our wheels. Josh could be anywhere."

"What have you told him to do if he ever gets lost like this?" Nick asked.

"To look for a security guard or policeman, then stay put and wait for me to find him."

"Do you think the lesson took? Has he ever gotten lost before?"

"No, he's usually very good about sticking close to me."

"Would he talk to strangers?"

"Not unless it's a policeman or somebody like that. I

know he's listened to me and his dad about that. He never answers the door unless he knows who it is. And he absolutely wouldn't get in a car with anyone he doesn't know. He even asks for permission before he'll accept a ride home with a friend's parent."

Nick nodded. "That's good. Would he kick up a fuss if someone approached him that he didn't know?"

"Absolutely," she said with confidence. It was the one thing she was sure of. No one would snatch Josh from the mall without someone noticing a struggle of some kind. Outlining all the safety measures they'd taught Josh reassured her.

"You know, I'm beginning to think you're right about him shopping," she told Nick, clinging to her newfound conviction. "He probably doesn't even think he's lost and he's probably completely forgotten about the time. I'll bet something in some store caught his attention and off he went without a second thought. Maybe it's not even me he's shopping for, but Emma. I saw a baby store somewhere. And there was a toy store when we first came in the mall."

Nick gave her an encouraging smile. "Let's hope you're right. We'll work our way back to those. If what you say is true, if he's just gotten distracted, he could still find his way over to Santa's village very soon."

"Yes," she said eagerly, ready to seize on the slim hope. "I'll bet that's exactly what will happen."

They went into another half-dozen stores with no luck, then started down the other side of the corridor. The canned Christmas music, barely discernible over the hum of conversation, seemed to mock their somber mission.

"How did you end up in Charlotte?" Nick asked as they walked past a wall of display windows for a department store.

Amy regretted more than ever that Josh wasn't with them as she glimpsed the elaborate displays of snow-covered villages and mechanical elves and reindeer. She dragged her gaze away and concentrated on answering Nick.

"Things were pretty bad after my divorce," she told him. "I'd been working for a bank that has headquarters here. My boss knew what I'd been going through and asked if I'd be interested in a transfer. I grabbed at the chance."

"Was Josh happy about the move?"

"No," she admitted. "He misses his dad. I've tried not to let him know how I feel about my ex, because I don't think it's fair for a kid to be caught in the middle between parents."

"I couldn't agree more," Nick said with feeling. "You'd

be surprised how many times I see parents using their children as weapons in their grown-up wars. It's always the kids who suffer most." He studied her intently. "I'm a little surprised, though, that your ex-husband agreed to let you bring the kids this far away."

"I never said he deserved the love Josh has for him," she said wryly. "He was reasonably attentive when Josh was underfoot. The same with Emma. But he's remarried and he has another baby on the way. Our kids are extraneous to his new life. I figured in the long run Josh and Emma would be better off in North Carolina, than they would be in Michigan where they'd experience their dad's growing disinterest on a daily basis."

"He sounds like a real jewel, this ex of yours," Nick said with evident disgust.

"He was that and worse," Amy confirmed. "But he gave me two great kids, so I can't hate him completely." She met his gaze. "Why were you so worried earlier that my ex-husband might be involved in Josh's disappearance?"

"It happens sometimes in divorces," he said. "Custody might be settled in a courtroom, but parents don't always agree with the decision. Then the noncustodial parent decides to do something about it."

His answer was too pat and the way he avoided meeting Amy's gaze told her there was more to it. "Have you handled some of these custody battles?"

"From time to time," he affirmed, his expression more strained than ever.

"How ugly have they gotten?" she pressed.

"Pretty damn ugly," he said. "Let's not go there, okay? Your ex is back in Michigan, so that's one less thing for us to worry about."

Amy recognized that he'd closed down the subject, but that only made her want to pursue it more. Before she could, Nick deftly changed the subject.

"It must be hard being in a new place at Christmas," he suggested. "Especially with kids."

Amy gave him a knowing look, but decided to let him get away with it.

"I don't think I realized until today how hard it would be," she admitted. "The Santa thing was a big tradition with us, at least for Josh. And we always went to church on Christmas Eve to the children's service, then went home and had hot chocolate, put out cookies and milk for Santa, and watched Christmas movies till Josh fell asleep. Then Ned would carry him upstairs and we'd put all the presents under the tree, then eat the cookies."

Nick smiled. "You didn't drink the milk?"

Amy wrinkled her nose. "Warm milk? Yuck. We

dumped it out and left the glass sitting there with the empty cookie plate." She sighed suddenly. "I wonder what traditions we'll have now."

"You'll make new ones," Nick said. "And keep the old ones that work, just like coming to the mall today to see Santa." He hesitated, then said, "You know, you could come to church with my family tonight if you wanted to. I wasn't going to go, but I will if you think Josh would enjoy going and keeping another tradition alive."

Amy's eyes turned misty at the suggestion, as well as at his confidence that Josh would be safely back with her before long. "You'd do that? You don't even know Josh and you can't have a very good impression of him—or me—after what's happened today."

"He got lost. He didn't commit a crime," Nick told her. "As for you, there's no mistaking the fact that you're a loving mom. Even the best mothers can't stop kids from slipping away in the blink of an eye."

"Thank you, but I'd hate to have you change your plans for us. You said you hadn't planned on going. What were you going to do?"

"Nothing in particular," he revealed.

Amy regarded him with surprise. "You were going to spend Christmas Eve alone?"

"People do," he said gruffly. "It's no big deal."

"Of course, it is. Surely you'd rather be with your family."

"Thus the invitation to church," he said wryly. "I'd definitely get points with my folks. Besides, I think maybe going to church would be as good for me as it would be for Josh. Maybe I need to stick with tradition, too."

She studied him curiously. "Why is that?"

"Just some demons that need to be laid to rest," he said evasively.

Amy sensed they were finally cutting close to whatever Nick was struggling with. He'd been so kind to her today, she wanted to return the favor. "I don't want to pry, Nick, but is it anything you want to talk about? You've been dancing around something ever since we started searching for Josh."

For an instant it looked as if he might open up and tell her, but just then the color washed out of his face and he abruptly whirled around as if he were trying to avoid someone.

"Nick?" she said, startled by his behavior. "What is it? Did you see someone you know? Someone you'd rather not see?"

"Let's check out this place," he said brusquely, dragging her inside a men's shoe store.

Amy scanned the faces outside to see if she could figure out who had sent Nick fleeing. All she noticed were families, some laughing, some obviously stressed by the mad rush. A few men hurried by looking thoroughly harried. And a few women—young and old—passed, laden down with packages. There was even one group of teenage girls who seemed more intent on looking for boys than shopping. They preened and pretended nonchalance whenever a boy passed by. No one jumped out at Amy as the possible cause of Nick's sudden panic, and that's what it had been, she realized. He'd been thoroughly spooked by whomever he'd spotted.

She turned back to Nick, who was chatting with the clerk behind the counter, his actions now briskly professional again.

Only after they were outside and walking toward the next store did she meet his gaze. "What happened back there, Nick?"

He regarded her with a neutral expression. "I don't know what you mean."

"You're not a good liar," she accused. "Was it an old girlfriend? A current one?"

"Not that it's any of your business, but it was nothing like that," he snapped.

His tone was like a slap. She felt oddly saddened by his refusal to confide in her, but what had she expected? He was right. She hardly knew him. He was a policeman helping her out in a crisis. She had no right to pry into his personal life.

And what about his questions, she asked herself. Were all of those strictly professional, the mark of a thorough detective? She didn't think so.

Nor was the invitation to church. No, there was something between them, some spark that might be explored sometime in the future. That spark went beyond the intensity of the situation. It was definitely personal. The surprise was that after all her vows to concentrate on her new job and her kids, she'd wanted to see where that spark led.

Or, she amended, she'd wanted to until the moment when Nick had deliberately lied and shut her out. She'd already been with a man who'd been a master at keeping her in the dark. She wouldn't knowingly get involved with another one who was capable of the same kind of deceit. It hurt to think that there might be any comparison whatsoever between her ex-husband and this man who'd been only decent and kind to her, but she couldn't take the chance.

Not that she could spend even one more second worrying about such things when Josh was still missing. Nick was her best hope for finding her son. She needed his help. And when Josh was safely with her, then she and Nick DiCaprio would go their separate ways.

Even with her mind made up, though, she couldn't help feeling as if she'd just lost something important, something good that had almost been within her grasp.

Six

Nick knew he'd been too abrupt and sharp with Amy. He'd immediately recognized the hurt in her eyes when he'd dismissed her well-meaning questions, but what other choice had he had? How could he explain to her that he'd just seen the mother of a child who'd died while he was supposed to be rescuing him? Not only was it something he could barely stand to remember, but it would be the worst possible testimonial to his skills as a police officer. Amy would be justified in demanding that someone else take over the search for her son.

For reasons he didn't care to examine too closely, Nick didn't want that to happen. As he'd told his sister, he wanted to see this through. Not only did he want to spend more time with Amy, but he needed redemption and this seemed like fate's way of giving him a chance for it. He needed to prove to himself that he could find this boy and return him safely to his mother, that the tragedy with Tyler Hamilton hadn't destroyed him. Otherwise he'd never be able to go back on active duty on the force. And if he wasn't a cop, who the hell was he?

Okay, so his motives were partly selfish. He admitted that without shame. He didn't want his career going up in flames. He knew in his gut he was *still* one of the best cops in the department. All modesty aside, his skills were superior. He had the citations and job performance reviews to prove it. He just had to tamp down his anger and get his confidence back. The shrink was right about that much. But finding Josh—not endless hours baring his soul—was the answer.

Although he believed wearing this hot and bulky Santa outfit would work to their advantage eventually, he had to admit that right this second he would have preferred being in street clothes so he could blend in and move more quickly. Then, again, the costume may have been the only thing that had kept Tyler Hamilton's mom from recognizing him and for that he was grateful. A confrontation with Mitzi Hamilton was the last thing he needed. He still had nightmares about the bleak expression on her face when he'd had to tell her that Tyler was dead.

"Nick?"

He gazed down into Amy's troubled eyes. "What?"

"Are you okay?"

He forced a reassuring smile. "Fine. Let's get back to work."

Once again, she looked disappointed by his response, as if she'd been expecting—or hoping for—something more. Unfortunately, until they found Josh, he was fresh out of revelations he could make without having her doubt him and scaring her to death.

Amy reevaluated her earlier dismay over Nick's reticence. It was evident he was genuinely troubled by something, something more than their unproductive search. Maybe she should force the issue, no matter how reluctant he seemed. Maybe it would do them both good to think about something other than her son. Whatever those demons were that Nick had mentioned, maybe she could help him deal with them.

"You know, Nick," she began casually. "You can talk to me."

He glanced at her with a questioning look. "We've been talking."

"Not about anything significant," she said.

"Oh, I don't know about that," he protested. "You've told me all about your son and about your divorce. I know about how hard it is being away from your family for the holidays. I'd say we've scratched below the surface."

"Up to a point, that's right," she agreed. "You know all that about me, but I know very little about you, other than how many siblings you have and that your folks don't like you being a cop."

"That's my life in a nutshell," he said glibly.

She looked away and thought back over their conversation. One comment stood out. She was pretty sure it held the key to understanding Nick.

"I don't think your life can be summed up so easily," she said quietly. "For instance, I think there's a very specific reason you planned to stay away from church tonight." She stared directly into his eyes. "Are you mad at God? Has something happened to make you question your faith?"

He turned away, but not before she saw that her questions had struck home.

"What was it?" she prodded. She connected the dots and realized that whatever it was that had happened was somehow work related. "Did something go wrong on a case you were handling?"

His hard expression, a stark contrast to the rosy tint of his cheeks and thick white beard of his Santa costume, told her she'd hit on it. Somehow, though, she didn't have the sense that Nick admired her detecting skills.

"Leave it alone," he commanded, his tone like ice. "I'm not discussing it with you or anyone else, especially not when we're in the middle of a search for your son."

"Something tells me this is exactly the time you should talk about it," she countered. "It's weighing on you now. Is it interfering with your ability to help me find Josh?"

"Absolutely not. I don't let anything interfere with my job, not even a woman asking too many pesky questions about things that are none of her business. Now will you get your priorities in order? Stop trying to dig around in my psyche and pay attention to the people around us. You could walk right on by Josh and never see him."

The harsh accusation stung, but unfortunately Amy couldn't deny it. She'd needed a temporary distraction and she'd seized on fixing Nick, whether he needed it or not. She still believed he did, but that wasn't the point and it wasn't her job, particularly not this afternoon.

"Okay," she said softly. "I apologize for prying."

"Whatever," he said, avoiding her gaze.

Nick's attention was deliberately focused on scanning the crowds around them. Amy sighed, then followed suit, looking into the face of every child they passed. With each one that wasn't Josh, she grew more and more discouraged. With each second that passed without a call from one of the security guards or Trish, her heart ached a little more.

Then, just when she was losing all hope, she spotted a familiar-looking shock of brown hair sticking up on the back of a boy's head. He was too far away for even a glimpse of his face. Even so, a faint spark of recognition made her spirits soar. She tried to tamp down her excitement. Too many times before her hopes had been dashed seconds later.

Then her eyes locked on a red and green scarf that had come unwound from around the boy's neck. It was dragging on the ground behind him. There was no mistaking that scarf. She'd knit it for Josh herself just last Christmas.

"There!" she screamed, seizing Nick's arm and pointing across the mall. "I see him, Nick. He's right over there, going into that store. You were right all along. He is shopping."

Nick stared in the direction she was pointing. "Where did you see him, Amy? Are you sure it was Josh?"

By then Josh had disappeared into the store, so rather than answer she started to dash across the mall, dragging Nick with her. Trying to cut through the crowd bordered on impossible until Nick cupped a hand under her arm and guided her through. Whether it was his size, his determination or the Santa costume, the crowd gave him room to pass.

"Which shop?" he asked when they reached the other side. "I still don't see him."

"Right here," Amy said, her cheeks burning as she stopped in front of a display window filled with mannequins clad only in lacy underwear. "He went into the lingerie shop."

Nick gave her an odd look. "Your five-year-old son went into a lingerie shop?"

"Hey, you asked what he might buy me for Christmas. His dad used to give me fancy lingerie. It never occurred to me when you asked, but I suppose Josh got the idea from that."

Nick still looked vaguely disconcerted. "I see."

As they reached the store's entrance, she sensed Nick's hesitation and thought she knew the cause. Most men loved to see women in sexy, lacy undergarments, but they'd rather be caught dead than be seen shopping for them. Amused, she looked into his eyes. "You're not scared of a few bras and panties, are you?"

He frowned at the question. "Nope, just the women swarming around in there buying them."

"It's Christmas Eve," she reminded him. "Take another look inside. Most of the shoppers today are desperate men. I'm the one who ought to be embarrassed."

"You're absolutely sure Josh went in there?" he asked, still hanging back, though his alert gaze continued to scan the customers.

Even amidst the crush of much taller men inside the shop, she could see Josh...or at least the tail end of that dragging scarf. Filled with relief at the realization that her boy was safe and sound, she nodded. Then the crowd parted and she saw him clearly, head to toe, totally absorbed by a table full of sale items.

"I can see him from here," she said excitedly. "Right there, Nick! He has a pair of red thong panties in his hand."

At her claim, rather than looking into the store, Nick's gaze sought hers and never left her face. His eyes darkened with unmistakable heat. "Red, huh?"

Amy couldn't help it. She laughed. "It's not becoming for Santa to drool. You look a little like I must have looked in the candy store. Will you come on? Let's not let him slip away from us."

"It's probably not a good idea for Santa to be seen ogling ladies' lingerie, either," he commented. "Why don't I just stand right here blocking the doorway with Miss Emma, while you retrieve your son? I'll be backup in case he tries to scoot off again."

"Chicken," she accused lightly, able to tease because the nightmare was almost over.

"Damn straight," he agreed without apology.

Amy didn't waste another second arguing. She made her way through the mobbed store till she was right beside Josh. For a second she simply stood there, drinking in the precious sight of him. Finally she spoke.

"Young man, you are in so much trouble," she said, hunkering down to draw him into her arms in a fierce embrace. She was so relieved, she wanted to never let go.

"Mom!" he protested, pulling away. "You're not supposed to see me."

She shook her head. He was oblivious to her distress and to the relief that was now spilling through her.

"And why shouldn't I see you?"

"'Cause I'm buying your present," he said reasonably. "It's supposed to be a surprise."

As desperately as she wanted to hug him and hold on forever, she had to make him understand that what he'd done was not acceptable.

Keeping her expression stern, she demanded, "Present or no present, Joshua Riley, did you stop to think for one second that you might scare the living daylights out of me by running off to go shopping?"

He blinked hard. "You were scared?"

"Well, of course, I was," she said, giving him a gentle shake. "When have I ever let you go off shopping all by yourself? More than that, you've never been to this mall before. When you let go of my hand, I thought you were going straight to see Santa, but you never showed up. I had no idea where you were. You've been missing for a very long time."

He regarded her earnestly. "I did go to see Santa, but the line was really, really long and I wanted to get you a surprise, you know, something like Dad would get you so you wouldn't be sad."

Touched more than she wanted to admit, she asked, "How did you know where to look?"

"I knew the kind of store, 'cause I went with Dad last year," he explained. "First I had to find the directory thing, because I knew you'd be mad if I asked a stranger. I looked and looked, but I couldn't find one, so I just kept looking for the store. There are lots of stores and it's hard to move 'cause there are so many people. It took a really long time, but this is just like the one where Dad used to shop."

He sounded so proud of himself, it made Amy want to cry. She blinked back tears. "Oh, sweetie, I don't need a present like that. Besides, where did you get that kind of money? Even on sale, these things are expensive."

"I saved the money Dad gave me before we left Michigan." He held out the red thong panties. "Do you like these?"

In Amy's opinion they looked uncomfortable, just as the ones Ned had given her through the years had been. Those had stayed tucked in her lingerie drawer most of the time. She was not letting her son waste money on another pair that would be consigned to the bottom of her dresser.

"What I think is that you are an amazing boy to want to buy me a present like that, but I want you to save that money for something special for you, just like your dad intended." She regarded him seriously. "Though, it will be a very long time before you get to spend it, because after this stunt you're going to be grounded till you're thirty."

His expression faltered. "But, Mom, I just went shopping for you," he protested. "I thought you'd be happy."

"While buying a present is a thoughtful thing to do, running away to do it is not. A policeman and an entire mall security team have been searching for you for more than an hour," she responded.

For the first time, Josh seemed to grasp the magnitude of what he'd done. "Uh-oh," he whispered. "Are they gonna be mad at me?"

"I think they're going to be relieved that you're okay," she said. "And I know they'll appreciate it when you apologize to each and every one of them."

"Okay," he said meekly. "I'll tell 'em I'm really sorry.

Maybe we could go home and get some Christmas cookies for them."

Her point seemed to have sunk in, at least enough for now. She'd spend the next ten years driving it home. With a boy this precocious, she was sure she'd have lots of opportunities.

"Now that you understand that what you did was wrong, I think there's somebody here you might want to meet. He needs to see for himself that you're safe and then let everyone know we've found you. Put those panties back, and let's go."

Josh parted with the panties reluctantly, then dutifully took the hand she held out.

"Who is it?" he asked as they walked through the store. "Who wants to see me?" His eyes widened. "Is it Dad? Did Dad come for Christmas?"

She was seized by momentary anger at her ex, who hadn't even made a phone call to Josh for over a week now. But what was the point? Ned was Ned. She was tired of covering for his lack of consideration.

"No, sweetie," she consoled Josh, biting back the desire to make excuses. "It's not your father."

"Oh," he said, his tone flat with disappointment.

"Come on now. I think this will be just as good," she told him.

"Grandma and Grandpa?" he asked, but without as much enthusiasm.

Before Amy could reply, Josh spotted Santa holding Emma. His cheeks turned pink and his eyes lit up. Whatever disappointment he'd felt that it wasn't his dad vanished in a split second of recognition.

"Santa!" he shouted, clearly thrilled. "You brought me Santa!"

For the second time that day he jerked free of Amy's grip and made a dash for it, but this time Santa was right there to scoop him close in a hug.

Seven

Nick's gaze had locked on Amy as she'd traveled through the store and reunited with her son. Emma had laughed and pointed, clearly recognizing her big brother and delighted to see him. Something inside Nick melted as he watched the reunion.

This was what should have happened with Tyler Hamilton. His mom should have had a joyous moment just like this, but she hadn't. Instead, there had been only the awful news that her boy was dead, news Nick had insisted on delivering himself. He had to stand by helplessly as the color had drained from her face. He'd caught her as her knees gave way and she'd been racked by grief-stricken sobs. He couldn't imagine that memory ever fading, not even with this far happier memory to replace it.

When Josh spotted him, whooped joyously, and let loose of Amy's hand, Nick dropped to his knees so he could catch the boy as he barreled straight into his knees. For at least a fraction of a second, all he felt was relief. *This* search had ended well. *This* boy was back with his mother and Nick had played at least a small part in making it happen.

His gaze stayed on Amy's. She looked as if she'd been given the very best Christmas present ever.

"Thank you," she mouthed.

Before Nick could respond, Josh wiggled free and studied him intently. "I met Santa last year," he said. "You don't look like him."

Nick bit back a smile. "Santa had a rough year. I'm older."

Josh didn't look convinced. "You don't sound like him, either. You sound funny, like you live around here instead of at the North Pole."

"Well, you see, Josh, that's the thing. Santa has to adapt to his environment," Nick improvised as Amy chuckled. "I've been here at this mall for a while now and everyone talks like this. They expect me to sound just like them."

"I guess," Josh said doubtfully. Then his expression brightened. "Can I tell you what I want for Christmas right now? That way I won't have to wait forever in line.

That's how come I got lost, 'cause the line was too long and I didn't want to wait in it."

Nick exchanged a glance with Amy, who looked as if she'd give the boy the sun, moon and stars now that he was safely back with her. He wasn't inclined to be as lenient.

"Let's talk about this," he suggested to Josh. "Man to man."

"Okay," Josh said eagerly.

Nick barely contained a grin. "I'm not so sure little boys who run away and scare their moms ought to be getting presents from Santa," he said. "What do you think?"

"You're asking me to decide if I should get presents?" Josh asked incredulously.

"Yep."

Josh's expression turned serious as he pondered Nick's—*San*ta's—question. *"Okay, here's what I think,"* he told Nick earnestly. *"I didn't mean to scare Mom. And I only went to buy her a present. That's a good thing, right? Mad as she was, even Mom said I was amazing."*

Nick swallowed a laugh. Amy must have her hands full with this one. He had well-developed reasoning powers for a boy his age, or else it was just a strong sense of self-preservation. Nick had been very much like that as a kid, able to fast-talk himself out of most trouble.

And his mother had been every bit as tolerant as Amy. His father had been the disciplinarian. Josh didn't have anyone around to fill that role. For today, at least, maybe Nick could do it.

He looked Josh in the eye. "It was a very unselfish thing to want to do," he agreed. "So, yes, that does count as a good thing. But running away, even with the best intentions, is never good. Lots of people have been very worried about you."

The boy regarded him with genuine dismay. "I know. Mom said." Then his expression brightened with hope. "But I'm going to apologize, so it'll be okay."

Nick glanced up at Amy. "I'm sure an apology will be appreciated, but I want to be sure you understand why what you did was wrong."

"Because I scared Mom," Josh said at once.

"That's one reason," Nick confirmed.

He tried to find a way to drive his point home without scaring Josh and robbing him of his astonishing fearlessness. It would be a good trait later in life, though in the meantime it was likely to give Amy frequent anxiety attacks.

He regarded Josh with a somber expression. "But there's another one and it's just as important. It's very dangerous for someone your age to be alone in a crowd like this. All sorts of things can happen to children when there's not an adult around to keep an eye on them."

Josh studied him intently, absorbing his words, but clearly not ready to take them at face value. "Like what?"

Nick debated how specific to get, then decided on another tack. "You believe in Santa, right?"

"Sure."

"Well, Santa sees a lot of things, like when boys and girls are good and bad."

Josh nodded. "That's why I'm really, really good." He glanced at his mom, then amended, "Well, most of the time, anyway. Until today."

Nick hid a grin. "Okay, then, if you understand that Santa knows a lot about what happens all over the world, then could you just take my word for it that it's dangerous for you not to be with an adult in a busy mall like this?"

Josh still looked vaguely skeptical. "But nothing bad happened," he protested.

"This time," Nick emphasized. "You were very lucky today, Josh, but it's not a chance you should ever take again. Do you understand that?"

"I guess so."

"Then here's the deal. If you want Santa to reconsider discussing presents with you, you have to promise never to do anything like this again."

With presents on the line, Josh nodded solemnly.

"Okay. I promise." He turned to his mother. "I'm sorry, Mom."

"Santa will know if you go back on your word," Nick warned him. "So you have to keep that promise forever."

Josh gazed at him with dismay. "Like, till I'm a teenager or something?"

"No, forever is even longer than that. It's till you're all grown-up and even then you should never do anything that might make your mom worry. Okay?"

"I guess," Josh said. "I'll try, but that sounds like a long time to be good." He studied Nick closely. "Do you have a mom?"

Nick nodded.

"Does she still worry about you?"

"Oh, yeah," Nick said fervently. And unfortunately he worried her all the time, though he wasn't about to tell Josh that.

"But you're Santa!"

"Moms never stop worrying, no matter who you are or how old you get," Nick told him. "I know forever seems like way too long, but I think you can do it."

"Maybe," Josh said, his voice filled with doubt.

"Why don't you think about it for a while and we'll talk about it again when you come through the line to tell me what you want for Christmas?"

Josh started to break away. "I'll get in line right now," he said, clearly about to make a dash for Santa's village.

Nick snagged his hand. "Hey there, what did we just talk about?"

Josh winced. "Oh, yeah. Mom, can we get in line now?"

Before Amy could reply, Nick glanced at the endless line. He figured if he was going to have to deal with all these kids who'd been waiting patiently to see him for more than an hour, there should be a reward for him at the end of it. Besides, something compelled him to make sure he had a chance to spend more time with this family. He wanted time to persuade Amy to go to church with his family this evening. He sensed that with them beside him tonight, he might start down the path to something special.

"Tell you what," he said to Josh. "Since the line's so long, why don't you, your mom and Emma here, go grab a snack and then come back? Then you can tell me what you want for Christmas."

"Will there still be time?" Josh asked worriedly.

"I won't leave till you've come back," Nick promised. He glanced at Amy. "Is that okay with you? You look as if you could use something to eat. The food court's right across the way. I highly recommend the pizza."

She seemed uncertain for a moment, then her expression brightened. "Actually I'm starving. I had a touch of the flu earlier, but it seems to be gone. To my amazement, pizza sounds great. Can we bring you anything?"

Nick shook his head.

"Then we'll see you in a little while," Amy concluded.

She started away with Emma in one arm and Josh holding her other hand, then turned and came back. Before Nick realized her intention, she stood on tiptoe and pressed a kiss to his cheek.

"Thank you for helping me find Josh," she whispered, her eyes damp with tears. "You have no idea…" Her voice broke.

He touched a finger to her cheek, wiped away a single tear. "I think I do," he responded. "And I'm glad I was able to help."

Her gaze locked with his. "I'll never forget what you did for us." Then her lips slowly curved. "Or all the unanswered questions I asked you."

Nick knew she'd meant it as a mild threat, but he couldn't help chuckling. "You may be the most persistent person I know."

She grinned. "Remember that. Now, are you sure you don't want me to bring something back for you? A soda? A slice of pizza?"

"Nothing," he said again.

Not until she was moving through the crowd did he murmur, "Just yourselves."

He uttered the telling words just in time for Trish to overhear them.

"Find something more than a lost boy, big brother?" she taunted.

"Who knows?" he said, sounding only slightly defensive. "I might have."

"I saw the kiss, by the way. And I couldn't miss the thunderstruck expression on your face." She smiled. "Apparently, it's a season for miracles, after all."

Just then their mother, Laura DiCaprio, rushed through the crowd and joined them. "There you are," she said, sounding slightly winded as if she'd run through the mall. She looked Nick over from head to toe. "Nicky, you make a wonderful Santa," she said approvingly.

His mother's arrival was not a development he'd anticipated. Nor was he particularly overjoyed to see her. He couldn't help wondering what had brought her here, especially since she looked as if she'd interrupted her Christmas baking to come. He frowned at his sister, convinced she was somehow behind this, but Trish merely shrugged.

"Don't look at me," she said. "I haven't spoken to her all day."

He turned back to his mother. "What are you doing

here, Mom? Don't tell me it's a coincidence, because I know you finished your Christmas shopping a month ago."

"I finished in September, as a matter of fact," she informed him.

"Not a direct answer," he accused.

"And I'm not some suspect," she retorted.

"Mother!"

"Okay, if you must know, Maylene Kinney called me. She told me about the missing boy…" Her voice trailed off as she studied him intently. "Well, I'm sure you understand why I had to come, Nicky. I wanted to see for myself that you're okay. Your father's outside cruising around looking for a parking place. I imagine he'll be in here eventually." She regarded him hesitantly. "Is it over? Is the boy okay?"

"He's fine," Nick said tersely.

None of this was good, Nick thought wearily. If news of another missing boy, even one that had been found already, got out, the mall was going to be crawling with reporters. He pinned his sister with a look. "If any of the media show up, keep them away from me, okay? Tell them it was a false alarm. Or tell them the truth, that Josh is back with his mom and it's all over, but leave me out of it."

Trish regarded him with dismay. "I'll do my best, but

Nicky, there's a reporter here already, doing a story about the last-minute holiday shoppers. I'll talk to her, but you know she may not give up easily. It's a great story. Family reunited by Santa on Christmas Eve."

"If that's all there was to it, it would be one thing, but we both know better," he said.

"But Nicky you'll be a hero," his mom spoke. "Wouldn't that be a good thing after…well, after what happened before?"

"I don't want to be a hero and it would take more than this to turn me into one. Hell, I don't even want to be Santa." He shook his head. "I never should have answered my phone this morning."

Then he thought of meeting Amy and that precocious boy of hers. He remembered how it felt to have sweet Emma in his arms. He wouldn't have missed that for anything.

He caught the expression in his sister's eyes and knew she understood. "I'm going back to work before these kids start a riot," he said grimly.

Then he was struck by another thought. "Trish, maybe you ought to find Amy and warn her about that reporter. I don't know if anyone would recognize her or Josh and point them out, but she ought to be prepared. Tell her to stay in the food court till you come back for her. I promised Josh he could visit with Santa before the mall closes."

His mother's eyes brightened with curiosity. "Amy? Is that the woman whose boy you found? Maylene said she was lovely and that she's new in town and a single mom. And Josh must be her son."

"That's right," Nick said, aware of the matchmaking wheels spinning into action.

"I'll go with you, Trish," his mother declared. "I'd like to meet her. Maybe she'd like to bring her family to Christmas dinner tomorrow."

Trish couldn't seem to hide her amusement. He doubted she'd even tried.

"Any comment, big brother?" she inquired.

He sighed. "What would be the point? You two never listen to a word I say, anyway."

"That is not true, Nicholas DiCaprio," his mother scolded, then winked. "Sometimes we just read between the lines, too. Come, Trish. Let's go find this woman. Nicky, when your father turns up, you tell him where to find me."

Nick watched them go. He swallowed hard. If it weren't for the jostling throng of kids waiting for him, he would have tried to stop his mom and sister, or at least gone with them to protect Amy. He had a hunch she'd be safer with a whole battalion of news-hungry reporters than she would be with his mom and sister when they were on a mission to give him the priceless Christmas gift of a new romance.

Amy bought slices of pizza and soft drinks for herself and Josh, then searched for a place to sit. Every table was jammed with shoppers taking a break from the frenzy. She could barely maneuver Emma's stroller, between the chairs. She watched with her heart in her throat as Josh tried to balance the tray with their food.

"Over here," Trish said, waving and greeting her with a smile. "My mom's holding a table for you."

"Thank you so much," Amy said, relieved. "Did Nick get back on Santa duty okay?"

"He's on the job, but he wanted me to warn you to stay put here till I come back for you."

Amy paused in midstride. "Oh?"

"I'm so sorry," Trish apologized. "We think word may have gotten out about the missing child. Because of Nick's involvement, it could turn into kind of a big story. I'm going to do what I can to fend off any reporters, including the one who's already here on a different assignment, but Nick didn't want you guys to get dragged into the middle of it." She gave Amy a questioning look. "I'm assuming he's right, that you'd prefer not to be interviewed?"

"He's absolutely right," Amy said, filled with dread at the prospect. Now that the incident was over, she didn't even want to think about it again.

Unfortunately Josh overheard them. "But Mom, we could be on TV," he said excitedly. "That would be so awesome! We could tape it and send it to Dad and Grandma and Grandpa."

"You don't get a say in this," Amy said firmly. "Besides, do you really want your dad to know you ran away? You're in trouble, remember? You have a lot of apologies to deliver."

"But I could say I'm sorry on TV and then everyone would know," Josh countered.

Amy merely shook her head as Trish tried to stifle a grin.

"Let's just sit here and eat our pizza, and be grateful things turned out okay," Amy told him. "And I need to feed Emma."

"My mom will be glad to help with that," Trish offered. "She's great with kids. She's right over here."

Trish led the way to an empty table that was being held by a woman who looked to be in her midfifties, about the same age as Amy's mother. She looked as if she'd run out of the house in the midst of baking. She still wore an apron over her slacks and sweater and there were streaks of flour on her clothes. The coat she'd flung on looked as if it might be her husband's hunting jacket. Her hair was mussed, as if it had curled while she was working around a hot stove. Despite her disheveled appearance, she gave Amy a warm smile.

"You must be Amy," she said as they approached. "Maylene Kinney described you perfectly." She beamed at Josh. "And you must be the little boy who got away."

Josh nodded. "I'm in trouble," he said, awkwardly balancing the tray of pizza and drinks.

"I imagine you are," she said. "But you're safe and that's what counts."

Mrs. DiCaprio rescued the tray of food and set it on the table. "Oh, that looks good. I think I'll run and get a slice for myself. I've been baking all day and haven't had a minute to eat anything. Don't wait for me."

Amy stared after her. She felt as if she'd been caught up in a whirlwind, then set back down in the calm that followed. "Is she always like this?"

Trish chuckled. "Pretty much. Look, is it okay if I leave you in her hands? I need to go and check on Santa. He was a bit surly before."

"Sure," Amy said, then thought of her earlier conviction that something had happened to Nick on the job recently. That fit with what Trish had mentioned about his involvement in Josh's search being newsworthy. "Trish, before you go, can I ask you something?"

Trish's expression turned cautious. "About?"

"Your brother." She moved away from the table and out of Josh's hearing so she wouldn't completely destroy his illusion of Nick as Santa. "Is there some reason reporters would be all over this story, other than it being Christmas Eve and Santa helping to find Josh?"

Trish hesitated a long time before answering. "You'll have to ask Nicky about that," she said finally. "I really do have to go now. He'll be over to get you soon, I'm sure. Or I'll come back myself. In the meantime, Mom will be around if you need anything."

She took off, leaving Amy's question unanswered. But even without Trish's confirmation, she knew she was right. There was something about Nick she needed to know before things went any further between them. Everything pointed to the fact that he was a great guy and he was certainly surrounded by a wonderful family, if Trish and his mom were anyone to judge by. But he had a secret and she'd had her fill of men with secrets.

Eight

It had been a day of astonishing ups and downs, Amy thought as she and Mrs. DiCaprio slowly ate their slices of pizza and listened to Josh going on and on about everything he'd seen while he was on his own in the mall. Nick's mom seemed highly amused by his nonstop chatter, which was all Josh needed. He liked nothing more than an appreciative audience. More worrisome to Amy was the fact that he sounded as if he still thought it was all a huge adventure.

"You do remember what you promised Santa, right?" she asked eventually.

"That I won't ever run away from you again," he said at once. "But Mom, I wasn't lost, not really. You were right here."

"But I didn't know where *you* were," she explained. "That's what counts."

"I get it," he said impatiently as he stuffed the last of his pizza into his mouth. "Can we go back now?"

Amy thought of Trish's warning and cast a helpless look toward Mrs. DiCaprio, who immediately grasped her dilemma.

"Josh, I think your mom needs to rest a bit longer," Nick's mother said. "She wasn't feeling well this morning and then she had quite a scare when you disappeared."

His expression turned into a pout that set Amy's teeth on edge.

"Young man, don't give me a look like that or we'll leave this mall and you won't see Santa at all," Amy threatened. "You need to sit here and behave yourself while I feed Emma. Thank goodness I thought to stick some baby food and a bottle in my bag when we left home. I must have had some instinct that seeing Santa wouldn't go as planned."

"Can't I go see Santa while you feed her?" he pleaded. "Mrs. DiCaprio could take me." Apparently he recognized his mother's exasperated expression, because he sighed heavily. "Okay, okay, I'll wait."

"Smart decision," she commended him.

"Josh, what's on your list for Santa?" Mrs. DiCaprio asked him.

"I can't tell," he said. "It's like a birthday wish. If you tell, it won't come true."

She grinned at him. "But I happen to know Santa very well," she confided in him. "Maybe I could put in a good word for you."

Josh's expression turned thoughtful, but then he shook his head. "That's okay. I think me and Santa are pals. I'll just tell him myself."

Mrs. DiCaprio chuckled. "You know something, Josh. You are a very self-possessed, confident young man. You remind me of another boy."

"Your son?" he guessed.

"Exactly." She pointed to the strands of gray in her hair. "You see all this gray hair? He's the reason I have it. Every time I turned around, he was getting into some kind of mischief. I have four children, all grown now, but only one of them threatened to turn me old before my time." She winked at Amy. "He still has that effect on me, thanks to that job of his."

"What kind of job is it?" Josh asked, regarding her with a rapt expression. "Maybe I could do the same thing when I grow up."

"He's a police detective, as a matter of fact," Mrs. DiCaprio said. "And while he's very good at it, I worry about him."

"Santa says all moms worry about their kids, no matter how old they get," Josh told her.

"That's very true," Mrs. DiCaprio confirmed.

"Do you worry about Trish, too?" he asked.

"Sometimes," she told him. "She works too hard and she could use a little more fun in her life, but at least her work isn't dangerous like my son's."

Amy thought of Nick and envisioned him as a mischievous boy a lot like Josh. It gave her a whole other perspective on the man. She considered asking Mrs. DiCaprio about whatever might be troubling him these days, but decided Trish was right. The answers needed to come from Nick himself.

"Amy?"

Startled, she met Mrs. DiCaprio's gaze. "I'm sorry. Did you say something?"

"I asked if you and your children have plans for tomorrow."

"It's Christmas!" Josh said, interrupting. "We're opening presents."

The older woman smiled. "I meant after that, of course," she assured him, then met Amy's eyes. "Would you like to spend the afternoon at our house and have dinner with us? It'll be a madhouse, but Rob's sons are about Josh's age. I think he'd enjoy meeting them, don't you? And he has a little girl—Annie—who's only a little older than your Emma."

Amy appreciated the woman's kindness, but surely their presence would be an intrusion. "I'm sure Josh would love meeting them sometime, but we wouldn't want to impose on your family's holiday."

"Don't be silly," Mrs. DiCaprio said at once. "It's no imposition at all. I always cook enough for an army. The turkey's huge, so everyone can take home leftovers. And I've been baking for a month now." She cast a chagrined glance at her flour-covered clothes. "I'm still at it, as you can see. I'm hoping to get one more batch of cookies done before church tonight. There's a reception after the early service."

"Then we shouldn't keep you," Amy said. "We'll be fine here till Trish comes back for us."

"A little while longer won't make a bit of difference," Mrs. DiCaprio responded. "The dough's in the refrigerator chilling. All I need to do is slice the cookies and put them in the oven, while I get dressed for church."

"We used to go to church on Christmas Eve," Josh said.

"Aren't you going to a service tonight?" Mrs. DiCaprio asked.

"Actually we haven't had a chance to find a church since we moved here," Amy admitted. "Nick mentioned something about us coming with you."

"Really?" she said, a speculative glint in her eyes.

"What a wonderful idea! Then you'll get to meet everyone before tomorrow, so you'll have no excuse not to join us for Christmas dinner."

"Can we, Mom? Please!" Josh begged.

Amy recognized that Mrs. DiCaprio had an agenda, but Josh looked so excited that she couldn't bring herself to say no. "If you're sure it's no trouble, we'd love to. The prospect of just the three of us for Christmas dinner didn't hold a lot of appeal."

"I'm sure it didn't," Mrs. DiCaprio sympathized. "The holidays are meant for families to celebrate together." She glanced up. "Ah, here comes Trish now." She stood up. "I'll leave you in her hands and see you this evening. If my husband's still circling around in the parking lot after all this time, he may never bring me here again."

To Amy's surprise, she leaned down and gave her a warm hug. "It was wonderful to meet you, Amy. I think fate had a hand in everything that happened today."

With that, she gathered up their trash, tossed it away, then rushed off with a merry wave in their direction.

Trish gave Amy a speculative look. "I imagine we'll be seeing you at her house tomorrow."

Amy nodded. "She doesn't take no for an answer."

"Not when it's for the greater good," Trish agreed.

"Which is?"

"Giving my brother exactly what he needs for Christmas."

Amy blushed when she realized that Trish was referring to her. To change the subject, she asked, "How did it go with the reporter?"

"She understands," Trish said. "Everything should be fine."

Amy smiled. "Is it okay for Josh to visit with Santa?"

Trish nodded. "That's why I came back for you now. With a half hour to go till the mall closes, there's still a short line. I figure you guys will blend right in. There's no reason for anyone to link you to the big story of the day."

"What about Nick? Was he interviewed?"

"Nope," Trish said grimly. "I told her he'd refused. He had a lot going on as it was—the kid on his lap was screaming bloody murder." She grinned at the memory.

Amy smiled. "How did Nick take that?"

"Stayed right on script," Trish said proudly. "He never missed a beat with the ho-ho-ho's and asking what the kid wanted for Christmas."

"Mom!" Josh interrupted, clearly tired of waiting. "Can we go *now!*"

"Okay, okay," she said, regarding Trish ruefully. "Let's go."

As she put an exhausted and unprotesting Emma back

into her stroller, Amy was filled with an unexpected sense of anticipation. It had been a lot of years since she'd been this eager to pay a visit to Santa.

The line was shorter now and they were at the end of it. No one came along to wait behind them. Exhausted shoppers were leaving the mall now in droves.

When Josh's turn came, he was still the last in line. The instant he climbed onto Santa's knee and Amy had placed Emma beside him, the photographer snapped their picture, then handed the instant photo to Amy. "No charge," he said as he packed up his things and left in a rush for whatever holiday festivities awaited him.

Emma leaned contentedly against Nick's chest and closed her eyes. The sight of her daughter in Nick's arms brought an odd tightness to Amy's heart. She had a feeling this image would linger inside her long after the photo had faded.

"So, young man," Nick said to Josh in his booming Santa voice, "What do you want Santa to bring you for Christmas?"

She tuned out the sound of her son's words as he recited not only his own list, one with which she was thoroughly familiar, but Emma's. It was a modest enough list by most standards and she knew that everything on it would be under the tree. The only wish she couldn't grant was his longing to see his dad on Christmas morning.

When Josh's consultation with Santa was over, Nick left the village with Emma in his arms and joined her. "Are we still on for church tonight?" he asked. "I can give you directions and meet you there, and then introduce you to the rest of my family." He gave her a hard look. "Or was meeting my mother more than enough?"

"Your mother is incredible," she told him. "She's invited us for Christmas dinner tomorrow."

He didn't look all that surprised. "I had a hunch that would come up."

"You didn't put her up to it?"

"My existence as a bachelor is enough to put her up to it," he said dryly. "Keep in mind she's scheming."

"I gathered as much," Amy admitted.

"And?"

"And what?" she asked.

"How do you feel about her scheme?"

"I told her we'd be there tomorrow." Her gaze locked with his. "How do *you* feel about her agenda?"

A grin spread across his face. "Better than I did a few minutes ago," he revealed. "How about giving me a moment to get out of this costume and I'll walk out with you?"

Amy glanced pointedly at Josh. "Not a good idea," she said succinctly.

"Of course not," he said at once. "What was I thinking?"

He looked around till he spotted Trish. "Sis, any problem if I wear this home?"

Laughing, she merely waved him away. "Go."

Josh looked from Nick to Trish and back again. "Is she your sister?" he asked, his expression puzzled.

Nick winced. "She is."

"Then that lady, Mrs. DiCaprio, is your mom, too?" Josh pressed.

Nick nodded.

Amy held her breath as Josh absorbed that information.

Finally Josh looked Nick in the eye. "Awesome! I know Santa's real mom! The kids back in Michigan will freak when I tell 'em. Can I call tonight, Mom? Can I? They're not going to believe this."

"Sure, you can call as soon as we get home," Amy told him, relieved that the whole Santa illusion hadn't been ruined. If anything, it had been reinforced and improved on.

"Then let's go," Josh said, trying to hurry her along. "I'll push Emma's stroller."

"Just don't get too far head of us, okay?"

"Okay," he said, glancing repeatedly over his shoulder to make sure she and Santa were close on his heels.

"I guess your lecture got through to him," she told Nick. "I think it made more of an impact coming from you."

"He'll forget it soon enough," Nick said. "I'll have to stick around to keep reminding him."

"I imagine I could remind him," Amy said, though the thought of Nick being around to do it held a whole lot of appeal.

"You don't have the Santa factor on your side," he told her.

"And you'll look pretty strange wearing that costume in July," she countered.

"Think I'll be around you guys in July?" he asked.

"I guess we'll just have to wait and see."

"You know, there's something I forgot to ask you earlier," he said.

"Oh?"

"What do you want for Christmas, Amy?"

She met his gaze and her heart gave a little lurch. "I have everything I need," she told him. "My kids are safe and happy."

"And that's enough?"

"It is for now," she told him, unable to tear her gaze away from the intensity and heat in his eyes.

He leaned down and brushed a kiss across her lips, then came back and lingered a second longer.

"Then maybe that will give you a few other ideas for your list," he said when he finally pulled away.

Oh, yeah, she thought. It most certainly did. But having X-rated ideas on Christmas Eve would shove her out of nice and straight into naughty. She wondered what Santa would have to say about that.

One glance into Nick's mischievous eyes told her the answer to that. They were working from the very same list.

Before she could examine how she felt about that, a woman tapped Nick on the shoulder. When he turned around, his expression froze. It was exactly the look he'd had on his face earlier, when he'd dragged Amy inside that shoe store.

"Nick," the woman said softly. "Could I please speak to you for a second?"

"Sure," he said, but there was no mistaking his reluctance.

The woman cast an apologetic look in Amy's direction. "I'm sorry to interrupt, but this is the first chance I've had to speak to Nick since..." Her voice caught. She shook her head. "Sorry. I still can't talk about it."

"It's okay," Nick soothed. "Really, you don't have to say anything."

To Amy, he sounded almost desperate, as if he were willing the woman to remain silent.

The woman drew in a deep breath. "No, it's important. I tried to call you at the station, but they said you were on leave."

Nick nodded.

"Because of what happened," she guessed.

"Yes," he said tightly.

"I'm so sorry," she told him. "It's all my fault."

Nick regarded her incredulously. "Your fault? How can you say that?"

"If I'd told you right away about my ex-husband, if I'd warned you..." Her voice fell to a whisper. "Maybe things would have gone differently."

Nick put his hands on her shoulders and looked into her eyes. "No, Mitzi, nothing that happened was your fault. If anything, it was mine. I just stood by..."

"No," she said harshly. "That's just it, that's why I had to talk to you. I knew you were blaming yourself."

"Who else should I blame?" he asked heatedly.

The woman sighed heavily. "Maybe it was no one's fault, not even my ex-husband's. He had to be sick, right? To think that taking our boy and hurting him would somehow make me love him again." She shuddered. "Or even that it was a way to pay me back for leaving him. That's not right. He needs help."

"Hopefully he'll get it while he's locked up," Nick told her. "The important thing is that he'll never get another chance to hurt anyone else."

Amy listened to the exchange with mounting horror. She realized now why Nick had been so desperate to find Josh, so determined to stay right by her side until her son was safe. He was trying to make up for not being able to help another little boy, this woman's son. No wonder he was tormented. No wonder he'd asked so many questions about Ned. The search for Josh must have dredged up a thousand terrifying moments for him.

The woman spoke to Amy, "I'm sorry to intrude, but when I saw that Nick was here, I wanted to tell him that I don't blame him for anything that happened. I thought he might need to know that."

Nick did, indeed, look as if a huge weight had been lifted from his shoulders. "You have an amazingly generous heart," he told her.

"If I do, it's because I had an incredible boy in my life for a few brief years. I'm so grateful for that. It was far too short, but he taught me so much. That's what I want to remember. Not the way he died, but the way he lived." She hugged Nick fiercely. "Merry Christmas, Detective."

"Merry Christmas," he whispered, his voice choked.

After she'd gone, Amy reached up and touched the

tears on his cheeks. "I am so sorry that you had to relive all that today."

He met her gaze. "I'm not," he said eventually. "Not if it brought you, Josh and Emma into my life. How could I possibly regret that?"

He turned to Josh, who was rolling a laughing Emma in circles nearby. "Hey, guys, let's get going. It's Christmas Eve and Santa's got a very busy night ahead. I have toys to deliver."

His gaze shifted to Amy and he lowered his voice. "And maybe, if I'm lucky, I can even sneak a kiss or two under the mistletoe."

Amy laughed. "You can try. I've been wondering all day if that beard tickles. I couldn't tell earlier."

Grinning, Nick called out to Josh. "Don't look, okay?"

"Don't look at what?" Josh asked.

"Do as you're told," Amy instructed, laughing. "Mommy's gonna kiss Santa Claus."

Josh's expression immediately brightened. "Cool!"

Yeah, Amy thought, as Nick's mouth settled on hers. It was definitely cool. No, she concluded an instant later, actually, it was hot. Very, very hot.

Outside the mall, the air was icy and snow was falling, but Amy was still overheated from that kiss. North Carolina might be in for some sort of rare blizzard, but for her this was quickly turning into the hottest Christmas on record.

Epilogue

Christmas, one year later

"So, young man," Nick said to Josh in his booming Santa voice, "What do you want Santa to bring you for Christmas?"

Amy had no idea how Trish had persuaded Nick to play Santa for a day once again this year. He still claimed he'd hated every minute of it when she'd coerced him into it the year before. Maybe it had something to do with knowing that Amy would once again be bringing Josh and Emma to the mall for their Christmas Eve visit.

Josh studied Santa intently, then seemed to reach some sort of decision. He cast a quick glance toward Amy, then pulled Santa's head down so he could whisper in his ear.

Nick immediately glanced at Amy, a grin spreading

across his face. "Well, now, I don't know about that, son. Maybe your mom should have a say about something that important."

Amy sighed. A puppy? He'd asked for a puppy. Josh knew they couldn't have one where they were living. What was she supposed to do now?

"Sweetie, I told you we can't have a puppy till we move to a house," she said, which oddly enough only seemed to make Nick's smile grow. She regarded him with confusion. "He didn't ask for a puppy?"

"Nope," Nick said, carrying Emma down to join her.

"What then?"

"A new dad," he told her. "And he seems to think having Santa for a dad would be pretty awesome."

Amy's cheeks flooded with heat. "Oh, no. I am so sorry."

"Don't be. I'm thinking it's something to consider."

She stared at him in shock. "Excuse me?"

"Not today, of course, but you know, down the road."

"Say sometime after you've actually had a chance to think about it?" she asked dryly.

He laughed, not the fake, booming laugh of Santa, but the amused chuckle of a man she'd discovered had a wonderful sense of humor.

"Oh, I've been thinking about it for some time now,"

he told her. "How about you? Has the thought crossed your mind?"

It was her turn to chuckle. "How could it not, with your folks and Trish pressuring me every chance they get?"

"So, what do you think?" Josh demanded impatiently. "Is he gonna be my new dad or not?"

"I think maybe we ought to give your mom a little more time to think about this," Nick told him. "She might even want a real, romantic proposal."

"What's that?" Josh asked.

"Candlelight and stuff," Nick told him. "Keep it in mind. You might need to know about things like that later. In the meantime, why don't I walk you all to your car. I've heard a rumor and I want to check it out."

"What kind of rumor?" Amy asked, confused by the hint of mystery in his voice.

"You'll see."

They walked to the same exit where Amy, Josh and Emma had entered the mall on that fateful day a year ago. When Nick pushed open the door, she immediately saw what he'd been talking about. Once again, snow was falling. It had already covered the ground and turned the rapidly emptying parking lot into a winter wonderland.

"Snow!" Josh screamed, running ahead and twirling around, his head thrown back and his mouth open so he could catch the fat snowflakes on his tongue. Suddenly he ran over and threw his arms around Nick's huge, padded waist. "Thank you, thank you, thank you."

Nick winked at Amy. "Sorry, kid, Santa can't take credit for this."

Maybe not, she thought, but he had a lot to do with the joyous expression on her son's face. He was also responsible for the amazingly lighthearted feeling inside her.

As far as she was concerned, Santa—*Nick*—had given them everything they needed and the promise of much more.

* * * * *

Midnight Confessions

Robyn Carr

One

Sunny Archer was seriously considering a legal name change.

"Come on, Sunny," her uncle Nathaniel said. "Let's go out on the town and see if we can't put a little of that legendary sunshine back into your disposition!"

Out on the town? she thought. In *Virgin River?* A town of about six hundred? "Ah, I think I'll pass…"

"C'mon, sunshine, you gotta be more flexible! Optimistic! You can't lick this wound forever."

Maybe it was cute when she was four or even fourteen to say things like "Sunny isn't too sunny today!"

But this was December 31 and she had come to Virgin River to spend a few quiet days with her uncle Nate and his fiancée Annie, to try to escape the reality of a heart that wouldn't heal. And if the hurt wasn't bad enough, her heart had gone cold and hard, too. She looked at her watch—4:00 p.m. Exactly one year ago at this time she was having her hair and makeup done right before slipping into a Vera Wang wedding gown, excited, blushing and oblivious to the fact that her fiancé Glen was getting blitzed and ready to run for his life.

"I'm not really in the mood for a New Year's Eve bash, Uncle Nate," she said.

"Aw, sweetheart, I can't bear to think of you home alone, brooding, feeling sad," Nathaniel said.

And feeling like a big loser who was left at the altar on her wedding day? she wondered. But that's what had happened. How was she supposed to feel?

"Nate," Annie said under her breath, "this might be a bad night to push the party idea...."

"Ya think?" Sunny said sarcastically, noting to herself that she hadn't been so irritable and sarcastic before becoming an abandoned bride. "Listen, you guys, please go. Party like rock stars. I actually have plans."

"You do?" they both asked hopefully.

"I do. I'm planning a ceremonial burning of last year's calendar. I should probably burn three years' worth of them—that's how much time and energy I invested in the scumbucket."

Nate and Annie were speechless for a moment; they exchanged dubious looks. When Nate recovered he said,

"Well all-righty then! We'll stay home and help with the ceremonial burning. Then we'll make some popcorn, play some monopoly, make some positive resolutions or something and ring in a much better new year than the last."

And that was how Sunny, who wasn't feeling at all accommodating, ended up going to the big Virgin River blast at Jack's Bar on New Year's Eve—because she just couldn't let her uncle Nate and sweet, funny Annie stay home to watch her sulk and whimper.

There had been a long history in Sunny's family of returning to the Jensen stables for a little rest and rejuvenation. Sunny and her cousins had spent countless vacations around the barn and pastures and trails, riding, playing, inhaling the fresh clean air and getting a regular new lease on life. It had been Sunny's mother's idea that she come to Virgin River for a post-Christmas revival. Sunny's mom was one of Nate's three older sisters, and Sunny's grandpa had been the original owner and veterinarian of Jensen's Clinic and Stable. Now Uncle Nate was the vet and Grandpa was retired and living in Arizona.

Sunny was her mama's only child, age twenty-five; she had one female cousin, Mary—who it just so happened had managed to get *her* groom to the church.

Since Uncle Nate was only ten years older than Sunny at thirty-five, she and her cousin had had tragic crushes on him. Nate, on the other hand, who had grown up with three older sisters, thought he was cursed with females.

Until he was thirty, anyway. Then he became a little more avuncular, patient and even protective. Nathaniel had been sitting in the church on New Year's Eve a year ago. Waiting, like everyone else, for the groom to show, for the wedding to begin.

The past year had passed in an angry, unhappy blur for Sunny. Her rather new and growing photography business had taken off—a combination of her kick-ass website and word of mouth—and rather than take a break after her personal disaster, she went right back to work. She had scheduled shoots, after all. The catastrophic twist was that she specialized in engagement, wedding, anniversary, belly and baby shots—five phases of a couple's life worth capturing for posterity. Her work, as well as her emotional well-being, was suffering. Although she couldn't focus, and she was either unable to sleep or hardly able to pull herself out of bed, she pressed on the best she could. The only major change she'd made in her life was to move out of the town house she had shared with Glen and back into her mom and dad's house until she could afford something of her own. She had her workroom in the basement of her parents' place anyway, so it was just a minor shift in geography.

During the past year at her parents', Sunny had a revelation. The driving reason behind most young women her age wanting their own space, their independence and privacy, was their being involved in a serious relationship. Since she was determined not to repeat past mistakes by allowing another man into her life, there was no need to leave the comfort, security and economy of her parents' house.

She was trying her hand at photographing sunrises, sunsets, landscapes, seascapes and pets. It wasn't working—her images were flat and uninteresting. If it wasn't bad enough that her heart was broken, so was her spirit. It was as if her gift was lost. She'd been brilliant with couples, inspired by weddings—stills, slideshows, videos. She saw the promise in their eyes, the potential for their lives. She'd brought romance to the fat bellies of pregnant women and was a veritable Anne Geddes with babies! But now that she was a mere observer who would never experience any of those things firsthand, everything had changed. Not only had it changed, it pierced her heart each time she did a shoot.

When she confessed this to Annie, Annie had said, "Oh, darling, but you're so young! Only twenty-five!

The possibilities ahead are endless if you're open to them!"

And Sunny had said, "I'm not upset because I didn't make the cheerleading squad, Annie. My fiancé dumped me on our wedding day—and my age doesn't matter a damn."

The town was carpeted in a fresh blanket of pretty white snow, the thirty-foot tree was lit and sparkling as gentle flakes continued to fall, and the porch at Jack's Bar, strung with lights and garlands, was welcoming. There was a friendly curl of smoke rising from the chimney and light shone from the windows.

Nate, Annie and Sunny walked into the bar at 8:00 p.m. and found the place packed with locals. Jack, the owner, and Preacher, the cook, were behind the bar. There was a festive table set up along one whole wall of the room, covered with food, to which Annie added a big plate of her special deviled eggs and a dill-speckled salmon loaf surrounded by crackers.

"Hey, looks like the whole town is here," Nate said.

"A good plenty," Jack said. "But I hope you don't see anyone here you want to kiss at midnight. Most of these folks won't make it that long. We have a strong skeleton crew that will stay late, however. They're busy getting all the kids settled back at Preacher's house with a sitter—it's going to be a dormitory. Vanessa and Paul's two are bunking in with Preacher's little Dana, my kids are sleeping in Preacher's room, Cameron's twins are in the guest room, Brie and Mike's little one is borrowing Christopher's room because he's planning on sitting up until midnight with the sitter. Oh, and to be very clear, the sitter is there for all the *little* kids—not for Chris," Jack added with a smile. "He's eight now. All man."

"Jack, Preach, meet my niece Sunny. Sunny, this is Jack and Preacher, the guys who run this place."

She gave them a weak smile, a nod and a mumbled nice to meet you.

"Hop up here, you three. As soon as you contribute your New Year's resolution, you get service," Jack said. "The price of admission is a food item and a resolution."

Sunny jumped up on a bar stool, hanging the strap of her large bag on the backrest. Jack leaned over the bar and eyed the big, leather shoulder bag. He peered at her with one brow lifted. "Going on a long trip right after the party?"

She laughed a little. "Camera equipment. I never leave it behind. Never know when I might need it."

"Well, by all means, the first annual New Year's Eve party is your canvas," Jack said. He slid a piece of paper and pen toward her.

Sunny hovered over it as if giving it careful thought.

She knew if she said her resolution was to get this over with as soon as possible, it would open up the conversation as to why she now and would forever more find New Year's Eve the most reprehensible of holidays.

"Make it a good one, Sunny," Jack said. "Keep it generic and don't sign it—it's anonymous. There's a surprise coming right after midnight."

Sunny glanced at her watch. God, she thought. At least four hours of this? I'll never make it! She wrote on her slip of paper. "Give up men."

Drew Foley was a second-year orthopedic resident at UCLA Medical and had somehow scored ten days off over Christmas, which he'd spent in Chico with his two sisters, Marcie and Erin, their guys Ian and Aiden and his new nephew. The three previous Christmases he'd spent with his family, and also his former fiancée, Penny. That somehow seemed so long ago.

When surgical residents get days off, they aren't *real* days off. They're merely days on which you're not required in surgery, clinic, class, writing reports or being verbally beaten to death by senior residents and attending physicians. But there was still plenty of studying to do. He'd been hitting the books straight through Christmas even with the distraction of family all around, including Marcie's new baby who was really starting to assert himself. With only a few days left before he had to head back to Southern California, he borrowed the family's isolated cabin on the ridge near Virgin River so he could study without distraction. He'd managed to focus completely for a couple of days and had impressed himself with the amount of academic ground he'd covered. As he saw it, that bought him a New Year's Eve beer or two and a few hours of satellite football on New Year's Day. On January 2 he'd head back to Erin's house in Chico, spend one more evening with the family, then throw himself back into the lion's den at UCLA Medical.

He grabbed his jacket. It was New Year's Eve and he'd spent enough time alone. He'd swing through town on his way to Fortuna to collect his beer, just to see what was going on. He'd be surprised if the only bar and grill in town was open, since Jack's Bar wasn't usually open late on holidays. In fact, the routine in Virgin River on regular days was that Jack's shut down before nine, open till ten at the latest, and that was only if there were hunters or fishermen in the area. This was a town of mostly farmers, ranchers, laborers and small-business owners; they didn't stay out late because farm chores and animals didn't sleep in.

But to his surprise, once in town he found that the little bar was hopping. It made him smile—this was going to save him some serious mountain driving and he'd get to have a beer among people. When he walked into the packed bar he heard his name shouted. "Ho! Doc Foley! When did you hit town?"

This was the best part about this place. He'd only been up here maybe a half dozen times in the past couple of years, but Jack never forgot anyone. For that matter, most of Jack's friends and family never did either.

He reached a hand across the bar in greeting to Jack. "How's it going, Jack?"

"I had no idea you were up here!" Jack said. "You bring the family along?"

"Nah, I was with the family over Christmas and came up to get a little studying done before I have to get back to residency. I thought I'd better escape the girls and especially the baby if I intend to concentrate at all."

"How is that baby?" Jack asked.

Drew grinned. "Red-headed and loud. I'm afraid he could be a little rip-off of Marcie. Ian should be afraid. Very, very afraid."

Jack chuckled. "You remember my wife, Mel."

"Sure," he said, turning toward the town's renowned midwife and accepting a kiss on the cheek. "How are you?"

"Never better. I wish we'd known you were up here, Drew—I'd have made it a point to call you, invite you."

Drew looked around. "Who knew you folks ripped up the town on New Year's Eve. Is everyone here?"

"Pretty good number," Jack said. "But expect this to change fairly quick—most of these folks will leave by nine. They start early. But I'm hanging in there till midnight," he assured Drew. "I bet I can count on one hand the number of Virgin River residents willing to stay up for a kiss at midnight."

And that's when he spotted her. Right when Jack said *kiss at midnight* he saw a young woman he'd be more than willing to accommodate when the clock struck twelve. She was tucked back in a corner by the hearth, swirling a glass of white wine, her golden hair falling onto her shoulders. She seemed just slightly apart from the table of three women who sat chatting near her. He watched as one of those women leaned toward her to speak, to try to include her, but she merely nodded, sipped, smiled politely and remained aloof. Someone's wife? Someone's girl? Whoever she was, she looked a little unhappy. He'd love to make her happier.

"Drew," Jack said. "Meet Nate Jensen, local vet."

Drew put out his hand, but didn't want to take his eyes off the girl. He said, "Nice to meet you," but what he was thinking was how long it had been since just looking at a beautiful woman had zinged him in the chest and head with almost instant attraction. Too long! Whoa, she was a stunner. He'd barely let go of Nate's hand, didn't even catch the guy's response because his ears were ringing, when he asked Jack, "Who is that blonde?"

"That's my niece," his new acquaintance said. "Sunny."

"Married? Engaged? Accompanied? Nun? Anything?"

Nate chuckled. "She's totally single. But—"

"Be right back," Drew said. "Guard my beer with your life!" And he took off for the corner by the hearth.

"But..." Nate attempted.

Drew kept moving. He was on automatic. Once he was standing right in front of her and she lifted her eyes to his, he was not surprised to find that she had the most beautiful blue eyes he could have ever imagined. He put out his hand. "Hi. I'm Drew. I just met your uncle." She said nothing, didn't even shake his hand. "And you're Sunny. Sunny Jensen?" he asked.

Her mouth fixed and her eyes narrowed. "Archer," she corrected.

Drew gave up on the shake and withdrew his hand. "Well, Sunny Archer, can I join you?"

"Are you trying to pick me up?" she asked directly.

He grinned. "I'm a very optimistic guy," he said pleasantly.

"Then let me save you some time. I'm not available."

He was struck silent for a moment. It wasn't that Drew enjoyed such great success with women—he was admittedly out of practice. But this one had drawn on him like a magnet and he was unaccountably surprised to be shot down before he'd even had a chance to screw up his approach. "Sorry," he said lamely. "Your uncle said you were single."

"Single and unavailable." She lifted her glass and gave him a weak smile. "Happy New Year."

He just looked at her for a moment, then beat a retreat back to the bar.

Jack and Nate were watching, waiting for him. Jack pushed the beer toward him. "How'd that work out for you?"

Drew took a pull on his beer. "I must be way out of practice," he said. "I probably should'a thought that through a little better...."

"What? Residency doesn't leave time for girls?" Jack asked with a twist of the lip.

"A breakup," Drew explained. "Which led to a break from women for a while."

Nate leaned an elbow on the bar. "That a fact? Bad breakup?"

"You ever been around a good one?" Drew asked. Then he chuckled, lifted an eyebrow and said, "Nah, it wasn't that it was so bad. In fact, she probably saved my life. We were engaged, but shouldn't have been. She finally told me what I should've known all along—*if we got married, it would be a disaster.*"

"Bad fit?"

"Yeah, bad fit. I should have seen it coming, but I was too busy putting titanium rods in femurs to pay attention to details like that, so my bad. But what's up with Sunny Archer?"

"Well," Nate said. "I guess you probably have a lot in common."

"Uh-oh. Bad breakup?"

"Let's just say, you ever been around a good one?"

"I should've known. She didn't give me a chance. And here I thought I'd bungled it."

"Gonna go for round two?" Jack asked him.

Drew thought about that a minute. "I don't know," he said with a shrug. "Maybe I should wait until she gets a little more wine in her."

Nate slapped a heavy hand on Drew's shoulder. "That's my niece, bud. I'll be watching."

"Sorry, bad joke. I'd never take advantage of her, don't worry about that," Drew protested. "But if she shoots me down twice, I could get a serious complex!"

Two

Drew nursed his beer slowly and joked around with Jack and Nate over a plate of wings, but the subject of breakups had him thinking a bit about Penny. There were times he missed her, or at least he missed the idea of what he thought they would be.

He had met her while he was in med school. She was a fellow med student's cousin and it had been a fix up. The first date had gone smoothly; the next seven dates in as many weeks went even better and before he knew it, he was dating Penny exclusively. They had so much in common, they grew on each other. She was an RN and he was studying medicine. She was pretty, had a good sense of humor, understood his work as he understood hers and in no time at all they had settled into a comfort zone that accommodated them both. And it didn't hurt that the sex was satisfying. Everything seemed compatible.

Penny had been in charge of the relationship from the start and Drew didn't have to think about it much, which suited him perfectly. He was a busy guy; he didn't have a lot of time for flirtation or pursuit. Penny was very well-equipped to fill him in on their agenda and he was perfectly happy to go along. "Valentine's Day is coming up," she would say. "I guess we'll be doing something special?"

Ding, ding, ding—he could figure that out easy. "Absolutely," he would say. Then he'd get a reservation, buy a gift. Penny thought he was brilliant and sensitive and all was right with his world.

It had been working out effortlessly until he asked her to go to Southern California with him, to live with him. His residency in orthopedic surgery was beginning, he'd dated Penny exclusively for a couple of years and it seemed like the natural progression of things. "Not without an engagement ring," she'd said. So he provided one. It had seemed reasonable enough.

But the move from Chico changed everything. It hadn't gone well for Penny. She'd been out of her element, away from her job, friends and family, and Drew had been far too stressed and overworked to help her make the transition. She was lonely, needed attention, time, reassurance. And he had wanted to give it to her, but it was like squeezing water out of a rock. It wasn't long before their only communication was in the form of arguing—make that fighting. Fights followed by days of not speaking or nights in which she cried into her pillow and wouldn't take comfort from him, if he could stay awake long enough to give it.

Drew shook off the memory and finally said to Nate, "So, tell me about Sunny, who, if you don't mind me saying, might be better named Stormy...."

"Well, for starters, jokes about her name don't seem to be working just now," Nate replied.

"Ahh," he said. Drew was distracted by a sudden flash and saw that it was none other than Stormy Sunny herself with the camera, getting a shot of a couple in a toast. "What's with the camera?"

"She's a photographer, as a matter of fact. A good one," Nate said. "She started out studying business in college but dropped out before she was twenty-one to start her own business. My sister Susan, her mother, almost had a heart attack over that. But it turned out she knew exactly what she was doing. There's a waiting list for her work."

"Is that a fact?" he said, intrigued. "She seems kind of young..."

"Very young, but she's been taking great pictures since she was in high school. Maybe earlier."

"Where?"

"She lives in L.A. Long Beach, actually."

Long Beach, Drew thought. Like next door! Of course, that didn't matter if she wouldn't even talk to him. But he wasn't giving anything away. "Is she a little artsy-fartsy?" Drew asked.

Nate laughed. "Not at all—she's very practical. But lately she's been trying some new stuff, shooting the horses, mountains, valleys, roads and buildings. Sunrises, sunsets, clouds, et cetera." Nate looked over at Sunny as she busily snapped pictures of a happy couple. "It's kind of nice to see her taking pictures of people again."

Drew watched Sunny focus, direct the pair with one hand while holding her camera with the other. Her face seriously lit up; her smile was alive and whatever it was she was saying caused her subjects to laugh, which was followed by several flashes. She was so animated as she took five or six more shots, then pulled a business card out of the pocket of her jeans and handed it to the couple. She was positively gorgeous when she wasn't giving him the brush. Then she retreated to her spot by the hearth and put her camera down. He noticed that the second she gave up the camera, her face returned to its seriousness. The sight of her was immediately obscured by partiers.

He wanted one of those business cards.

"Hey, buddy, you didn't make out your resolution," Jack said, passing him a slip of paper and pen. "That's the price of admission."

"I don't usually do resolutions," Drew said. "Well, except every morning when I resolve to fly under the radar of the senior residents."

"Because?" Jack asked.

Sometimes Drew forgot that few people knew what the life of a junior resident was like. "Because they're sociopaths with a mean streak."

"Ah," Jack said as if he bought that. "Maybe that's your resolution—to avoid sociopaths? When you've written one, it goes in the pot here."

"And then?" Drew asked.

"When you're getting ready to leave, you can draw one—maybe you'll get a better one than you wrote. Give you something new to strive for."

Drew laughed. "I dunno. This is such a crazy idea," he said. "What if the one I draw is to bike across the U.S.?"

Jack looked around. "Nah," he said. "No danger of that around here. You could draw one that says to remember your annual mammogram, however. Now get on it," he said, tapping the paper on the bar.

Chuckling, Drew wrote. Then he scratched it out. Thinking about the grumpy but beautiful woman in the corner he wrote "Start the new year by giving a new guy a chance." Then he folded it in half and shoved it in his pocket; he asked for a new piece of paper. On his second try he wrote "Don't let past hurts ruin future possibilities."

Then he took a bolstering swallow of his beer and said, "Excuse me a second." And off he went to the other side of the room.

He stood in front of Sunny, smiled his handsomest smile and said, "So. You're a photographer."

She looked up at him, her expression deadpan. "Yes," she said.

"You like being a photographer?" he asked.

Again there was that pregnant pause before she said, "Yes."

"What do you like best about it?"

She thought for a moment. Then she said, "The quiet."

He had to ask himself why in the world he was interested. She was beautiful, but Drew had never been drawn by beauty alone. He'd known lots of gorgeous women who fell short in other areas, thus killing his interest instantly. For a woman to really intrigue him she had to be fun, smart, good natured, energetic, driven by something besides her looks and above all, *positive*. So far this one, this Sunny, had only looks going for her and it was not enough. Still, for unknown reasons, he lingered. "The quiet," he repeated. "Anything else?"

"Yes. It doesn't require any other people. I can do it alone."

"Just out of curiosity, are you always this unapproachable, or is it just at New Year's Eve parties?"

She shrugged. "Pretty much always."

"Gotcha. One last question. Will you take my picture?"

"For what occasion?" she asked.

Nothing came to mind. "Passport photo?" he attempted.

"Sorry. I don't do passport photos."

He smiled at her. "Well, Sunny—you're in luck. Because that's all I got. You are, as you obviously wish to be, on your own."

Oh, I'm such a bitch, she thought as she watched Drew's back weave through the people to return to the bar. When he sat up on the stool beside her uncle, she cringed in embarrassment. She adored her uncle Nate and knew how much he cared about her, how it had hurt him to see her in pain on what was supposed to have

been her wedding day, how it killed him to see her struggle with it for so long afterward. But while she knew
Nate had nothing but sympathy for her, she realized he
was running short on patience with her bitterness and
what could only be described as attitude a full year later.

He wasn't the only one. Friends had tried to encour-
age her to let go of the heartache and move on. If she
didn't want to date again, fine, but being pissed off all
the time was not only wearing on friendships, it was
hurting business. And she was hearing a lot about the
fact that she was only twenty-five! She wasn't sure if
twenty-five was so young it excused her for making such
a mistake on Glen or if that meant she had decades left
to find the right guy!

Then, right after she arrived in Virgin River, Annie
had taken her aside, sat her down and said, "This rage
isn't going to help you get on with your life in a positive way, Sunny. You're not the only one who's been
dumped. I found out the man I was supposed to marry
had three full-time girlfriends he lived with—each of
us part time, of course."

"How'd he manage that?" Sunny had asked, intrigued
and astonished.

"He obviously kept a very careful calendar. He was
in sales and traveled. When I thought he was selling

farm equipment, he was actually with one of the other girlfriends."

"Oh, my God! You must have wanted to *kill* him!"

"Sure. I was kind of hoping my dad or one of my brothers would do it for me, but when they didn't I got past it. I realize I wasn't left at the altar with a very expensive, non-refundable wedding to pay for, like you were. I can't imagine the pain and humiliation of that, but even so, I was very angry. And now I'm so grateful that I found a way to get beyond that because if I hadn't, I would never have given Nate a chance. And your uncle Nate is the best thing that ever happened to me."

What Sunny wanted to tell Annie was that the pain and humiliation wasn't the worst part—it was that her friends and family *pitied* her for being left. What was wrong with her, that he would do that?

She knew what was wrong, when she thought about it. Her nose was too long, her forehead too high, her chest small and feet big, her hips too wide, she hadn't finished college and she took pictures for a living. That they were good pictures didn't seem to matter—it wasn't all that impressive. She sometimes veered into that territory of "if I had been a super model with a great body, he'd never have left me." Intellectually she knew that was nonsense, but emotionally she felt lacking in too many ways.

Instead she said to Annie, "Did you know? Did you ever have a hint that something was wrong?"

She shook her head. "Only when it was over, when I looked back and realized he never spent a weekend with me, and I was too trusting to wonder why he hadn't ever asked me to join him on a business trip to one of the other towns where he stayed overnight on business. Oh, after it was all over, I had lots of questions. But at the time?" She shook her head. "I didn't know anything was wrong."

"Me either," Sunny said.

"I probably didn't want to know anything was wrong," Annie added. "I don't like conflict."

Sunny didn't say anything. She was pretty well acquainted with her own denial and that hurt just about as much as the hard truth.

"Well, there was one thing," Annie corrected. "After it was all over I wondered if I shouldn't have been more desperate to spend every moment with *him,* if I loved him so much. You know—Nate gets called out in the middle of the night pretty often, and I never make a fuss about it. But we both complain if we haven't had enough time together. We need each other a lot. That never happened with Ed. I was perfectly fine when he wasn't around. Should have tipped me off, I guess."

No help there, Sunny thought. Glen had complained

constantly of her Fridays through Sundays always being booked with shoots. There were times she worked a sixteen-hour day on the weekends, covering three weddings and receptions and a baptism. Slip in some engagement slide shows, photos of babies, whatever had to be done for people who worked Monday through Friday and who only had weekends available. Then from Monday through Thursday she'd work like a dog editing and setting up proofs.

Glen was a California Highway Patrolman who worked swing shifts to have weekends off and she was always unavailable then.

She revisited that old argument—wait a minute! Here was a clue she hadn't figured out at the time. Glen had a few years seniority with CHP, so why would he work swings just to have those weekends off when he knew she would be tied up with her clients the entire time? She'd been rather proud of the fact that it hadn't taken her long to develop a strong clientele, to make incredibly good money for a woman her age—weddings were especially profitable. But she'd had to sacrifice her weekends to get and keep that success.

So why? It would have been easy for him to get a schedule with a Tuesday through Thursday, her lightest days, off. In fact, if he had been willing to take those days off, and work the day shift regularly, they could have gone to bed together every night. He said at the time that it suited his body clock, that he wasn't a morning person. And he *liked* to go out on the weekends. He went out with "the boys." The *boys?* Not bloody likely....

After being left at the church a couple of his groomsmen had admitted he'd been having his doubts about the big, legal, forever commitment. Apparently he'd worried aloud to them, but all he ever did was argue with her about it. *We don't need all that! We could fly to Aruba, get married there, take a week of sailing, scuba diving...* He hadn't said the commitment was an issue, just the wedding—something Sunny and her mom were having a real party putting together. So she had said, "Try not to worry so much, Glen—you'll get your week in Aruba on the honeymoon. Just be at the church on time, say your lines and we'll be diving and sunning and sailing before you know it."

Sunny shook her head in frustration. What was the point in figuring it out now? She grabbed her coat, her camera and headed out the door. The snow was still gently falling and she backed away from the town Christmas tree, snapping photos as she went. She zoomed in on some of the military unit patches used as decorations, caught snowflakes glistening against gold balls and white lights, captured angles of the tree until, finally, far enough away, she got the whole tree. If these came out the way she hoped, she might use them for something next Christmas—ads or cards or something.

Then she turned and caught a couple of good shots of the bar porch, the snow drifting on the rails and steps and roof. Then of the street with all the houses lit for holiday cheer. Then the bar porch with a man leaning against the rail, arms crossed over his chest—a very handsome man.

She lowered the camera and walked toward Drew. There was no getting around the fact that he was handsome—tall and built, light brown hair, twinkling brown eyes, and if she remembered right, a very sexy smile. He stood on the porch and she looked up at him.

"Okay, look, I apologize," she said. "It's not like me to be so rude, so 'unapproachable' as you call it. I got dumped, okay? I'm still licking my wounds, as my uncle Nathaniel puts it. Not a good time for me to respond to a come-on from a guy. I'm scared to death to meet a guy and end up actually liking him, so I avoid all males. That's it in a nutshell," she added with a shrug. "I used to be very friendly and outgoing—now I'm on guard a lot."

"Apology accepted. And I had a bad breakup, too, but it was a while ago. Water under the bridge, as they say."

"You got dumped?"

He gave a nod. "And I understand how you feel. So

let's start over. What do you say? I'm Drew Foley," he said.

She took another step toward the porch, looking up at him. "Sunny Archer. But when? I mean, how long ago did you get dumped?"

"About nine months, I guess."

"About?" she asked. It must not have impacted him in quite the same way if he couldn't remember the date. "I mean—was it traumatic?"

"Sort of," he said. "We were engaged, lived together, but we were arguing all the time. She finally told me she wasn't willing to have a life like that and we had to go our separate ways. It wasn't my idea to break up." He shrugged. "I thought we could fix it and wanted to try, but she didn't."

"Did you know?" she asked. "Were you expecting it?"

He shook his head. "I should have expected it, but it broadsided me."

"How can that be? If you should have expected it, how could it possibly have taken you by surprise?"

He took a deep breath, looked skyward into the softly falling flakes, then back at her. "We were pretty miserable, but before we lived together we did great. I'm a medical resident and my hours were…still are hideous. Sometimes I'm on for thirty-six hours and just get enough time off to sleep. She needed more from me than that. She…" He looked down. "I don't like calling her *she* or *her*. *Penny* had a hard time changing her life in order to move in with me. She had to get a new job, make new friends, and I was never there for her. I should have seen it coming but I didn't. It was all my fault but I couldn't have done anything to change it."

"Where are you from?" she asked him.

"Chico. About four hours south of here."

"Wow," she said. "We actually do have some things in common."

"Do we?" he asked.

"But you're over it. How'd you get over it?"

He put his hands in his front pants pockets. "She invited me to her engagement party three months ago. To another surgical resident. Last time I looked, he was on the same treadmill I was on. Guess he manages better with no sleep."

"No way," she said, backing away from the bar's porch a little bit.

"Way."

"You don't suppose…?"

"That she was doing him when she was supposed to be doing me?" he asked for her. "It crossed my mind. But I'm not going there. I don't even want to know. All that aside, she obviously wasn't the one. I know that now. Which means it really *was* my fault. I was hook-ing up with someone out of inertia, not because I was insanely in love with her. Bottom line, Sunny, me and Penny? We both dodged a bullet. We were not meant to be."

She was speechless. Her mouth formed a perfect O. Her eyes were round. She wished she'd been able to take her own situation in such stride. "Holy crap," she finally said. Then she shook her head. "I guess you have to be confident to be in medicine and all."

"Aw, come on, don't give the study all the credit. I might actually have some common sense." He took a step down from the bar porch to approach her, his heel slid on the step and he went airborne. While he was in the air, there were rapid flashes from her camera. Then he landed, flat on his back, and there were more flashes.

Sunny stood over him, camera in hand. She looked down at him. "Are you all right?"

He narrowed his eyes at her. It took him a moment to catch his breath. "I could be paralyzed, you know. I hope I was hallucinating, but were you actually taking my picture as I fell?"

"Well, I couldn't catch you," she said. Then she smiled.

"You are sick and twisted."

"Maybe you should lie still. I could go in the bar and

get the pediatrician and the midwife to have a look at you. I met them earlier, before you got here."

He looked up at her; she was still smiling. Apparently it didn't take much to cheer her up—the near death of a man seemed to put her in a better mood. "Maybe you could just show them the pictures...."

She fell onto her knees beside him and laughed, her camera still in hand. It was a bright and happy sound and those beautiful blue eyes glittered. "Seriously, you're the doctor—do you think you're all right?"

"I don't know," he said. "I haven't moved yet. One wrong move and I could be paralyzed from the neck down."

"Are you playing me?"

"Might be," he admitted with a shrug of his shoulders.

"Hah! You moved! You're fine. Get up."

"Are you going to have a drink with me?" he asked.

"Why should I? Seriously, we're a couple of wounded birds—we probably shouldn't drink, and we certainly shouldn't drink together!"

"Get over it," he said, rising a bit, holding himself up on his elbows. "We have nothing to lose. It's a New Year's Eve party. We'll have a couple of drinks, toast the New Year, move on. But give it a try not so pissed off. See if you can have some fun." He smiled. "Just for the heck of it?"

She sat back on her heels and eyed him warily. "Is this just more inertia?"

His grin widened. "No, Sunny. This is part chivalry and part animal attraction."

"Oh, God.… I just got dumped by an animal. So not looking for another one."

He gave her a gentle punch in the arm. "Buck up. Be a big girl. I bet you haven't let an interested guy buy you a drink in a long time. Take a chance. Practice on me. I'm harmless."

She lifted one light brown brow. "How do I know you're harmless?"

"I'm going back to sacrifice myself to the gods of residency in two days. They'll chew me up and spit me out. Those chief residents are ruthless and they want revenge for what was done to them when they were the little guys. There won't even be a body left. No one will ever know you succumbed to having a beer with me." And then he smiled with all his teeth.

She tsked and rolled her eyes at him.

He sat up. "See how much you like me? You're putty in my hands."

"You're a dork!"

He got to his feet and held out a hand to her, helping

her up. "I've heard that, but I'm not buying it yet. I think if you dig deep enough, I might be cool."

She brushed off the knees of her jeans. "I'm not sure I have that kind of time."

Three

Once Drew got up and moved, he limped. He claimed a wounded hip and leaned on Sunny. Since she couldn't be sure if he was faking, she allowed this. But just as they neared the steps, the doors to the bar flew open and people began to spill out, laughing, shouting, waving goodbye.

"Careful there," he yelled, straightening up. "I just slipped on the steps. They're iced over. I'll get Jack to throw some salt on them, but take it slow and easy."

"Sure," someone said. "Thanks, Drew."

"Be careful driving back to Chico," someone else said.

"Say hello to your sisters," a woman said. "Tell them to come up before too long, we miss them."

"Pinch that cute baby!"

"Will do," Drew said in response, and he pulled Sunny to the side to make way for the grand exodus. The laughing, joking, talking people, some carrying their plates and pots from the buffet table, headed for their cars.

"What the heck," Sunny said. "It's not even nine o'clock!"

Drew laughed and put his arm back over her shoulder to lean on her. "This is a little town, Sunny. These folks have farms, ranches, orchards, vineyards, small businesses and stuff like that. The ones who don't have to get up early for work—even on holidays—might stay later. And some of the folks who are staying are on call—the midwife, the cop, the doctor." He grinned. "Probably the bartender. If anyone has a flat on the way home, five gets you ten either Jack or Preacher will help out."

"Do you know all these people?"

"A lot of them, yeah. I'll give you the short version of the story—my sister Marcie was married to a marine who was disabled in action and then later died. She came up here to find his best friend and sergeant—Ian Buchanan. She found him in a run-down old cabin up on the ridge, just over the county line, but the nearest town was Virgin River. So—she married him and they have a baby now. My oldest sister, Erin, wanted a retreat up here, but she couldn't handle a cabin with no indoor bathroom or where you'd have to boil your bath water and chop your wood for heat, so she got a local builder to renovate one into something up to her standards with electricity, indoor plumbing and a whirlpool tub." He laughed. "Really, Marcie's pretty tough, but if Erin risked breaking a nail, that would make her very cranky." He looked at Sunny and smiled. "It used to be a lean-to, now it should be in *Architectural Digest.* Anyway, I've been up here several times in the past couple of years, and Jack's is the only game in town. You don't have to drop into Jack's very many times before you know half the town. I'm hiding out in the cabin for a few days to get some studying done, away from my sisters and the baby. I have to go back on the second. I just swung through town for a beer—I had no idea there was a party."

They just stood there, in front of the porch, his arm draped across her shoulder. It was kind of silly—she was only five foot four and he was easily six feet, plus muscular. He didn't lean on her too heavily.

"Is it very hard, what you do? Residency?"

"It doesn't have to be. It could be a learning experience, but the senior residents pile as much on you as they can. It's like a dare—who can take it all and keep standing. That's the part that makes it hard." Then he sobered for a second. "And kids. I love working with the kids, making them laugh, helping them get better, but it's so tough to see them broken. Being the surgeon who puts a kid back together again—it's like the best and worst part of what I do. Know what I mean?"

She couldn't help but imagine him taking a little soccer player into surgery, or wrapping casting material around the arm of a young violinist. "Your sister was married to a soldier who was killed...?"

"She was married to a marine. Bobby was permanently disabled by a bomb in Iraq. He was in a nursing home for a few years before he died, but he never really came back, you know? No conscious recognition—the light was on but no one was home. They were very young."

"Were you close to him?"

"Yeah, sure. He was two years older and we all went to high school together. Bobby went in right after graduation. Ian was a little older, so I didn't know him until Marcie brought him home." He laughed sentimentally. "She's something, Marcie. She came up here to find Ian, make sure he was all right after the war and to give him Bobby's baseball card collection. She brought him home on Christmas eve and said, 'This is Ian and I'm going to marry him as soon as he can get used to the idea.'"

"This is why," she said softly. "This is why you can move on after getting dumped by your fiancée. You've seen some rough stuff and you know how to count your blessings. I bet that's it."

He turned Sunny so she faced him. Of course he couldn't lean on her then, but he got close. "Sunny, my family's been through some stuff... Mostly my sisters, really—they had it toughest. But the thing that keeps me looking up instead of down—it's what I see at work everyday. I'm called on to treat people with problems lots bigger than mine—people who will never walk again, never use their arms or hands, and sometimes worse. Orthopedic pain can be terrible, rehab can be extended and dreary.... Tell you what, Sunshine—I'm upright, walking around, healthy, have a brain to think with and the option to enjoy my life. Well, I'm not going to take that for granted." He lifted a brow, tilted his head, smiled. "Maybe you should spend a little time in my trauma center, see if it fixes up all those things you think you should worry about?"

"What about your chief residents?" she asked, showing him her smile.

"Oh, them. Well, I pretty much wish them dead. No remorse, either. God, they're mean. Mean and spiteful and impossible to please."

"Will you be a chief resident someday?"

His smile took on an evil slant. "Yes. But not soon enough. Watch yourself on these stairs, honey." Before opening the door for Sunny, he stopped her. "So—want to find a cozy spot by the fire and tell me about the breakup that left you so sad and unapproachable?"

She didn't even have to think about it. "No," she said, shaking her head. "I'd rather not talk about it."

"Fair enough. Want to tell me how you got into photography?"

She smiled at him. "I could do that."

"Good. I'll have Jack pour you a glass of wine and while he's doing that I'll scatter some salt on those icy steps." He touched her pink nose. "Your mission is to find us a spot in that bar where we can talk. If I'm not mistaken, we're the only two singles at this party."

Sunny went back to the place near the fire where she had left her camera bag and put her camera away. She glanced over at Drew. He stood at the bar talking with Jack; Jack handed him a large canister of salt.

And suddenly it was someone else standing at the bar, and it wasn't this bar. Her mind drifted and took her back in time. It was Glen and it was the bar at their rehearsal dinner. Glen was leaning on the bar, staring morosely into his drink, one foot lifted up on the rail. His best man, Russ, had a hand on his back, leaning close and talking in Glen's ear. Glen wasn't responding.

Why hadn't she been more worried? she asked herself in retrospect. Maybe because everyone around her had been so reassuring? Or was it because she *refused* to be concerned?

Sunny wasn't very old-fashioned, but there were a few traditional wedding customs she had wanted to uphold—one was not seeing her groom the day of her wedding. So she and her cousin Mary, who was also her matron of honor, would spend the night at Sunny's parents' house after the rehearsal dinner. Even still, she remembered thinking it was a little early when Glen kissed her goodnight that evening.

"I'm going out with the boys for a nightcap, then home," he said.

"Is everything all right?" she asked.

"Sure. Fine." His smile was flat, she knew things were not fine.

"You're not driving, are you?"

"Russ has the keys. It's fine."

"I guess I'll see you tomorrow." She remembered so vividly that she laid her palm against his handsome cheek. "I can't wait for tomorrow."

He didn't move his head, but his eyes had darted briefly away. "Me, too."

When Russ came over to her to say good-night, she had asked, "What's bothering Glen?"

"Oh, he'll be fine."

"But what is it?"

Russ had laughed a bit uncomfortably. "Y'know, even though you two have been together a long time, lived together and everything, it's still a pretty big step for a guy. For both of you, I realize. But guys... I don't know what it is about us—I was a little jittery the day before my wedding. And it was absolutely what I wanted, no doubt, but I was still nervous. I don't know if it's the responsibility, the lifestyle change..."

"What changes?" she asked. "Besides that we're going to take a nice trip and write a lot of thank-you notes?"

"I'm just saying... I've been in a bunch of weddings, including my own, and every groom I've ever known gets a little jumpy right before. Don't worry about it. I'll buy him a drink on the way home, make sure he gets all tucked in. You'll be on your way to Aruba before you know it." Then he had smiled reassuringly.

"Will you ask him to call me to say good-night?" she asked.

"Sure. But if he's slurring by then, don't hold it against me!"

She'd been up late talking to Mary; they'd opened another bottle of wine. By the time they fell asleep it was the wee hours and they'd slept soundly. In the morning when she checked her cell phone, she found a text from

Glen that had come in at three in the morning. *Going to bed. Talk to you tomorrow.*

She wanted to talk to him, but she thought it would probably be better if he slept till noon, especially if there was anything to sleep off, so he'd be in good shape for the ceremony. All she wanted was for the wedding to be perfect! She had many bridely things to do and was kept busy from brunch getting a manicure and pedicure, surrounded by the women in her family and her girlfriends.

The New Year's Eve wedding had been Sunny's idea. It had been born of a conversation with the girls about how they'd never had a memorable New Year's Eve— even when they had steady guys, were engaged or even married. Oh, there'd been a few parties, but they hadn't been special in any way. Sunny thought it would be fantastic—a classy party to accompany her wedding, something for everyone to remember. An unforgettable event.

Little did she know.

She'd been so busy all day, she hadn't worried that she never heard from Glen. She assumed he was as occupied with his guys as she was with her girls. In fact, it hadn't really bothered her until about five, still a couple of hours till the wedding. She called him and when he didn't pick up, she left him a voice mail that she loved him, that she was so happy, that soon they would be married and off on a wonderful honeymoon.

It's very hard for a photographer to choose a photographer; almost no one was going to measure up to Sunny's expectations. But the very well known Lin Hui was trying her best, and started snapping shots as soon as the girls showed up at the church with hairdressers and professional makeup artists in tow. Her camera flashed at almost every phase of preparation and in addition captured special memories—shiny, strappy heels against flowers, female hands clutching white satin, mothers of the bride and groom embracing and dabbing each other's eyes. But the poor thing seemed very nervous. Sunny assumed it was because of the challenge of shooting another professional. She had no idea it was because Lin couldn't find the groom for a photo shoot of the men in the wedding party.

It happened at six forty-five, fifteen minutes before the ceremony was to start. Sunny's father came into the wedding prep room with Russ. Both of them looked as if someone had died and she immediately gasped and ran to her father. "Is Glen all right?"

"He's fine, honey." Then he sent everyone out of the room including Sunny's mom and the mother of the groom. He turned to Russ and said, "Tell her."

Russ hung his head. He shook it. "Don't ask me what's got into him, I really can't explain. There's no good reason for this. He said he's sorry, he just isn't ready for this. He froze up, can't go through with it."

She had never before realized how fast denial can set in or how long it can last. "Impossible. The wedding is in fifteen minutes," she said.

"I know. I'm sorry—I spent all day trying to get through this with him. I even suggested he just show up, do it, and if he still feels the same way in a few months, he can get a divorce. Honest to God, it made more sense to me than this."

She shook her head and then, inexplicably, laughed. "Aw, you guys. This is not funny. You got me, okay? But this isn't funny!"

"It's not a joke, baby," her father said. "I've tried calling him—he won't pick up."

"He'll pick up for me," she said. "He always picks up for me!"

But he didn't. Her call was sent to voice mail. Her message was, "Please call me and tell me I'm just dreaming this! Please! You can't really be ditching me at the church fifteen minutes before the wedding! Not you! You're better than this!"

Russ grabbed her wrist. "Sunny—he left his tux in my car to return. He's not coming."

Sunny looked at her father. "What am I supposed to do?" she asked in a whisper.

Her father's face was dark with anger, stony with fury. "We'll give him till seven-fifteen to call or do something honorable, then we make an announcement to the guests, invite them to go to the party and eat the food that will otherwise be given away or thrown out, and we'll return the gifts with apologies. And then I'm going to kill him."

"He said he'll pay back the cost of the reception if it takes his whole life. But there's no way he can pay me back for what he asked me to do today," Russ said. "Sunny, I'm so sorry."

"But *why?*"

"Like I said, he doesn't have a logical reason. He can't, he said." Russ shook his head. "I don't understand, so I know you can't possibly."

Sunny grabbed Russ's arm. "Go tell his mother to call him! Give her your cell phone so he'll think it's you and pick up!"

But Glen didn't pick up and his mother was left to growl angrily into the phone's voice mail right before she fell apart and cried.

Before they got even close to seven-fifteen everyone nearby was firing questions at Sunny like it was her fault. Why? Did he talk to you about this? Was he upset, troubled? Did you suspect this was coming? You must have noticed something! How can you not have known? Suspected? Were you having problems? Arguing about something? Fighting? Was his behavior off? Strange? Was there another woman? It didn't take long for her to erupt. "You'll have to ask *him!* And he's not even here to ask! Not only did he not show up, he left me to try to answer for him!"

At seven-ten, right before her father made an announcement to the wedding guests, Sunny quietly got into the bridal limo. She took her bouquet—her beautiful bouquet filled with roses and orchids and calla lilies—made a stop at her parents' house for her purse and honeymoon luggage and had the driver take her home.

Home. The town house she shared with Glen. Her parents were frantic, her girlfriends were worried, her wedding guests wondered what went wrong. She wasn't sure why she went home, maybe to see if he'd moved out while she was having a manicure and pedicure. But no—everything was just as she'd left it. And typical of Glen, the bed wasn't made and there were dirty dishes in the sink.

She sat on the edge of their king-size bed in her wedding gown, her bouquet in her lap and her cell phone in her hand in case he should call and say it was all a bad joke and rather than pulling out of the wedding he was in the hospital or in jail. The only calls she got were from friends and family, all worried about her. She fended off most of them without saying where she was, others were forced to leave messages. For some reason she couldn't explain to this day, she didn't cry. She let herself fall back on the bed, stared at the ceiling and asked herself over and over what she didn't know about this man she had been willing to commit a lifetime to. She was vaguely aware of that special midnight hour passing. The new year didn't come in with a kiss, but with a scandalous breakup.

Sunny hadn't had a plan when she went home, but when she heard a key in the lock she realized that because she'd taken the bridal limo and left her car at her parents', Glen didn't know she was there. She sat up.

He walked through the bedroom door, grabbing his wallet, keys and change out of his pockets to drop onto the dresser when he saw her. Everything scattered as he made a sound of surprise and he automatically reached for his ankle where he always kept a small, back-up gun. Breathing hard, he left it there and straightened. Cops, she thought. They like always having *something,* in case they happen to run into someone they put away...or a pissed-off bride.

"Go ahead," she said. "Shoot me. It might be easier."

"Sunny," he said, breathless. "What are you *doing* here?"

"I *live* here," she said. She looked down at the bou-

quet she still held. Why had she clung to that? Because
it was sentimental or because it cost 175 dollars and she
couldn't return it? "You can't have done this to me," she
said almost weakly. "You can't have. You must have a
brain tumor or something."

He walked into the room. "I'm sorry," he said, shaking his head. "I kept thinking that by the time we got
to the actual date, the wedding date, I'd be ready. I really thought that."

"Ready for what?" she asked, nonplussed.

"Ready for that life, that commitment forever, that
next stage, the house, the children, the fidelity, the—"

She shook her head, frowning in confusion. "Wait a
minute, we haven't found a house we like and can afford,
we agreed we're not ready for children yet and I thought
we already had commitment…" His chin dropped. "Fidelity?" she asked in a whisper.

He lifted his eyes and locked with hers. "See, I haven't
really done anything wrong, not really. I kept thinking,
I'm not married yet! And I thought by the time—"

"Did you sleep with other women?" she asked, rising to her feet.

"No! No! I swear!"

She didn't believe him for a second! "Then what *did*
you do?"

"Nothing much. I partied a little. Had drinks, you

know. Danced. Just went out and sometimes I met girls, but it didn't get serious or anything."

"But it did get to meeting, dancing, buying drinks. Talking on the phone? Texting little messages? Maybe having dinner?"

"Maybe some of that. A couple of times."

"Maybe kissing?"

"Only, maybe, twice. At the most, twice."

"My God, have I been brain damaged? To not know?"

"When were we together?" he asked. "We had different nights off, we were like roommates!"

"You could have fixed that easy! You could have changed your nights off! I couldn't! People don't get married or have fiftieth anniversary parties on Tuesday nights!"

"And they also don't go out for fun on Tuesday nights! I guess I'm just a bad boy, but I enjoy a ball game or a run on a bar or club on a weekend when people are out! And you were never available on a weekend! We talked about it, we *fought* about it! You said it would never change, not while you took pictures."

"This isn't happening," she said. "You stood up two hundred wedding guests and a trip to Aruba because I work weekends?"

"Not exactly, but... Well... Look," he said, shaking his head. "I'm twenty-six. I thought you were probably the best thing for me, the best woman I could ever hook up with for the long haul except for one thing—I'm not ready to stop having fun! And you are—you're all business. Even that wedding—Jesus, it was like a runaway train! Planning that astronomical wedding was like a second job for you and I never wanted anything that big, that out of control! Sunny, you're way too young to be so old."

That was one way to deliver what she could only describe as a punch to the gut. Of all the things she thought she knew about him, she hadn't given enough credence to the fact that even at twenty-six, he was younger than she. More immature. He wanted to have *fun.* "And you couldn't tell me this last month? Or last week? Or *yesterday?*" She stared at him, waiting.

"Like I said, I thought I'd work it out in my head, be ready in time."

Talk about shock and awe. "You're an infant. How did I not realize what a liability that could be?"

"Excuse me, but I lay my life on the line every day! I go to work in a bulletproof vest! And you're calling me an *infant?*"

"Oh, I'm so sorry, Glen. You're an infant with a dick. With a little, tiny brain in it." She took a breath. "Pack a bag. Take some things and see if you can find a friend who will take you in for a few days. I'll move home to my mom and dad's as soon as I can. I hope you can make the rent alone. If I recall, I was making more money with my boring old weekend job than you were with your bulletproof vest."

Sunny sat back on the bed, then she lay down. Still gowned in a very big wedding dress, holding her valuable bouquet at her waist, Sunny closed her eyes. She heard Glen rustling around, finding clothes, his shaving kit, the essentials. Her mind was completely occupied with thoughts like, will the airline refund the money for the first-class tickets because the groom didn't show? How much non-refundable money had her parents wasted on a wedding that never happened? Would the homeless of L.A. be eating thousands of dollars worth of exquisite food discarded by the caterer? And since her name was also on the lease to this townhouse, would fun-man Glen stiff her there, too? Hurt her credit rating *and* her business?

"Sunny?" Glen said to her. He was standing over her. "Wake up. You look so… I don't know… *Funereal* or something. Like a dead body, all laid out." He winced. "In a wedding dress…"

She opened her eyes, then narrowed them at him. "Go. Away."

Sunny gave her head a little shake to clear her mind and looked up to see Drew standing in front of her. He held a glass of wine toward her. "I salted the steps, got you a wine and me a beer. Now," he said, sitting down opposite her. "About this photography of yours…"

"It happened a year ago," she said.

"Huh? The picture taking happened a year ago?" he asked.

"The wedding that never was. Big wedding—big party. We'd been together three years, engaged and living together for one, and all of a sudden he didn't show. I was all dressed up in a Vera Wang, two hundred guests were waiting, little sausages simmering and stuffed mushrooms warming, champagne corks popping…and no groom."

Total shock was etched into his features. "Get out!" he said in a shocked breath.

"God's truth. His best man told me he couldn't do it. He wasn't ready."

Suddenly Drew laughed, but not unkindly, not of humor but disbelief. He ran his hand through his hair. "Did he ever say *why?*"

She had never told anyone what he'd said, it was too embarrassing. But for some reason she couldn't explain, she spit it right out to Drew. "Yeah. He wasn't done having fun."

Silence reigned for a moment. "You're not serious," Drew finally said.

"Deadly. It was all so stunning, there was even a small newspaper article about it."

"And this happened when?" he asked.

"One year ago. Today."

Drew sat back in his chair. "Whoa," was all he could say. "Well, no wonder you're in a mood. Fun?" he asked. "He wasn't done having *fun?*"

"Fun," she affirmed. "That's the best explanation he could come up with. He liked to party, go to clubs, flirt, dance, whatever... He's a Saturday-night kind of guy and just wasn't ready to stop doing that and guess what? Photographers work weekends—weddings, baptisms, et cetera. Apparently I'm a real drag."

Drew rubbed the back of his neck. "I must be really backward then. I always thought having the right person there for you, listening to your voice mails and texting you to pick up her dry cleaning or saying she'd pick up yours, someone who argued with you over what sushi to bring home or what went on the pizza, someone who would come to bed naked on a regular basis—I always thought *those things* were fun. Sexy and fun."

She grinned at him. "You find dry cleaning sexy?"

"I do," he said. "I really do." And then they both laughed.

Four

Sunny sat forward, elbows on her knees, a smile on her face and said, "I can't wait to hear more about this— the things you find sexy. I mean pizza toppings and dry cleaning? Do go on."

He took a sip of his beer. "There is a long list, Miss Sunshine, but let's be clear—I am a boy. Naked tops the list."

"Yes, there are some things all you *boys* seem to have in common. But if I've learned anything it's that show-ing up naked regularly apparently isn't quite enough."

"Pah—for men with no imagination maybe. Or men who don't have to push a month's worth of work into a day."

"Well, then…?" she asked. "What?"

"I like working out a budget you'll never stick to.

There's something about planning that together, it's cool. Not the checkbook, that's not a two-person job—it's dicey. No two people add and subtract the same, did you know that? And the chore list, that turns me on like you wouldn't believe. Picking movies—there's a real skill to that. If you can find a girl who likes action then you can negotiate three action movies to every chick flick, and you can eventually work up to trading chick flicks for back rubs." He leaned close to whisper. "I don't want this to get out, but I actually like some of the chick flicks. I'm picky, but I do like some."

"Shopping?" she asked.

"I have to draw the line there," he said firmly. "That just doesn't do it for me. If I need clothes or shoes I take care of it as fast as I can. I don't like to screw around with that. It's boring and I have no skills. But I get that you have to look at least half decent to get a girl to like you." He smiled. "A pretty girl like you," he added.

"Then how do you manage that? Because tonight, you weren't even aware there was a party and you don't look that terrible."

"Why, thank you," he said, straightening proudly. "I either ask my oldest sister, Erin, to dress me—the one who made the lean-to into a showplace—or failing that I just look for a gay guy working in clothing."

She burst out laughing, not realizing that Nate, Annie,

Jack and a few others turned to look. "That's awful, shame on you!"

"Gimme a break—I have gay friends. You can say anything you want about them but the common denominator is—they have fashion sense. At least the guys I know do."

"Then why not ask a gay friend to go shopping with you?"

"I don't want to mislead anyone," he said with a shrug.

"Sure you're not just a little self-conscious about your…um…somewhat *flexible* status?"

He leaned so close she could inhale the Michelob on his breath. His eyes locked on hers. "Not flexible about that. Ab. So. Lutely. Not." Then he smiled. "I only swing one way."

She couldn't help it, she laughed loudly. Happily.

"You gotta stop that, my sunshine. You're supposed to be miserable. You were left at the altar by a juvenile idiot a year ago tonight. We're grieving here."

"I know, I know," she said, fanning her face. "I'm going to get back into depression mode in a sec. Right now, tell me another thing you find impossibly sexy, and keep in mind we've already covered that naked thing."

"Okay," he said. He rolled his eyes skyward, looking for the answer. "Ah!" he said. "Her lingerie in the bathroom! It's impossible. Hanging everywhere. A guy can't even pee much less brush his teeth or get a shower. I hate that!" And there was that wicked grin again. "Very sexy."

"Okay, I'm a little confused here. You hate it? And it's very sexy?"

"Well, you have to be a guy to get this. A guy goes into the bathroom—which is small like the rest of your house or apartment until you're at least an evil senior resident—and you put your face into all the satin and lace hanging all over the place. You rub it between your palms, wear a thong on your head for a minute, have a couple of reality-based fantasies, and then you yell, 'Penny! Get your underwear out of here so I can get a shower! I'm late.'"

She put her hands over her face and laughed into them.

His eyes glowed as he looked at her. "Be careful, Sunny. You're enjoying yourself."

She reached across the short space that separated them and gave him a playful slug. "So are you! And your breakup was more recent."

"Yeah, but—"

He was about to say *but not more traumatic*. At least he wasn't left in a Vera Wang gown hiding from two hundred wedding guests. But the door to the bar opened and in came the local Riordans—Luke, Shelby and little

Brett, their new baby. Luke was holding Brett against his chest, tucked under his jacket. Drew jumped to his feet. "Hey! Son of a gun!" Then he grabbed Sunny's hand and pulled her along. He turned to her and said, "Kind of family. I'll explain."

Leaving Sunny behind him a bit, he grabbed Shelby in a big hug and kissed her cheek. He grabbed Luke, careful of the baby and Luke scowled at him and said, "Do *not* kiss me!"

"All right, but gee, I'll have to really hold myself back," Drew said with a laugh. He winked at Sunny before he pulled her forward. "Meet Sunny, here visiting her uncle. Sunny, remember I told you about the sister who turned the shack into a showplace? That's Erin—and while she was up here finding herself, she also found Luke's brother Aiden. They're engaged. That makes me almost related to these guys and little Brett."

Shelby reached out to shake Sunny's hand. "I heard you'd be visiting, Sunny. We know Nate and Annie. I sometimes ride with Annie."

"Hey, I thought you said you weren't coming out tonight," Jack said from behind the bar. "Baby sleeping and all that."

"We should'a thought that through a little better," Luke said. "Brett prefers to sleep during the day and is a regular party animal at night."

Mel moved closer and said, "Aww, let me have him a minute." She pulled the little guy from Luke and indeed, his eyes were as big as saucers—he was wide awake at nine-thirty. Mel laughed at him. "Well, aren't you something!"

Shelby said to Sunny, "Mel delivered him. She gets really invested in her babies."

"Let's have your resolutions," Jack said. "Then I'll set you up a drink and you can graze the buffet table."

"What resolutions?" Luke wanted to know.

Jack patted the fishbowl full of slips of paper on the bar. "Everyone has contributed their number one, generic resolution. You know the kind—quit smoking, lose ten pounds, work out everyday. We're going to do something fun with them at midnight. A kind of game."

"I don't do games," Luke said.

"Lighten up, it's not like charades or anything. It's more like cracking open a fortune cookie."

"I don't do resolutions," Luke said.

"I'll do his," Shelby said, sitting up at the bar. "I have some ideas."

"Easy, baby," Luke said. "You know you don't like me too perfect. Rough around the edges caught you in the first place."

Shelby glanced over her shoulder and smiled at him. Nate, who was sitting beside her, leaned in and pretended to read her resolution. "No more boys' nights out or dancing girls?" he said. "Shelby, isn't that a little strict for our boy Luke?"

Luke just laughed. So did Shelby.

Sunny took it all in. She had always liked to be around couples who were making that whole couple thing work—understanding each other, give and take, good humor, physical attraction. She'd done a lot of weddings. They weren't all easy and pleasant. A lot of the couples she photographed she wouldn't give a year.

Drew whispered in her ear. "Shelby is a full-time nursing student. She and Luke run a bunch of riverside cabin rentals and while Shelby goes to school and studies, Luke not only takes care of the cabins and house, but Brett, too. I think dancing girls are way in the past for Luke."

"Hmm," she said. She went for her camera and started taking pictures again, and while she did so she listened. Sunny could see things through the lens that were harder to see with the naked eye. For her, anyway.

She learned that Vanessa and Paul Haggerty were more conventional. She was home with the children while he was a general contractor who did most of the building and renovating around Virgin River, including the reconstruction of that old cabin for Drew's sister, the cabin Drew was staying in. Abby Michaels, the local doctor's wife, had a set of toddler twins and was overseeing the building of a house while her husband, Cam, was at the clinic or on call 24/7. The situation was a bit different for Mel and Jack Sheridan. The local midwife was always on call and Jack had a business that was open about sixteen hours a day—they had to shore each other up. They did a lot of juggling of kids and chores—Jack did all the cooking and Mel all the cleaning. If all the jokes could be believed, apparently Mel could burn water. Preacher and Paige worked together to raise their kids, run the kitchen and keep the accounting books at the bar. Brie and Mike Valenzuela had a child and two full-time jobs—she was an attorney, he was the town cop. And Sunny already knew that Uncle Nate and Annie were partners in running the Jensen Clinic and Stable. Their wedding was scheduled for May.

Lots of interesting and individual methods of managing the realities of work, family, relationships. She wondered about a couple who would split up because one of them wasn't available to party on Saturday nights. She already knew that wasn't an issue among these folks.

While she observed and listened, she snapped pictures. She instructed Mel to hold the Riordan baby over her head and lower him slowly to kiss his nose. She got a great shot of Jack leaning on the bar, braced on strong arms spread wide, wearing a half smile as he watched his wife with a baby she had delivered, a proud glow in his eyes. Preacher was caught with his huge arms wrapped around his little wife, his lips against her head. Paul Haggerty put a quarter in the jukebox and danced his wife around the bar. Cameron Michaels was clinking glasses with Abby Michaels and couldn't resist nuzzling her neck—Sunny caught that. In fact, she caught many interesting postures, loving poses. Not only was there a lot of affection in the room, but plenty of humor and happiness. God, she never used to be the type that got dragged down.

When Sunny was focusing the camera, she didn't miss much. Maybe she should have been looking at Glen through the lens because clearly she missed a lot about him. Or had she just ignored it all?

She wondered if this was all about it being New Year's Eve, being among friends and the promise of a brand-new start, a first day of a new year. That's what she'd had in mind for her wedding—a new beginning.

Then she spotted Drew, apart from the crowd, leaning against the wall beside the hearth, watching her with a lazy smile on his lips. He had one leg crossed over the other, one hand was in his front jeans pocket and he lifted his bottle of Mich, which had to be warm by now since he'd been nursing it for so long. She snapped, flashed the camera, making him laugh. He posed for her, pulling that hand out of his pocket and flexing his muscles. Of course it was impossible to see his real physique given the roomy plaid flannel shirt. He put his leg up on the seat of a nearby chair, gave her a profile and lifted the beer bottle—she liked it. He grinned, scowled, stuck his tongue out, blew raspberries at the camera—she snapped and laughed. Then he crooked his finger at her for her to come closer and she took pictures as she went. When she got real close he pulled the camera away.

"Let's get out of here," he whispered. "Somewhere we can talk."

"Can't we talk here?" she asked.

He shook his head. "Listen," he said.

She listened—the jukebox. Only the jukebox. He turned her around. Every single eye was on them. Watching. Waiting. She turned back to Drew. "Everyone knows," she said. "We are the only single people, we're both single and miserable—"

"Single," he said. "I'm not miserable and I know you intended to be miserable, but that's not really working out for you. So?" he asked with a shrug. "Wanna just throw caution to the wind and see if you can enjoy the rest of the evening?"

"I can't enjoy it here?"

"With all of them watching you? Listening?" he asked
with a lift of the chin to indicate the bar at large.

When she turned around to look, she caught everyone quickly averting their eyes and it made her laugh.
She laughed harder, putting her hand over her mouth.

"Don't do that," he said, pulling her hand away. "You
have an amazing smile and I love listening to you laugh."

"Where would we go?"

"Well, it's only ten. I could take you to Eureka or Fortuna—there's bound to be stuff going on, but I'd prefer
to find somewhere there's not a party. I could show you
the cabin Erin turned into a showplace, but I don't have
any 'before' pictures. Or we could take a drive, park in
the woods and make out like teenagers." He grinned at
her playfully. Hopefully.

"You're overconfident," she accused.

"I've been told that. It's better than being under-
confident, in these circumstances at least."

"I have to speak to Uncle Nathaniel," she said.

He touched her cheek with the knuckle of one finger.
"Permission?"

She shook her head a little. "Courtesy. I'm his guest.
Grab our coats."

The walk across the bar to her uncle was very short
and in that time she realized that Drew wasn't overconfident—*Glen* was overconfident. He preened, and

had always managed to strike a pose that accentuated his height, firm jaw, strong shoulders. Drew clowned around. Laughed. Drew seemed to be pretty easygoing and took things as they came. But she'd known him for two whole hours. Who knew what secrets he harbored?

But what the hell, Sunny thought. I can experiment with actually letting a male person get close without much risk—I'm never going to see him again. Who knows? Maybe I'll recover after all.

"Uncle Nate," she said. "I'm going to go with Drew to see if anything fun is happening in Fortuna or Eureka. If you're okay with that."

"Well," he said. "I don't actually know—*ow!*"

Annie slugged him in the arm. "That's great, Sunny," she said. "Will you come back here or have Drew take you home?"

She shrugged and shook her head. "I don't know. Depends on where we are, what's going on, you know. Listen, if the cells worked up here, I'd call, but…"

"Your cell from Fortuna or Eureka to my home phone works. Or to Jack's land line. We'll be here till midnight," Nate said. Then he glared briefly at Annie. "Jack, can you give her your number?"

"You bet," Jack said, jotting it on a napkin. "I've known Drew and his family a couple of years. You're in good hands, Sunny."

"Does he have four-wheel drive?" Nate asked.

Sunny grinned. "Oh, you're going to be a fun daddy, yessir." Then she walked back to Drew and let him help her slip on her jacket.

"Where did you say we were going?" Drew asked.

"I said Fortuna or Eureka, but I want to see it—the cabin."

He grabbed his own jacket. "Hope I didn't leave it nasty."

"And is that likely?" she wanted to know.

"Depends where my head was at the time," he said. He rested her elbow in the palm of his hand and began to direct her out of the bar. As they were leaving he put two fingers to his brow and gave the gawkers a salute.

Sunny was trying to remember, what was the first thing Drew had said to her? She thought it was something simple, like "Hi, my name is Drew." And what had been Glen's opening line? With a finger in her sternum he had said, "Yo. You and me."

Five

"I'm not sure that was the best thing to do," Nate Jensen said right after Sunny and Drew left. "I'm supposed to be looking after her, and I let her go off with some guy I don't even know."

"She was *laughing!*" Annie stressed. "Having fun for the first time in so long! She didn't need your permission, Nate. She was being polite, telling you where she was going so you wouldn't worry."

"You did fine," Jack said. "Drew's a good guy. A doctor, actually—in his residency now."

"But is he the kind of guy who will take advantage of a girl with a broken heart?" Nate asked. "Because my sister…"

"I don't know a thing about his love life," Jack said. "He said he'd had a breakup, so that might make them sympathetic to each other. I'll tell you what I know. Every time I've talked to him he's seemed like a stand-up guy. His brother-in-law was a disabled marine in a nursing home for a few years before he died, and Erin said that Drew, along with the rest of the family, helped take care of him. Erin thinks that had an impact on him, drew him to medicine. And...he has four-wheel drive. That should put your mind at ease."

"She *was* smiling," Nate admitted. "You should'a been there last year. Sitting in that church, waiting for the wedding to start. Just like in all things, the rumors that the groom didn't show started floating around the guests, maybe before Sunny had even heard it. It was awful. How do you not know something like that is coming? How could she not know?"

Jack gave the bar a wipe. "You can bet she's been asking herself that question for about a year."

"Tell me about the photography business," Drew said as they drove.

"You don't have to ask that," she said. "I can tell you're a gentleman and that's very polite, but you don't have to pretend to be interested in photography. It bores the heck out of most people."

He laughed at her. "When I was a kid, I took pictures sometimes," he said. "Awful pictures that were developed at the drugstore, but it was enough to get me on the yearbook staff, which I only wanted to be on because Bitsy Massey was on it. Bitsy was a cute little thing, a cheerleader of course, and she was on the yearbook committee—most likely to been sure the lion's share of the pictures were of her. I was in love with her for about six months, and she never knew I was alive. The only upside to the whole thing? I actually like taking pictures. I admit, I take a lot with my cell phone now and I don't have any aspirations to go professional, but I wasn't just being polite. In fact," he said, reaching into his pocket for his cell, "I happen to have some compound fractures, crushed ankles, ripped out shoulders and really horrible jaw fractures if you'd like to—"

"Ack!" she yelled, fanning him away with her hand. "Why in the world would you have those?"

"Snap 'em in E.R., take 'em to report and explain how we treated 'em and have the senior residents shoot us down and call us fools and idiots. So, Sunny—how'd it happen for you—picture taking? A big thug named Rock who liked to pose for you?"

"Nothing of the sort," she said indignantly. "I got a camera for Christmas when I was ten and started taking pictures. It only takes a few good ones before you realize you *can*. Take good pictures, that is. I figured out early what they would teach us about photography in college later—to get four or forty good pictures, just take four hundred. Of course, some subjects are close to impossible. Their color, angles, tones and shadows just don't work, while others just eat the camera, they're so photogenic. But..." She looked over at him. "Bored?"

"Not yet," he answered with a grin.

"It was my favorite thing," she said. "My folks kept saying there was no real future in it and I'd better have a backup plan, so I majored in business. But friends kept asking me to take pictures because I could. Pretty soon I had the moxie to ask them to at least pay the expenses—travel costs like gas for the car, film, developing, mounting, that sort of thing. Me and my dad put a darkroom in the basement when I was a junior in high school, but right after that we went digital and got a really good computer, upscale program and big screen. I built a website, using some of my stock for online advertising, and launched a price list that was real practical for people on a budget—but the product was *good*. My darkroom became a work room. I could deliver finished portraits in glossy, matte, texture, whatever they wanted, and I could do it quickly. Friends told friends who told friends and by my sophomore year I was booked every weekend for family reunions, birthday parties, christenings, weddings, engagement parties, you name it. The only thing I didn't have when I dropped out of school to do this full-time was a studio. Since I did all my shooting on location at the site, all I needed in a studio was a desk, computer, big-screen monitor, DVD player and some civilized furnishings, plus a whole lot of albums and DVDs and brochures of photo packages. The money was good. I was set up before I was set up. I was lucky."

"I bet you were also smart," Drew said.

She laughed a bit. "Sort of, with my dad running herd on my little business all the time. He wasn't trying to make me successful, he was looking out for me, showing me the pitfalls, helping me not fail. When it became my means of income, I think he was a little ambivalent about me quitting college. And my mom? Scared her to death! She's old-fashioned—go get a practical job! Don't bet on your ingenuity or worse, your talent!"

"Your guy," Drew asked. "What did he do?"

"Highway Patrol. He liked life on the edge."

"Did he like your photographs?"

Without even thinking she answered, "Of him. He liked being in front of the camera. I like being behind it."

"Oh, he was one of the photogenic ones?"

"He was," she admitted. "He could be a model. Maybe he is by now."

"You don't keep in touch?"

"Oh, no," she said with a mean laugh.

"Not even through friends?"

"Definitely not through friends." She turned to look at him. "You? Do you keep in touch?"

He shrugged but his eyes were focused on the road. "Well, she's going to marry one of the residents at the hospital. We're not in the same service—he's general surgery. But she turns up sometimes. She's polite. I'm polite." He took a breath. "I hate that. I don't know how she feels, but I don't feel polite."

"So you are angry," she said, a note of surprise in her voice.

"Oh, hell yes," he replied. "It's just that sometimes the line is blurred, and I get confused about who I'm angriest with—her or me. She knew what she was signing up for, that residents don't have a lot of time or money or energy after work. Why couldn't we figure that out without all the drama? But then, I'm guilty of the same thing—I was asking way too much of her. See? Plenty of blame to go around."

There was quiet for a while. The road was curvy, banked by very tall trees heavy with snow. The snow was falling lightly, softly. The higher they went, the more snow there was on the ground. There were some sharp turns along the road, and a few drop-offs that, in the dark of night, looked like they were bottomless. He drove slowly, carefully, attentively. If he looked at her at all, which was rare, it was the briefest glance.

"Very pretty out here," she said quietly.

He responded with, "Can I ask you a personal question?"

She sucked in her breath. "I don't know...."

"Tell you what—don't answer if it makes you the least bit uncomfortable," he suggested.

"But wouldn't my not answering tell you that—"

"Did you fall in love with him the second you met him? Like right off the bat? Boom—you saw him, you were knocked off your feet, dead in love?"

No! she thought. "Yes," she said. She looked across the front seat at him. "You?"

He shook his head first. "No. I liked her right away, though. There were things about her that really worked for me, that work for a guy. Like, for example, no guessing games. She was very up-front, but never in a bitchy way. Not a lot of games with Penny, at least up until we got to the breaking-up part of our relationship. For example, if we went out to dinner, she ordered exactly what she liked. If I asked her what she'd like to do, she came up with an answer—never any of that 'I don't care' when she really did care. I liked that. We got along, seemed like we were paddling in the same direction. I wanted to be a surgeon, and she was a nurse who liked the idea of being with a doctor, even though she knew it was never easy on the spouse. When I asked her if she wanted to move in with me before the residency started she said, 'Not without a ring.'" He shrugged. "Seemed reasonable to me that we'd just get married. I'm still real surprised it didn't work out that way. I really couldn't tell you exactly when it stopped working. That's the only thing that scares me."

She stared at his profile. At that moment she decided that if she ever broke a bone, she'd want him to set it. "But by then you were madly in love with her, right? By the time you got to the ring?"

"Probably. Yeah, I think so. The thing is, Penny seemed exactly right for me, exactly. Logical. Problems that friends of mine had with wives or girlfriends, I didn't have with Penny. Guys envied me. I thought she was the perfect one for me."

She heard Glen's voice in her head. *I thought you were the best thing for me, the best woman I could ever hook up with for the long haul....*

"Until all this fighting started," he went on. "Things had been so easy with us, I didn't get it. I thought it was all about her missing her friends, me working such long hours, that kind of thing. I'm still not sure—maybe it was about another guy and being all torn up trying to decide. But really, I thought everything was fine."

"What is it with you guys?" she said hotly. "You just pick out a girl who looks like wife material and hope by the time you get to the altar you'll be ready?"

Drew gave her a quick glance, a frown, then looked back at the road. And that's when it happened—as if it fell from the sky, he hit a buck. He knew it was a buck when he saw the antlers. He also saw its big, brown eyes. It was suddenly in front of the SUV—his oldest sister's SUV that he had borrowed to go up to the cabin. Though they weren't traveling fast, the strike was close, sudden, the buck hit the front hard, was briefly airborne, came down on the hood, and rolled up against the windshield with enough force for the antlers to crack it, splinter it.

Drew fought the car, though he could only see clearly out of the driver's side window. He knew that to let the SUV go off the road could be disastrous—there were so many drop-offs on the way to the cabin. He finally brought the car to rest on the shoulder, the passenger side safely resting against a big tree.

Sunny screamed in surprise and was left staring into the eyes of a large buck through the webbed and cracked windshield. The deer was lying motionless across the hood.

Drew turned to Sunny first. "Sunny…"

"We hit a deer!" she screamed.

"Are you okay? Neck? Head? Back? Anything?" he asked her.

She was unhooking her belt and wiggling out of it. "Oh, my God, oh, my God, oh, my God! He's dead! Look at him! He's dead, isn't he?"

"Sunny," he said, stopping her, holding her still. "Wait a second. Sit still for just a second and tell me—does anything hurt?"

Wide-eyed, she shook her head.

He ran a hand down each of her legs, over her knees. "Did you hit the dash?" he asked. "Any part of you?"

She shook her head. "You have to help the deer!" she said in a panic.

"I don't know if there's much help for him. I wonder why the airbags didn't deploy—the SUV must've swept the buck's legs out from under him, causing him to directly hit the grille, and since the car kept moving forward, no airbags. Whew, he isn't real small, either."

"Check him, Drew. Okay?"

"I'll look at him, but you stay right here for now, all right?"

"You bet I will. I should tell you—me and blood? Not a good combination."

"You faint?"

She nodded, panic etched on her face. "Right after I get sick."

He rolled his eyes. That was all he needed. "Do not get out of the car!"

"Don't worry," she said as he was exiting.

Drew assessed the deer before he took a closer look at the car. The deer was dead, bleeding from legs and head, eyes wide and fixed, blood running onto the white snow. There was some hood and grille damage, but the car might be driveable if he didn't have a smashed windshield. It was laminated glass, so it had gone all veiny like a spiderweb. He'd have to find a way to get that big buck off and then, if he drove it, he'd have a hard time seeing through the cracked glass.

He pulled out his cell phone and began snapping pictures, but in the dark it was questionable what kind of shots he'd get.

He leaned back in the car. "Can I borrow your camera? It has a nice, big flash, right?"

"Borrow it for what?"

"To get some pictures of the accident. For insurance."

"Should I take them?" she asked.

"I don't know if you'll have time before you get sick and faint."

Blood. That meant there was blood. "Okay—but let me show you how." She pulled the camera bag from the backseat, took the camera out and gave him a quick lesson, then sat quietly, trying not to look at the dead deer staring at her as light flashed in her peripheral vision.

But then, curious about where Drew was, she looked out the cracked windshield and what she saw almost brought tears to her eyes. With the camera hanging at his side from his left hand, he looked down at the poor animal and, with his right hand, gave him a gentle stroke.

Then he was back, handing her the camera. "Did you pet that dead deer?" she asked softly.

He gave his head a little nod. "I feel bad. I wish I'd seen him in time. Poor guy. I hope he doesn't have a family somewhere."

"Aw, Drew, you're just a tender heart."

"Here's what we have to do," he said, moving on. "We're going to have to walk the rest of the way. Fortunately it's only a couple of miles."

"Shouldn't we stay with the car? I've always heard you should stay with the car. What if someone comes looking for us?"

"It will be too cold. I can't keep it running all night. And if anyone gets worried by how long we're gone, they're going to look in Fortuna or Eureka. Or at least the route to those towns, which is where you told them we were going." He lifted a brow. "Why do you suppose you did that?"

She shook her head. "I didn't want my uncle Nate to

think we were going somewhere to be alone. Dumb. Very dumb."

"I need a phone, a tow truck and a warm place to wait, so here's what's going to happen. Hand me the camera case." She zipped it closed and he hung it over his shoulder. "There's a big flashlight in the glove box. Grab it—I'll have to light our way when we clear the headlights. Now slide over here and when you get out, either shield or close your eyes until I lead you past the deer, because the way my night's going if you get sick, it'll be on me."

She wrinkled her nose. "I smell it," she said. "Ick, I can *smell* it!"

"Close your eyes *and* your nose," he said. "Let's get past this, all right?"

She slid over, put her feet on the ground and stood. And her spike heels on her boots sank into the frozen, snowy ground. "Uh-oh," she said.

"Oh, brother. So, what if I broke the heels off those boots? Would you be able to walk in them?"

She gasped! "They're six-hundred-dollar Stuart Weitzman boots!"

He looked at her levelly for a long moment. "I guess the photography business is going very, very well."

"I had to console myself a little after being left at the

church. Giving them up now would be like another…
Oh, never mind…"

"You're right," he said. "I must have lost my mind."
He eased her backward, lifted her onto the seat with her
legs dangling out. Then he positioned the heavy camera
bag around his neck so it hung toward the front. Next
he turned his back to her, braced his hands on his knees
and bent a little. "Piggyback," he said. "Let's move it."

"I'm too heavy."

"No, Sunny, you're not."

"I am. You have no idea how much I weigh."

"It's all right," he said. "It's not too much."

"I'll go in my socks. It's just a couple of miles…"

"And get frostbite and from then on you'll be putting your prosthetic feet into your Stuart Weitzmans."
He looked over his shoulder at her. "The sooner we do
this, the sooner we're warm and with help on the way."

Sunny only thought about it for a second—she was
getting cold and she liked her feet, didn't want to give
them up to frostbite. She grumbled as she climbed on.
"I was just willing to leave Jack's so we could talk without everyone watching. I haven't really talked to a single guy in a year."

"Close your eyes," he said. "What does that mean,
'really talked to a single guy'?"

"Obviously I ran into them from time to time. Bag

boys, mechanics, cable repairmen, cousins to the bride or groom… But after Glen, I had sworn off dating or even getting to know single men. Just not interested in ever putting myself in that position again. You know?"

"I know," he said a bit breathlessly. He stopped trudging up the hill to catch his breath. Then he said, "You lucked out with me—there's no better way to see a person's true colors than when everything goes to hell. Wrecked car, dead dear, spiked heels—it qualifies." He hoisted her up a bit and walked on.

"I'd like to ask you something personal, if you're up for it," she said.

He stopped walking and slid her off his back. He turned toward her and he was smiling. "Sunny, I can't talk and carry you—this top-of-the-line camera is heavy. Here's what you can do—tell me stories. Any stories you want—chick stories about shopping and buying six-hundred-dollar boots, or photographer stories, or scary stories. And when we get to the cabin, you can ask me anything you want."

"I'm too heavy," she said for the umpteenth time.

"I'm doing fine, but I can't carry on much of a conversation. Why don't you entertain us by talking, I'll walk and listen." And he presented his back again so she could climb on.

She decided to tell him all about her family; how her

mother, two aunts and Uncle Nate had grown up in these mountains; and how later, when Grandpa had retired and left the veterinary practice to Uncle Nate, they all went back for visits. Grandma and Grandpa lived in Arizona as did Patricia and her two sons. Auntie Chris lived in Nevada with their two sons and one daughter and Sunny, an only child, lived in Southern California.

"Am I heavier when I talk?" she asked him.

"No," he said, stopping for a moment. "You make the walk shorter."

So she kept going. She talked about the family gatherings at the Jensen stables, about how she grew up on a horse like her mom and aunts had. But while her only female cousin and best friend since birth, Mary, had ridden competitively, Sunny was taking pictures. She spoke about fun times and pranks with her cousins.

She told him how Nate and Annie had met over an abandoned litter of puppies and would be married in the spring. "I'll be a bridesmaid. It will be my third time as a bridesmaid and a lot of my girlfriends are getting married. I've never before in my life known a single woman who was left at the altar. I keep wondering what I did wrong. I mean, Glen worked out like a madman and he wanted me to work out too, but you can't imagine the exercise involved in carrying a twenty pound camera bag, running, stooping, crouching, lifting that heavy camera for literally hours. I just couldn't get excited about lifting weights on top of that. He said I should think about implants. I hate surgical procedures of any kind. Oh, sure, I've always wanted boobs, but not that bad. And yes, I'm short and my butt's too big and my nose is pointy.... He used to say wide hips are good for sex and nothing else. That felt nice, hearing that," she said facetiously. "I tried to take comfort in the sex part—maybe that meant I was all right in the sack, huh? And I'm bossy, I know I'm bossy sometimes. I liked to think I'm efficient and capable, but Glen thought it was controlling and he said it pissed him off to be controlled by a woman. There you have it—the recipe for getting left at the altar."

Then she stopped talking for a while. When she spoke again, her voice was quiet and his tread actually slowed. "I'd like you to know something. When we first met and I was so snotty and rude, I never used to be like that. Really. I always concentrated on being nice. That's how I built my business—I was nice, on time, and worked hard—that's what I attribute most of my success to. Seriously. That whole thing with Glen.... Well, it changed me. I apologize."

"No apology necessary," he said breathlessly. "I understand."

Then she was embarrassed by all her talking, talking about boobs and hips and sex to a total stranger. Blessedly, he didn't make any further comment. It wasn't long before she could see a structure and some lights up ahead. He trudged on, breathing hard, and finally put her down on the porch that spanned the front of a small cabin.

She looked up at him. "It's amazing that you would do that. I would have left me in the car."

He gave her a little smile. "Well, you wanted to see the cabin. And now you will. We'll call Jack's, let everyone know what happened, that we're all right, and I'll light the fire, so we can warm up. Then I have a few things to tell you."

Six

Drew immediately started stacking wood in the fireplace on top of some very big pinecones he used as starters.

Sunny looked around—showplace, all right. She appreciated the plush leather furniture, beautiful patterned area rug, spacious stone hearth, stained shutters, large kitchen. There were two doors off the great room—bedrooms, she assumed. It wasn't messy, though books and papers were stacked on the ottoman and beside the long, leather sofa, and a laptop sat open on the same ottoman. There was a throw that looked like it might be cashmere that was tossed in a heap at the foot of the sofa.

"Should I go ahead and call Jack's?" she asked him.

He looked over his shoulder at her and smiled. "No hurry. No way I'm getting a tow truck tonight, on New

Year's Eve. In fact, I wouldn't count on New Year's Day either—I'm probably going to have to get my brother-in-law to drive up here in his truck to get me and tow Erin's car home. We're not late yet, so no one's worried." He lit a match to the starter cones and stood up as the fire took light. He brushed the dirt off his hands. "I hate to think about you being rescued too soon. I think we still have some things to talk about."

"Like?"

He stepped toward her. There was a softness in his eyes, a sweet smile on his lips. "You wanted to ask me something personal. And I have to tell you something." His hands were on her upper arms and he leaned down to put a light kiss on her forehead. "You're not too short. You're a good height." He touched her nose with a finger, then he had to brush a little soot off of it. "Your nose looks perfect to me—it's a very nice nose. And your chest is beautiful. Inviting, if you can handle hearing that from a man who is not your fiancé. I was never attracted to big boobs. I like to look at well-proportioned women. More than that, women in their real, natural bodies—implants might stay standing, but they're not pretty to me." His hands went to her hips. "And these?" he asked, squeezing. "Delicious. And your butt? One of the best on record. On top of all that I think you have the greatest laugh I've heard in a long time and your smile is infectious—I bet you can coax excellent smiles out of photo subjects with it. When you smile at me? I feel like I'm somebody, that's what. And the fact that you were a little ornery? I'm okay with that—you know why? Because when someone does something that bad to you, they shouldn't just get away with it. It hurts and turns you a little mean because it's just plain unfathomable that a guy, even a stupid guy, can be that cruel. I'm really sorry that happened, Sunny. And I hope you manage to get past it."

She was a little stunned for a moment. No one had ever talked to her like that, not that she'd given anyone a chance with the way she pushed people away. But he was so sexy and sweet it was *killing* her. "Just out of curiosity, what would you have done?"

"If I was left in my Vera Wang?" he asked, wide-eyed.

She laughed in spite of herself. "No, if you realized you didn't want to get married to the woman you were getting married to!"

"First of all, it would never have gotten that far if I wasn't sure. Invitations would never be mailed. Getting married isn't just some romantic thing—it's a lot of things, and one is a serious partnership. You have to be in the same canoe on at least most issues, but it's okay to be different, I think. Like my sisters and their guys? I would never have coupled them up, they're so different from their guys. But they're perfect for each other because they have mutual respect and a willingness to negotiate. They keep each other in balance. Plus, they love each other. Jesus, you wouldn't believe it, how much they're in love. It's almost embarrassing. But when they talk about being married, it's more about how they want their lives to go, how they want their partnership to feel."

"And you were that way with… Penny?" she asked.

"I thought I was," he said. "Thought she was, too."

"What if you're wrong next time, too?" Sunny asked.

"Is that what you're afraid of, honey?" he asked her gently.

"Of course! Aren't you?"

He stared at her for a second, then walked into the kitchen without answering. "Let's hope good old Erin stocked something decent for a cold winter night, huh?" He began opening cupboards. He finally came out with a dark bottle of liquid. "Aha! Brandy! Bet you anything this isn't Erin's, but Aiden's. But it's not terrible brandy—at least it's Christian Brothers." He lifted the bottle toward her.

"Sure, what the hell," she said, going over to the sofa to sit. She raised the legs of her jeans, unzipped her boots and pulled them off. She lifted one and looked at it. Now why would she bring these to Uncle Nate's stable? These were L.A. boots—black suede with pointy toes and spike heels. The boots she normally brought to the stable were low-heeled or cowboy, hard leather, well worn. The kind that would've made it up that hill so she wouldn't have to be carried.

She threw the boot on the floor. Okay, she had wanted to be seen, if possible, and judge the look on the face of the seer. Her confidence was pretty rocky; she needed to feel attractive. She wanted to see a light in a male eye like the one she had originally seen in Glen's—a light she would run like hell from, but still....

Drew brought her a brandy in a cocktail glass, not a snifter. He sat down beside her. "Here's to surviving a deer strike!" he said, raising his glass to her.

She clinked. "Hear, hear."

They each had a little sip and he said, "Now—that personal question? Since I can breathe and talk again."

"It's probably a dumb question. You'd never be able to answer it honestly and preserve your manhood."

"Try me. Maybe you're right about me, maybe you're not."

"Okay. Did you cry? When she left you?"

He rolled his eyes upward to find an answer. He shook his head just a bit, frowning. "I don't think so. Didn't cry, didn't beg." He leveled his gaze at her. "Didn't sleep either, and since I couldn't sleep I worked even more hours. I kept trying to figure out where I'd gone wrong. For two years we seemed to be fine and then once the ring was on the finger, everything went to hell."

"So what *did* you do?" she wanted to know.

"I did my chores," he said. "All the things she wanted me to do that when I didn't, drove her crazy. There were little rules. If you're the last one out of the bed, make it. If you eat off a plate, rinse it and put it in the dishwasher. If something you take off is dirty it doesn't go on the floor, but in the hamper. I thought if she came back, she'd see I was capable of doing the things that were important to her."

That almost broke her heart. "Drew…"

"In medicine we have a saying, if you hear hoofbeats, don't expect to see a zebra. I was thinking horses—it's pretty common for surgeons to have relationship problems because of the pressure, the stress, the time they have to spend away from home. Horses. I brought her with me to my residency program, took her away from her mom, away from her job and girlfriends, and then I had even less time for her than I'd had as a med student. And we fought about it—about my hours, her loneliness. But when she left me, she didn't go back home. It took me so long to figure that out. I thought it meant she was still considering us. She moved a few miles away. Not because I was still a consideration, but because there was a guy. I never suspected a guy. I didn't even know about him for six months after we broke up. It was a zebra all along."

"Ow. That must have hurt you bad."

He leaned toward her. "My pride, Sunny. At the end of the day, I missed her, hated giving up my idea of how we'd spend the rest of our lives, but it was mostly my pride that was hurt. I'm real grateful to Penny—she walked away while all we had at stake was some cheap, hand-me-down furniture to divide between us. If we weren't going to make it together, if she wasn't happy with me, I'm glad she left me before we invested a lot more in each other. See," he said, taking Sunny's hand in his, "I think I put Penny in charge and I went along, and that wasn't fair. When a man cares about a woman, he owes it to her to romance her, pursue her, *convince* her. I learned something there—you don't just move along toward something as serious as marriage unless just about every emotion you have has been engaged. Like I said, we grew on each other. Lots of times I asked myself why I thought that was enough."

"But what I want to know is, will you ever be willing to risk it again?" she asked.

"Yes, and I look forward to it," he answered.

"You're just plain crazy! A glutton for punishment!"

"No, I'm reformed. I always heard it was a good idea to fall in love with your best friend and I bought that. I thought if you could meet someone you really liked and she also turned you on, all the mysteries of life were solved. I still think you'd better be good, trusted friends with the person you marry, but by God, there had better be some mind-blowing passion. Not like when you're sixteen and carry your brain in your... Well, you know. But next time, and there will be a next time, I want it all—someone I like a lot, trust, someone I respect and love and someone I want so bad I'm almost out of my mind."

"Do you think you'll ever find that?" Sunny asked.

"The important thing is that I won't settle for less. Now, you've had a year to think about it—what's your conclusion about what happened?"

She pursed her lips and frowned, looked down for a second, then up. "I was about to marry the wrong guy and he bolted before he could make the biggest mistake of his life. But don't look at me to thank him for it— the mess he left was unbelievable. Over a hundred gifts had to be returned, my parents had paid for invitations, a designer gown, flowers and several big dinners—including the reception dinner. Flowers were distributed to the wedding party so they wouldn't just be wasted... It was horrendous."

"Have you ever wondered," he asked her, "what one thing would make that whole nightmare a blessing in disguise?"

"I can't imagine!" she said.

Funniest thing, he thought. *Before tonight, neither could I.*

He moved very slowly, scooting closer to her. He lifted the glass of brandy out of her hand and placed both hers and his on the coffee table. He put his hands on her waist and pulled her closer, leaning his lips toward hers. He hovered just over hers, waiting for a sign that she felt something, too; at least a stirring, a curiosity, that would be enough for now. Then slowly, perhaps reluctantly, her hands slid up his arms to his shoulders and that was just what he needed. He covered her mouth with his in a hot, searing kiss. He wanted to see her face when he kissed her, but he let his eyelids close and allowed his hands to wander around to her back, pulling her chest harder against his, just imagining what more could happen between them.

The kiss was warm and wet and caused his heart to thump. He'd had quite a few brief fantasies linked to desires. Earlier, out by the Christmas tree in town, he'd had a vision of kissing her and then licking his way down her belly to secret parts that would respond to him with powerful satisfaction. He wanted nothing as much as to lie in her arms, skin on skin, and explore every small corner of her beautiful body.

But that wasn't going to happen now. Not tonight. Not tomorrow.

He pulled away reluctantly.

"I haven't been kissed in a year," she whispered. "I had decided I wasn't ever going to be kissed again. It was too dangerous."

"No danger here, Sunny. And you'll be happy to know you haven't lost your touch. You're very good at it." He looked into those hypnotic blue eyes as he pushed a lock of her hair over her ear. "If I had married Penny, if Glen had shown up when he was supposed to, I wouldn't be kissing you now. And I have to tell you, Sunny, I can't remember ever feeling so good about a kiss…"

She could only sigh and let her eyes drift closed. "We are a bad combination," she whispered.

"I can't believe that…"

"Oh, believe it." She opened her eyes. "You were a guy who just went along with what a woman wanted and I was a woman who, without even thinking about it too much, pushed a man into a great big wedding he didn't want." She swallowed and her eyes glistened. "I hate to admit this to anyone, but Glen kept telling me things—like he just wasn't comfortable with the size of that wedding, and he wasn't sure our work schedules would be good for us, or this or that. I told him not to worry, but I never changed anything. I kept saying I couldn't—that photographers work weekends. But that's not really true, they don't have to work *every* weekend. Portraits for events like anniversaries and engagements can be done before the parties are held, belly shots and babies can be done on weekdays. But the important thing is that until five minutes ago, I wasn't willing to admit our breakup had anything to do with me. And I might be admitting it to you because I'll probably never see you again."

"Listen—I might have been a go-along kind of guy, but I was never that spineless. Glen let it go too far. He doesn't get off that easy."

She gave him a weak smile. "I'm glad I met you. I didn't want to meet a guy, get to know a guy, and I sure didn't want to like a guy, but… Well, I'm not sorry."

"You know what that means, don't you?"

She shook her head.

"After you go through something like a bad breakup and you meet someone new, you check it out and you either find someone better for you, or you recognize right off that you haven't found the right one yet. But at least you keep moving forward until the guy and the life that's right for you comes into focus. And until that happens, we get to kiss."

"You're an opportunist. I could smell it on you the second I met you."

"Now you call your uncle and tell him about the deer accident, tell him we're safe and warm and I'll be looking for a tow truck in the morning. If you want him to, you can ask him if he'll come and rescue you. He can come now or later. A little later or much, much later. You could even stay the night, if you felt like it."

"No I couldn't," she said with a laugh.

"Then will you ask him to wait till after midnight? It's not that far off."

"I think I'll just wait a while to call," she said. "If I know my uncle, he'll be on the road as soon as he gets my call."

That made Drew smile. "I know I'm probably a poor substitute for the guy you wanted to be kissing at midnight, but—"

"Actually, Dr. Foley, I think maybe you're a big improvement. And I might've gone a long time without knowing that."

Sunny waited a little bit and then called her uncle, letting him know where she was, what had happened and that she was fine. While she was on the phone, Drew quickly downloaded the pictures of the bloody deer onto his laptop and deleted them from her camera.

Then, while the fire roared, they sat on the leather sofa, very close together, with their feet propped up on the ottoman. At times their legs were on top of each other's. They kissed now and then. Other times they talked. Sunny didn't say too much more about Glen, and she didn't want to hear any more about Penny.

She didn't tell him that Glen wasn't always nice to her. Oh, it went a bit further than the comment about the wide hips. Glen was the kind of guy who stayed out too late "unwinding" after work, criticized her appearance as being not sexy enough for his tastes and when they did have time together, he was never happy with how they were going to spend it—almost as if he'd rather she be working. She had thought about snatching his phone and looking at old text messages, listening to voice mails, but she was a little afraid of what she might find so she convinced herself she was being paranoid. By the time she realized it wasn't such a positive match, she was wearing a ring and had made deposits on wedding stuff.

It was too late.

But what she did want to ask Drew was, "What makes you think you'll do any better the next time you have a relationship?"

He turned to her with a smile and said, "Good! I really wanted you to ask me that." He ran the knuckle of his index finger along her cheek. "Do you have any idea what attracts men and women to each other?"

She just shook her head. "I thought it was a learned behavior...."

"Maybe, but I bet it's more. I bet it's a real primal mating thing that has no logical explanation. Like you see someone and right away, *bam,* you gotta be with that person. And I bet sometimes all the other elements fall into place, and sometimes they don't. That kind of un-explainable thing—you see a woman on the other side of the room and your heart just about leaps out of your chest. You go brain-dead and you're on automatic. All of a sudden you're walking over to her and you don't know why, you just know you have to get closer. Every-thing about her pulls you like a magnet. You feel kind of stupid but you just walk up to her and say, 'Hi, my name is Drew' and hope for the best, even though she's looking at you like you're an idiot."

"Slick," she said. "Have you actually been able to use that technique very often?"

"I've never even tried it before, I swear. Listen, it's kind of embarrassing to admit this, but that never hap-pened with Penny. It was comfortable, nice, that's all. No fireworks, no mind-blowing passion…"

"But you said it was good with her! You said sex was good."

"I might be kind of easy to please in that department. The worst sex I ever had was actually pretty good. I want what *else* there is! How did what's his name reel you in?" he asked.

Yo. Me and you!

"He wasn't too slick, as a matter of fact. He thought he was. I never told him his great pick-up line didn't impress me. Thing was, he was cute. And I worked all the time. I hadn't been out on a date in a long time and he was..." She shrugged. "Handsome and interested." She tilted her head and smiled at him. "I think I'm telling you all these things because you're safe."

His large hand closed over her shoulder. "I don't want to be safe," he said. "And I want to see you again."

"Want to go off, live our solitary lives and meet back here for New Year's Eve every year...kind of like a take-off on *Same Time Next Year?*"

"Did you know what Jack had planned for midnight?" Drew asked. "Did you write your resolution?"

She shook her head, then nodded. "I wrote that I had to stay away from men. He put it in the fishbowl."

"At midnight everyone was going to pull out a resolution, ending up with someone else's. Really corny, don't you think?" he asked her, reaching into the pocket of his jeans. "It's going to be for laughs, not for real. Some skinny girl could get a resolution to lose twenty pounds.

But I wrote this one before I knew much about you." He presented a slip of paper. "Look, Sunny—it's midnight."

"No, it's not," she said. "It's like three minutes till."

"We can stretch it out," he said, handing her the paper. "I have no idea why I stuck this in my pocket. I put a different one in the fishbowl."

She took it, opened it and read, "Start the new year by giving a new guy a chance."

Her cheeks got a little pink. She was flattered, she was feeling lusty and attracted, but… "But Drew, I'm not going to see you again."

"If you want to, you will…"

"You're just looking for a replacement fiancée," she said. "And long-distance relationships are even harder to keep going than the close kind."

"We can start with football tomorrow. I have beer and wings. Unfortunately I have no car, but I bet you can wrangle one from the uncle."

"That's cute, but—"

"It's midnight," he said, closing in on her. His lips hovered right over hers. "Sunny, you just do something to me."

"Thanks," she said weakly. "Really, thanks. I needed to think I was actually attractive to someone."

"You're way more than that," he said, covering her mouth in a deep and powerful kiss. He put his arms around her waist and pulled her onto his lap, holding her against him. His head tilted to get a deeper fit over her mouth, their tongues played, her fingers threaded into his hair. At long last their lips parted. "Let's just give it a try, see where it goes."

"Can't work. I live in the south. L.A. area...."

"Me, too."

She jumped, startled. She slid off his lap. "You said Chico..."

"No, I didn't. My family is in Chico. I lived there while I went to med school, while I dated Penny, but I don't live there anymore. I'm in residency at UCLA Medical."

She slid away from him. "Uh-oh..."

He shook his head. "I'm just saying we keep getting to know each other, that's all. Neither one of us is likely to keep moving forward in a relationship that doesn't feel good. We're wiser—we know too much now. But for God's sake, Sunny, what if it's good? You gonna walk away from that?"

"I don't want to take any chances!"

"I don't blame you," he said. "It's midnight. Kiss in a new year. And just think about it."

She looked into his eyes for a long moment, then she groaned and put the palms of her hands on his bristly cheeks and planted a good, wide, hot one on his mouth.

Against her open mouth he said, *"Yeah!"* Then he moved against her mouth, holding her tight, breathing her in, memorizing the taste of her.

A car horn penetrated the night. "Awww," he groaned. "Your uncle broke every speed limit in Humboldt and Trinity Counties."

"I told him to stay at Jack's till midnight, but I knew he wouldn't listen," she said. She pulled away from him, slid down the couch and reached to the floor for her boots. Without looking at him she said, "Listen, thanks. Really, thanks. I needed to drop the rage for a while, have a real conversation with a guy, test the waters a little bit. Kiss—I needed to kiss." She zipped the first boot. Then she looked at him. "I'm just not ready for more."

"But you will be," he said. "I can hang loose until you're more comfortable."

"I'll think about that," she said, reaching for the other boot.

The horn sounded again.

"He's going to be pounding on the door real soon," she said, zipping the boot.

"Will you come back tomorrow?" he asked.

She shook her head. "I need to think. Please understand."

"But how will I find you? How will you find me?"

"Doesn't Jack know your family? Don't they know where you are?"

He grabbed her just as the horn blasted another time. He held her upper arms firmly but not painfully, and looked deeply into her eyes. "The second I saw you I lost my mind and wanted to sit right down by you and talk to you. I wanted a lot more than that, but I'm no caveman. Sunny, all I want is to know more about you, to know if there's an upside to our mistakes—like maybe the right ones were meant to come along just a little later. I'd hate to stomp on a perfectly good spark if it's meant to be a big, strong, healthy flame. I—"

There was a pounding at the door.

Sunny sighed and pulled herself from his grip. "Well, here's a bright side for you," she said. "I'm going to kill my uncle."

Seven

Sunny threw open the door and glared at her uncle Nathaniel. "Not real patient, are you?"

Nate had his hands plunged into his jacket pockets to keep warm. He glared back. "A—you didn't go where you said you were going to go. And B—you didn't come out when I honked. Something could have been *wrong!*"

"A—I'm twenty-five and can change my plans when it suits me. And B—something could have been *right!*" She turned toward Drew. "Thank you for everything. I'll get this lunatic out of here."

"Sunny," Drew said. "UCLA Medical. Orthopedics Residency. I stand out like a sore thumb. I'm the one the senior residents are whipping and screaming at."

She smiled at him. "I'll remember. I promise."

Sunny grabbed her jacket, her camera bag and pulled

the door closed behind her as she left. Nathaniel let her pass him on the porch. She stomped a little toward the truck until her skinny heels stuck into the snow covered drive and she had to stop to pull them out.

"Must've been tough, walking from that wrecked car to the cabin in those boots," Nate observed.

She glared over her shoulder at him. "He carried me."

"Are you kidding me?" Nate said. "It was two miles!"

"Piggyback," she said, trying to balance her weight on the balls of her feet until she got to the truck. She pulled herself up into the backseat of the extended cab with a grunt.

Annie, who sat in the front of the truck, had her arms crossed over her chest. When she looked into the back-seat, there was a frown on her face. "Are you all right?" she asked grimly.

"Of course, I'm all right," Sunny said. "Are you angry with me, too?"

"Of course not! I'm angry with Nathaniel!"

"Because...?"

"Because you were laughing with Drew Foley and I didn't want to crash your party!"

Sunny laughed lightly. "Oh, you two," she said. "It wasn't a party," she said just as her uncle was getting behind the wheel. "It was supposed to be a tour of the cabin, but it turned into a deer accident and a two-mile trek. Poor Drew. He had to carry me because of my stupid boots."

"But were you ready to leave?" Annie asked, just as Nate put the truck in gear.

No, Sunny thought. Not nearly ready. She loved everything about Drew—his voice, his gentle touch, his empathy for kids and animals, his scent.… Oh, his scent, his lips, his *taste*. But she said, "Yeah, sure. Thanks for coming for me. Sorry if I was a bother."

"Sorry if I was a lunatic," Nate said, turning the truck around. "I have a feeling if I have daughters, Annie will have to be in charge."

"First smart thing you've said in an hour," Annie informed him.

"Well, I have a responsibility!" he argued.

Sunny leaned her head forward into the front of the cab, coming between them. "You two didn't have your New Year's kiss, did you? Because whew, are you ever pissy!"

"Some people," Annie said, her eyes narrowed at Nate, "just don't listen."

Winter in the mountains is so dark; the sun wasn't usually up before seven in the morning. But Sunny was. In fact, she'd barely slept. She just couldn't get Drew out of her mind. She got up a couple of times to get something from the kitchen, but she only dozed. At five-thirty she gave up and put the coffee on.

By the time it was brewing, Annie was up. Before coming into the kitchen she started the fire in the great room fireplace. She shivered a bit even though she wore her big, furry slippers and quilted robe.

"Why are you up so early?" Sunny asked, passing a mug of coffee across the breakfast bar.

"Me? I'm always up early—we have a rigid feeding schedule for the horses."

"This early?"

"Well, I thought I heard a mouse in the kitchen," Annie said with a smile. "Let's go by the fire and you can tell me why *you're* up."

"Oh, Annie," she said a bit sadly, as she headed into the great room. "What's wrong with me?"

"Wrong?" Annie asked. She sat on the big leather sofa in front of the fire and patted the seat beside her. "I think you're close to perfect!"

Sunny shook her head. She sat on the sofa, turned toward Annie and pulled her feet under her. "I made up my mind I wasn't getting mixed up with another guy after what Glen did to me, then I go and meet this sweetheart. He's pretty unforgettable."

"Oh? The guy from the bar?"

Sunny sipped her coffee. "Sounds funny when you

put it that way. Drew—a doctor of all things. Not a guy from a bar. He was up at his sister's cabin to study and only came into town to get a New Year's Eve beer. I never should have run into him. And even though he's totally nice and very sweet, I promised him I'd never get involved again, with him or anyone else. I told him I just wasn't ready."

"Smart if you ask me," Annie said, sipping from her own steaming cup.

"Really?" Sunny asked, surprised. Wasn't this the same woman who lectured her about letting go of the anger and getting on with her life?

Annie gave a short laugh. "After what happened to you? Why would you take that kind of chance again? Too risky. Besides, you have a good life! You have work you love and your parents are completely devoted to you."

"Annie, they're my parents," she said. "They're wonderful and I adore them, but they're my parents! They don't exactly meet all my needs, if you get my drift."

Annie patted Sunny's knee. "When more time has passed, when you feel stronger and more confident, you might run into a guy who can fill some of the blank spots—and do that without getting involved. Know what I mean?"

"I know what you mean," Sunny said, looking down.

"Problem is, those kind of relationships never appealed to me much."

"Well, as time goes on..." Annie said. "I imagine you'll get the hang of it. You're young and you've been kicked in the teeth pretty good. I understand—you're not feeling that strong."

Sunny actually laughed. "I had no idea how strong I was," she said. "I got through the worst day of my life. I helped my mom return over a hundred wedding gifts..." She swallowed. "With notes of apology."

"You're right—that takes strength of a very unique variety. But you told me you don't feel too confident about your ability to know whether a guy is a good guy, a guy you can really trust," Annie said.

Sunny sighed. "Yeah, it's scary." Then she lifted her gaze and a small smile flitted across her mouth. "Some things are just obvious, though. You know what Drew said is the best and worst part of his job as an orthopedic surgery resident? Kids. He loves being able to help them, loves making them laugh, but it's really hard for him to see them broken. What a term, huh? Broken? But that's what he does—fixes broken parts."

"That doesn't mean you'd be able to count on him to come through for the wedding dance..." Annie pointed out.

But Sunny wasn't really listening. "When that deer

was lying on the hood of the SUV I tried not to look, but he was taking pictures for the insurance and I had to take a peek out the windshield. He gave the deer a pet on the neck. He looked so sad. He said it made him feel bad and he hoped the deer didn't have a family somewhere. Annie, you grew up around here, grew up on a farm—do deer have families?"

"Sort of," she said softly. "Well, they breed. The bucks tend to breed with several doe and they run herd on their families, keep 'em together. They—"

"He's got a soft spot," Sunny said. "If I ever gave a new guy a chance, it would be someone with a soft spot for kids, for animals...."

"But you won't," Annie said, shaking her head. "You made the right decision—no guys, no wedding, no marriage, no kids." Sunny looked at her in sudden shock. "Maybe later, when much more time has passed," Annie went on. "You know, like ten years. And no worries—you could meet a guy you could actually trust in ten years, date a year, be engaged a year, get married and think about a family... I mean, women are now having babies into their forties! You have lots of time!"

Sunny leaned toward her. "Did you hear me? He loves helping kids. He carried me to the cabin—two miles. He petted the dead dear! And he should have broken the heels off my Stuart Weitzmans so I could walk in the snow, but he carried me instead because I just couldn't part with—" Sunny looked at Annie with suddenly wide eyes. "What if he's a wonderful, perfect, loving man and I refuse to get to know him because I'm mad at Glen?"

Annie gave Sunny's hand a pat. "Nah, you wouldn't do that. You're just taking care of yourself, that's all. You don't have a lot of confidence right now. You're a little afraid you wouldn't know the right guy if he snuck up on you and kissed you senseless."

Sunny touched her lips with her fingertips. "He kisses *great*."

"Oh, Sunny! You let him *kiss* you?"

Sunny jumped up so fast she sloshed a little coffee on her pajamas. "I have plenty of confidence, I always have," she said. "I started my own business when I was twenty and it's going great. I know I get help from my dad, but I was never unsure. And I can't even think about being alone another ten years! Or sleeping with guys I don't care about just to scratch an itch—bleck!"

Annie shrugged and smiled, looking up at her. "All part of protecting yourself from possible hurt. I mean, what if you're wrong? Scary, huh?"

"Oh, crap, one hour with Drew and I knew what was wrong with Glen! I just couldn't…" She stopped herself. She couldn't stop that wedding!

"You said it yourself—you shouldn't get mixed up with another guy," Annie reminded her softly. "You wouldn't want to risk getting hurt." Annie stood and looked Sunny in the eyes. "Give it eight or ten years. I'm sure the right guy will be hanging around just when you're ready."

Sunny stiffened so suddenly she almost grew an inch. She grabbed Annie's upper arm. "Can I borrow your truck? I have something important to do."

"In your pajamas?" Annie asked.

"I'll throw on some jeans and boots while you find your keys," she said.

Sunny dashed to the kitchen, put her coffee mug on the breakfast bar and as she was sailing through the great room Annie said, "Sunny?" Sunny stopped and turned. Annie took a set of keys out of the pocket of her quilted robe and tossed them.

Sunny caught them in surprise, then a smile slowly spread across her face. Who carries their car keys in their robe? "You sly dog," she said to Annie.

Annie just shrugged. "There are only two things you have to remember. Trust your gut and take it one day at a time." Annie raised a finger. "One day at a time, sweetheart. Nice and easy."

"Will you tell Uncle Nate I had an errand to run?"

"You leave Uncle Nate to me," Annie said.

* * *

By the time Sunny was standing in front of the cabin door, it still was not light out. It was only six-thirty, but there were lights on inside and the faintest glow from the east that suggested sunrise. Drew opened the door.

"We never open the door that fast in L.A.," she said.

"There weren't very many possibilities for this part of town," he said. And he smiled at her. "I'm pretty surprised to see you. Coming in?"

"In a minute, if you still want me. I have to tell you a couple of things."

He lifted a light brown brow. "About my nose? My hips?"

"About me. First of all, I never lie. To anyone else or to myself. But my whole relationship with Glen? I wouldn't admit it to anyone, but it was one lie after another. I knew it wasn't going well, I knew we should have put on the brakes and taken a good, honest, deep look at our relationship. But I couldn't." She glanced down, then up into his warm brown eyes. "I couldn't stop the wedding. It had taken on a life of its own."

"I understand," he said.

"No, you don't. It was the wedding that had become a monster—a year in the making. Oh, Glen should take some responsibility for going along with it in the beginning, but it was entirely my fault for turning off my eyes, ears and *brain* when it got closer! I'd invested in it—passion and energy and money! My parents had made deposits on everything from invitations and gowns to parties! And there was an emotional investment, too. My friends and family were involved, praising me for the great job I was doing, getting all excited about the big event! Not only did I feel like I was letting everyone down, I couldn't give it up."

"I understand," he said again.

"No, you don't! The wedding had become more important than the marriage! I knew I should snoop into his text messages and voice mails because lots of things were fishy, but I didn't because it would ruin the wedding! I should have confronted our issues in counseling, but I couldn't because I knew the only logical thing to do was to postpone the wedding! The wedding of the century!" A tear ran down her cheek and he caught it with a finger. "I knew it was all a mistake, but I really didn't see him not showing up at the last minute as a threat, so that made it easy for me to lie when everyone asked me if there were any clues that it would happen." She shook her head. "That he would leave me at the altar? I didn't see that coming. That we weren't right for each other? I managed to close my eyes to that because I was very busy, and very committed. That's the truth about me. There. I traded my integrity for the best wedding anyone had ever attended in their life! And I've never admitted that to anyone, ever!"

"I see," he said. "Now do you want to come in?"

"Why are you awake so early?" she asked with a sniff.

"I don't seem to need that much sleep. I'd guess that was a real problem when I was a kid. Sunny, I'm sorry everything went to hell with your perfect wedding, but I'm not threatened by that. I'm not Glen and I have my own mistakes to learn from—that wouldn't happen with me. And guess what? You're not going to let something like that happen again. So the way I see it, we have only one thing to worry about."

"What's that?" she asked.

"Breakfast. I was going to have to eat canned beans till you showed up. I don't have a car. Now you can take me to breakfast." He grinned. "I'm starving."

"I brought breakfast. I grazed through Uncle Nate's kitchen for groceries," she explained. "I wasn't going to find anything open on the way over here."

"You are brilliant as well as beautiful. Now we only have one other thing to worry about."

"What?"

"Whether we're going to make out like teenagers on the couch, the floor or the bed after we have breakfast."

She threw her arms around him. "You should send me away! I'm full of contradictions and flaws! I'm as much to blame for that nightmare of a wedding day as Glen is!"

He grinned only briefly before covering her mouth in a fabulous, hot, wet, long kiss. And after that he said, "Look. The sun's coming up on a new day. A new year. A new life. Let's eat something and get started on the making out."

"You're not afraid to take a chance on me?" Sunny asked him.

"You know what I'm looking forward to the most? I can't wait to see if we fall in love. And I like our chances. Scared?"

She shook her head. "Not at all."

"Then come in here and let's see if we can't turn the worst day of your life into the best one."

* * * * *

Look out for another dazzling Christmas tale from
bestselling author Debbie Macomber!

1225 CHRISTMAS TREE LANE

featuring in the anthology

A MERRY LITTLE CHRISTMAS

Read on for a preview!

"Mom!"

The front door slammed and Beth Morehouse hurried out of the kitchen. Three days before Christmas, and her daughters were home from college—at last! Her foreman, Jeff, had been kind enough to pick them up at the airport while Beth dealt with last-minute chores. She'd been looking forward to seeing them for weeks. Throwing her arms wide, she ran toward Bailey and Sophie. "Merry Christmas, girls."

Squealing with delight, they dropped their bags and rushed into her embrace.

"I can't believe it's snowing. It's so beautiful," Bailey said, holding Beth in a tight hug. At twenty-one, she was the oldest by fourteen months. She resembled her father in so many ways. She was tall like Kent and had his dark brown hair, which she'd tucked under a knitted cap. Her eyes shone with a quiet joy. She was the thoughtful one and that, too, reminded Beth of her ex-husband. Three years after the divorce, she still missed him, although pride would never allow her to admit that. Even her budding relationship with Ted Reynolds, the local veterinarian, paled when she thought about her life with Kent and their history together.

"My turn." Displacing Bailey, Sophie snuggled into Beth's embrace. "The house looks fabulous, Mom. Really Christmassy." This child was more like Beth. A few inches shorter than her sister, Sophie had curly auburn hair and eyes so blue they seemed to reflect a summer sky. Releasing Beth, Sophie added, "And it smells wonderful."

Beth had done her best to make the house as festive and bright as possible for her daughters. She'd spent long hours draping fresh evergreen boughs on the staircase leading to the second-floor bedrooms. Two of the three Christmas trees were loaded with ornaments. The main tree in the family room was still bare, awaiting their arrival so they could decorate it together, which was a family tradition.

A trio of four-foot-tall snowmen stood guard in the hallway near the family room where the Nativity scene was displayed on the fireplace mantel. Decorating had helped take Beth's mind off the fact that her ex-husband would be joining them for Christmas. This would be the first time she'd seen him in three years. Oh, they'd spoken often enough, but every conversation had revolved around their daughters. Nothing else. No questions asked. No comments of a personal nature. Just the girls and only the girls. It'd been strictly business. Until now.

Until Christmas.

They both loved the holidays. It was Kent who'd first suggested they have several Christmas trees. Always fresh ones, which was one reason Beth had been attracted to the Christmas tree farm when she started her new life.

"I've got lunch ready," Beth said, trying to turn her attention away from her ex-husband. He still lived in California, as did the girls. He'd stayed in their hometown of Sacramento, while Bailey and Sophie both attended university in San Diego. According to their daughters, Kent had asked to come for Christmas. She'd known for almost two weeks that he'd made reservations at the Thyme and Tide B and B in Cedar Cove. The news that he'd be in town had initially come as a shock to Beth. He hadn't discussed it with her at all. Instead, he'd had their daughters do his talking for him. That made everything more awkward, because it wasn't as if she could refuse, not with Bailey and Sophie so excited about spending Christmas together as a family. But Kent's plans had left her with a host of unanswered questions. Was this his way of telling Beth he missed her? Was he looking for a reconciliation? Was she? The questions swarmed in her head, but the answers wouldn't be clear until he arrived. At least she'd be better able to judge his reasons. His intentions. And her own...

"Just like it used to be," Bailey finished. Beth had missed whatever she'd said before that, although it wasn't hard to guess.

Just like it used to be. These were magic words, but Beth had recognized long ago that the clock only moved forward. Yet the girls' eagerness, Kent's apparent insistence and her nostalgia for what they'd once shared swept aside her customary reserve.

"Mom?" Bailey said when she didn't respond. "We're talking.... Where are you?"

Beth gave a quick shake of her head. "Woolgathering. Sorry. I haven't had much sleep lately." Exhausted as she was, managing the tree farm and getting ready for Christmas with her daughters—and Kent—she'd hardly slept. She couldn't. Every time she closed her eyes, Kent was there. Kent with his boyish smile and his eyes twinkling with mischief and fun. They'd been happy once and somehow they'd lost that and so much more. Beth had never been able to put her finger on what exactly had gone wrong; she only knew that it had. In the end they'd lived separate lives, going their own ways. Their daughters had kept them together—and then they were off at college, and suddenly it was just Kent and Beth. That was when they discovered they no longer had anything in common.

"You're not sleeping?" Bailey's eyes widened with concern.

Sophie elbowed her sister. "Bailey, think about it. This is the busiest time of year for a Christmas tree farm. Then there's all this decorating. And, if we're really lucky—"

"Mom made date candy?" Bailey cut in.

"And caramel corn?" Sophie asked hopefully, hands folded in prayer.

"Yes to you both. It wouldn't be Christmas without our special treats."

"You're the best mom in the world."

Beth smiled. She'd had less than three hours' sleep, thanks to all the Christmas preparations, her dogs and… her incessant memories of Kent. Traffic at the tree farm had thinned out now that Christmas was only three days away. But families were still stopping by and there was quite a bit to do, including cleanup. Her ten-man crew was down to four and they'd coped just fine without either her or Jeff this morning. While he drove out to the airport, she'd been getting ready for her daughters' arrival. However, as soon as lunch was over, she needed to head back outside.

Beth and the girls had booked a skiing trip between Christmas and New Year's, and after the hectic schedule of the past two months, she was counting on a few relaxing days with her daughters. Their reservations were made and she was eager to go. Ted Reynolds, good friend that he was, had offered to take care of her animals, which reminded her of the one hitch in her perfectly planned holiday escape.

"Before we sit down to eat, I need to tell you we have special guests this Christmas."

"You mean Dad, right?" Bailey led the way into the other room, where there was more greenery and a beautifully arranged table with three place settings.

"Well, yes, your father. But he's not the only one…."

"Mom." Bailey tensed as she spoke. "Don't tell me you have a boyfriend. It's that vet, isn't it?"

"Ten guests, actually," she said, ignoring the comment about Ted, "and they aren't all boys."

"Puppies?" Sophie guessed.

"Puppies," Beth confirmed, not surprised that her daughter had figured it out. "Ten of them."

"Ten?" Sophie cried, aghast.

Without asking, Bailey went straight to the laundry room off the kitchen. "Where did you get ten puppies?" The instant she opened the door, all ten black puppies scampered into the kitchen, scrambling about, skidding across the polished hardwood floor.

"They're adorable." Sharing Beth's love for animals, both girls were immediately down on the floor, scooping the puppies into their arms. Before long, each held at least two of the Lab-mix puppies, the little creatures intent on licking their faces.

Unable to resist, Beth joined her daughters and gathered the remaining puppies onto her lap. One curled into a tight ball. Another climbed onto her shoulder and began licking her ear. The others squirmed until one wriggled free and chased his tail with determined vigor, completely preoccupied. They really were adorable, which was good because in every other way they were a nuisance.

Sophie held a puppy to her cheek. "Where'd you get them, Mom?"

"They were...a gift," she explained, turning her face away to avoid more wet, slurpy kisses.

"A gift?"

"But why'd you take all ten?" Bailey asked, astonished.

"I didn't have any choice. They showed up on my porch in a basket a week ago." Beth didn't say that discovering these puppies had been the proverbial last straw. They'd literally appeared on her doorstep the same day she'd learned Kent was coming here for Christmas. For an insane moment she'd considered running away, grabbing a plane to Fiji or Bora-Bora. Instead, she'd run over to the Hardings' and ended up spilling her heart out to Grace. Under normal conditions, Beth wasn't one to share her burdens with others. However, this was simply too much—an ex-husband's unexpected visit and the arrival of ten abandoned puppies, all during the busiest season of the year. The Hardings had given her tea and sympathy; Ted had been wonderful, too. Beth was grateful for his willingness to watch her animals but she refused to leave him with these ten additional dogs. So she'd made it her goal to find homes for all of them before Christmas. Which didn't give her a lot of time…

Make time for friends.
Make time for Debbie Macomber.

Look out for another sparkling Christmas romance from
bestselling author Sherryl Woods!

A CHESAPEAKE SHORES CHRISTMAS

Read on for a preview!

It was only the second time in the more than twelve years since her divorce that Megan O'Brien had been home in Chesapeake Shores during the holiday season.

Newly divorced and separated from her children, Megan had found the memories had been too bittersweet to leave New York and come back for Christmas. She'd tried to make up for her absence by sending a mountain of presents, each one carefully chosen to suit the interests of each child. She'd called on Christmas Day, but the conversations with the older children had been grudging and too brief. Her youngest, Jess, had refused to take her call at all.

The following year Megan had ventured back to town, hoping to spend time with the children on Christmas morning. Her ex-husband, Mick O'Brien, had agreed to the visit. She'd anticipated seeing their eyes light up over the presents she'd chosen. She'd even arranged for a special breakfast at Brady's, a family favorite, but the atmosphere had been so strained, the reaction to her gifts so dismissive, that she'd driven everyone back home an hour later. She'd managed to hide her tears and disappointment until she was once again alone in her hotel room.

After that, she'd made countless attempts to convince the children to come to New York for the holidays, but they'd stubbornly refused, and Mick had backed them up. She could have fought harder, but she'd realized that to do so would only ruin Christmas for all of them. Teenagers who were where they didn't want to be could make everyone's life miserable.

Now she parked her car at the end of Main and walked slowly along the block, taking it all in. Even though it was only days after Halloween, the town was all decked out. Every storefront along Main Street had been transformed with twinkling white lights and filled with enticing displays. The yellow chrysanthemums outside the doorways during the fall had given way to an abundance of bright red poinsettias.

Workers were stringing lights along the downtown streets and readying a towering fir on the town green for a tree-lighting ceremony that would be held in a few weeks. The only thing missing was snow, and since Chesapeake Shores hadn't had a white Christmas in years, no one was counting on that to set the scene.

The town created its own festive atmosphere to charm residents and lure tourists to the seaside community.

As she strolled, Megan recalled the sweet simplicity of going Christmas shopping with the kids when they were small, pausing as they stared in wonder at the window displays. There were a few new shops now, but many remained exactly the same, the windows gaily decorated in a suitable theme. Now it was her grandchildren who would be enchanted by the displays.

Ethel's Emporium, for instance, still had the same animated figures of Santa and Mrs. Claus in the window along with giant jars filled with the colorful penny candy that was so popular with the children in town. Once again, Seaside Gifts had draped fishing nets in the window, woven lights through them and added an exceptional assortment of glittering nautical ornaments, some delicate, some delightfully gaudy and outrageous.

At her daughter Bree's shop, Flowers on Main, lights sparkled amid a sea of red and white poinsettias. Next door, in her daughter-in-law Shanna's bookstore, the window featured seasonal children's books, along with a selection of holiday cookie recipe books and a plate filled with samples to entice a jolly life-size stuffed Santa. Inside, she knew, there would be more of the delectable cookies for the customers. The chef at her daughter Jess's inn was sending them over daily during the season, some packaged for resale as enticing gifts.

In fact, all along Main Street, Megan saw evidence of her family settling down in this town that had been the creation of her ex-husband, architect Mick O'Brien.

Though all of their children except Jess had fled for careers and college, one by one they had drifted back home and made lives for themselves in Chesapeake Shores. They'd made peace with their father and, to some extent, with her. Only Connor, now an attorney in Baltimore, had kept his distance.

It should have been gratifying to see an O'Brien touch everywhere she looked, but instead it left Megan feeling oddly out of sorts. Just like Connor, she, too, had yet to find her way home. And though her relationship with Mick had been improving—she had, in fact, agreed to consider marrying him again—something continued to hold her back from making that final commitment.

Megan shivered as the wind off the Chesapeake Bay cut through her. Though it was nothing like the wind that whipped between New York's skyscrapers this time of year, the bitter chill and gathering storm clouds seemed to accentuate her odd mood.

When she shivered again, strong arms slid around her waist from behind and she was drawn into all the protective warmth that was Mick O'Brien. He smelled of the crisp outdoors and the lingering aroma of a spicy aftershave, one as familiar to her as the scent of sea air.

"Why the sad expression, Meggie?" he asked. "Isn't this the most wonderful time of the year? You used to love Christmas."

"I still do," she said, leaning against him. Despite all those sorrowful holidays she'd spent alone, it was impossible for her to resist the hopeful magic of the season. "New York is always so special during the holidays. I'd forgotten that Chesapeake Shores has its own charm at Christmas."

She gestured toward the shop windows. "Bree and Shanna have a real knack for creating inviting displays, don't they?"

"Best on the block," he said proudly. There was nothing an O'Brien did that wasn't the best, according to Mick—unless, of course, it was an accomplishment by one of his estranged brothers, Jeff or Thomas. "Why don't we go to Sally's and have some hot chocolate and one of her raspberry croissants?"

"I was planning to start on my Christmas shopping this morning," she protested. "It's practically my duty to support the local economy, don't you think?"

"Why not warm up with the hot chocolate first?" he coaxed. "And then I'll go with you."

Megan regarded him with surprise. "You hate to shop."

"That was the old me," he said with the irrepressible grin she'd never been able to resist. "I'm reformed, remember? I want to do anything that allows me some extra time with you. Besides, I'm hoping you'll give me some ideas about what you really want for Christmas."

Given all the years when Mick had turned his holiday shopping over to her and later to his secretary, this commitment to finding the perfect gift was yet more evidence that he was truly trying to change his neglectful ways.

"I appreciate the thought," she began, only to draw a scowl.

"Don't be telling me you don't need anything," he

said as he guided her into Sally's. "Christmas gifts aren't about what you need. They're about things that will make those beautiful eyes of yours light up."

Megan smiled. "You still have the gift of blarney, Mick O'Brien." And over the past couple of years since they'd been reunited, his charm had become harder and harder to resist. In fact, she couldn't say for sure why she'd been so reluctant to set a wedding date when he'd shown her time and again how much he'd tried to change in all the ways that had once mattered so much to her.

When they were seated and held steaming cups of hot chocolate, topped with extra marshmallows, she studied the man across from her. Still handsome, with thick black hair, twinkling blue eyes and a body kept fit from working construction in many of his own developments as well as his recent Habitat for Humanity projects, Mick O'Brien would turn any woman's head.

Now when he was with her—unlike when they were married—he was attentive and thoughtful. He courted her as only a man who knew her deepest desires possibly could. There was an intimacy and understanding between them that could only come from so many years of marriage.

And yet, she still held back. She'd found so many excuses, in fact, that Mick had stopped pressing her to set a date. She had a feeling that a perverse desire to be pursued was behind her disgruntled mood this morning.

"You've that sad expression on your face again, Meggie. Is something wrong?" he asked, once more proving he was attuned to her every mood.

She drew in a deep breath and, surprising herself, blurted, "I'm wondering why you've stopped pestering me to marry you."

© Sherryl Woods 2010

Home, heart and family
Sherryl Woods knows what truly matters

Look out for another heart-warming Christmas story
from bestselling author Robyn Carr!

A VIRGIN RIVER CHRISTMAS

Read on for a preview!

Marcie stood beside her lime-green Volkswagen, shivering in the November chill, the morning sun barely over the horizon. She was packed and ready, as excited as she was scared about this undertaking. In the backseat she had a small cooler with snacks and sodas. There was a case of bottled water in the trunk and a thermos of coffee on the passenger seat. She'd brought a sleeping bag just in case the motel bedding wasn't to her standards; the clothes she'd packed in her duffel were mostly jeans, sweatshirts, heavy socks and boots, all appropriate for tramping around small mountain towns. She was itching to hit the road, but her younger brother, Drew, and her older sister, Erin, were stretching out the goodbyes.

"You have the phone cards I gave you? In case you don't have good cell reception?" Erin asked.

"Got 'em."

"Sure you have enough money?"

"I'll be fine."

"Thanksgiving is in less than two weeks."

"It shouldn't take that long," Marcie said, because if she said anything else, there would be yet another showdown. "I figure I'm going to find Ian pretty quick. I think I have his location narrowed down."

"Rethink this, Marcie," Erin said, giving it one last try. "I know some of the best private detectives in the business—the law firm employs them all the time. We could locate Ian and have the things you want to give him delivered."

"We've been over this," Marcie said. "I want to see him, talk to him."

"We could find him first and then you could—"

"Tell her, Drew," Marcie implored.

Drew took a breath. "She's going to find him, talk to him, find out what's going on with him, spend some time with him, give him the baseball cards, show him the letter, and then she'll come home."

"But we could—"

Marcie put a hand on her older sister's arm and looked at her with determined green eyes. "Stop. I can't move on until I do this, and do it my way, not your way. We're done talking about it. I know you think it's dumb, but it's what I'm going to do." She leaned toward Erin and gave her a kiss on the cheek. Erin, so sleek, beautiful, accomplished and sophisticated—so nothing like Marcie—had been like a mother to her since she was a little girl. She had a hard time leaving off the mothering. "Don't worry—there's nothing to worry about. I'll be careful. I won't be gone long."

Then she kissed Drew's cheek and said, "Can't you get her some Xanax or something?" Drew was in med school and, no, he couldn't write prescriptions.

He laughed and wrapped his arms around her, hugging

her tight for a moment. "Just hurry up and get this over with. Erin's going to drive me nuts."

Marcie narrowed her eyes at Erin. "Go easy on him," she said. "This was my idea. I'll be back before you know it."

And then she got in the car, leaving them standing on the curb in front of the house as she pulled away. She made it all the way to the highway before she felt her eyes sting with tears. She knew she was worrying her siblings, but she had no choice.

Marcie's husband, Bobby, had died almost a year ago, just before Christmas, at the age of twenty-six. That came after more than three years in hospitals and then in a nursing home—hopelessly disabled and brain damaged, with injuries incurred as a marine serving in Iraq. Ian Buchanan was his sergeant and best friend, a marine Bobby said would do twenty. But Ian exited the Marine Corps shortly after Bobby was wounded and had been out of touch ever since.

Since she knew that Bobby would never recover, since she had grieved his loss for a long time before he actually died, Marcie would have expected to feel a sense of relief in his passing—at least for him. She thought she'd be more than ready to step into a new life, one that had been put on hold for years. At the tender age of twenty-seven, already a widow, there was still plenty of time for things like education, dating, travel—so many possibilities. But it had been just shy of a year, and she was stuck. Unable to move forward. Wondering, always wondering, why the man Bobby had loved like a brother had dropped out of sight and had never called or written. He'd estranged himself from his marine brothers and his father. Estranged himself from her, his best friend's wife.

So there were these baseball cards. If she stretched her imagination to the limit she couldn't come up with anything her lawyer sister would find more ridiculous than wanting to be sure Ian had Bobby's baseball cards. But since she'd met Bobby at the age of fourteen, she knew how obsessed he was with his collection. There wasn't a player or stat he didn't have memorized. It turned out that Ian was also a baseball nut and had his own collection; she knew from Bobby's letters that they had talked about trading.

In the deserts and towns of Iraq, while they hunted insurgents and worried about suicide bombers and sniper fire, Bobby and Ian had talked about trading baseball cards. It was surreal.

Then there was this letter that Bobby wrote to her from Iraq before he was wounded. It was all about Ian and how proud it would make him to be like Ian. He was a marine's marine—the guy who got into the mess with his men, led them with strength and courage, never let them down, hung with them through everything—whether they were up to their necks in a fight or crying over a dear-John letter. He was a funny guy, who made them all laugh, but he was a tough sergeant who also made them work hard, learn and follow every rule to the letter so they'd be safe. It was in that letter that Bobby had told her he hoped she'd support him if he decided to make it a career. Like Ian Buchanan had. If he could be half the man Ian was, he'd be damn proud; all the men saw him as a hero, someone on his way to being a legend. Marcie wasn't sure she could part with the letter, even though it was all about Ian. But he should know. Ian should know how Bobby felt about him.

In the year since Bobby had moved into a quiet and peaceful death, she had passed his birthday, their anniversary, every holiday, and still, it was as though there was this unfinished business. There was a big piece missing; something yet to be resolved.

Ian had saved Bobby's life. He didn't make it out whole, but still—Ian had braved death to carry Bobby to safety. And then he'd disappeared. It was like a hangnail; she couldn't leave it alone. Couldn't let it go.

Marcie didn't have much money; she'd had the same secretarial job for five years—a good job with good people, but with pay that couldn't support a family. She was lucky her boss gave her as much time as she wanted right after Bobby was wounded, because she'd traveled first to Germany, then to D.C. to be near him, and the expenses had been enormous, far more than his paycheck could bear. As a third-year enlisted marine, he'd earned less than fifteen hundred dollars a month. She'd pushed the credit cards to the max and took out loans, despite the willingness of Erin and Bobby's family to help her. In the end, his military life insurance hadn't gone too far to pay those bills, and the widow's death benefit wasn't much either.

The miracle was getting him home to Chico, which was probably entirely due to Erin's bulldogging. Many families of military men who were 100 percent disabled and in long-term care actually relocated to be near the patient, because the government wouldn't or couldn't send the patient home to them. But Erin managed to get them into CHAMPUS, a private nursing home in Chico paid for by the Civilian Health and Medical Program of the Uniformed Services. Most soldiers were not so fortunate. It was a complicated and strained system, now heavy with casualties. Erin had taken care of everything—using her exquisite lawyer's brain to get the best benefits and stipend possible from the Corps. Erin hadn't wanted Marcie to be stressed by benefit or money worries on top of everything else. Erin had done it all, even paid all the household bills. In addition to all that, she was somehow managing the cost of Drew's medical college.

So, for this excursion, she couldn't take a dime from her sister. Erin had already given so much. Drew did have some pocket change, but being a poor medical student, he didn't have much. It would have been far more practical to wait till spring—until she'd had a chance to put aside a little more—to head into the small towns and mountains of Northern California looking for Ian Buchanan, but there was something about the anniversary of Bobby's death and Christmas approaching that filled her with a fierce longing to get the matter settled once and for all. Wouldn't it be nice, she kept thinking, if the questions could be answered and the contact renewed before the holidays?

Marcie meant to find him. To give peace to the ghosts. And then they could all get on with their lives....

Welcome to Virgin River.
The small town where dreams come true.

Special Offers

Every month we put together collections and longer reads written by your favourite authors.

Here are some of next month's highlights— and don't miss our fabulous discount online!

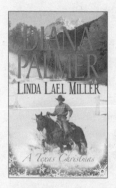

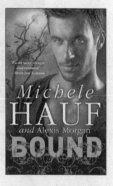

On sale 16th November   On sale 16th November   On sale 7th December

Sparkling Christmas kisses!

Bryony's daughter, Lizzie, wants was a *dad* for Christmas and Bryony's determined to fulfil this Christmas wish. But when every date ends in disaster, Bryony fears she'll need a miracle. But she only needs a man for Christmas, not for love…right?

Unlike Bryony, the last thing Helen needs is a man! In her eyes, all men are *Trouble*! Of course, it doesn't help that as soon as she arrives in the snow-covered mountains, she meets Mr Tall, Dark and Handsome *Trouble*!

www.millsandboon.co.uk

1112/MB391

Come home to the magic of *Nora Roberts*

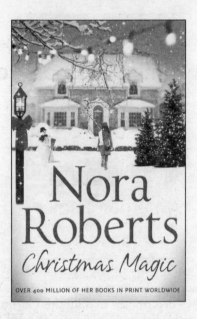

Identical twin boys Zeke and Zach wished for
only one gift from Santa this year: a new mum!
But convincing their love-wary dad that their
music teacher, Miss Davis, is his destiny and
part of Santa's plan isn't as easy as
they'd hoped...

Have Your Say

You've just finished your book.
So what did you think?

We'd love to hear your thoughts on our
'Have your say' online panel
www.millsandboon.co.uk/haveyoursay

- 🌹 Easy to use
- 🌹 Short questionnaire
- 🌹 Chance to win Mills & Boon®
  goodies